Jammy Dodgers get

Bowering Sivers comes from a long line of Londoners. There were members of her family living in Southwark at the same time as Shakespeare. Having travelled and worked in Africa and Canada, she is now happily settled by the English seaside, writing for both adults and children. This is her third Jammy Dodgers book. The first in the series, *Jammy Dodgers on the Run*, was shortlisted for the Stockport Children's Book Award.

The JAMMY DODGERS books
have received the following praise:

'A foray into the Victorian underworld . . .
A great deal of fun'
TES

'Heaps of scary stuff – wicked'
K-club magazine

'The books I like are usually funny or exciting,
but the Jammy Dodgers books are funny *and* exciting'
Sasha, aged 8

'I liked this book because there was a mystery in it.
It was exciting and brilliant too'
Joe, aged 9

Jammy Dodgers get Filthy Rich

BOWERING SIVERS

MACMILLAN CHILDREN'S BOOKS

First published 2006 by Macmillan Children's Books

This edition published 2007 by Macmillan Children's Books
a division of Macmillan Publishers Limited
20 New Wharf Road, London N1 9RR
Basingstoke and Oxford
www.panmacmillan.com

Associated companies throughout the world

ISBN: 978-0-330-44315-9

Text copyright © Bowering Sivers 2006
Illustrations copyright © Tony Ross 2006

The right of Bowering Sivers and Tony Ross to be identified as the
author and illustrator of this work has been asserted by them in
accordance with the Copyright, Designs and Patents Act 1988.

1 3 5 7 9 8 6 4 2

A CIP catalogue record for this book is available from
the British Library.

Typeset by Intype Libra Ltd
Printed and bound in Great Britain by Mackays of Chatham plc, Kent

For Alice, my aunt, who was only sixteen
when she died in the Spanish Flu epidemic
after the First World War

Acknowledgements

Thanks again to Sarah Dudman, the jammiest editor any writer could have, and to Talya Baker, my splendacious desk editor.

Contents

1

In the dead of a midsummer's night a cart pulled by a rough old nag trundled along a fashionable street in London's Mayfair. Although it was warm, both the driver and his companion wore oilskin coats and sou'wester hats pulled well down over their faces. A smaller figure, similarly dressed, walked alongside, occasionally stopping to pick up something from the pavement and put it in a box hung from a hook on the side of the cart.

As the driver tugged on the horse's mouth to steer him around a corner he caught sight of a man in a stiff-collared coat with a heavy belt from which were dangling a pair of handcuffs, a wooden truncheon and a cutlass in a scabbard. Attached to the middle of his belt was a bullseye lantern which the man held up in order to get a better look at the cart moving slowly towards him, for although the street was lit by gas lamps there were pools of darkness between them.

'Evenin', constable,' sang out the driver, touching his whip to his hat in a respectful gesture.

'Good evening,' replied the policeman.

'A fine night, sir.'

The policeman was about to reply when he caught a whiff of the foul cargo in the back of the cart, for these were night-soil men.

Beneath the buildings in London, and there were many buildings in this city of two and a half million people, were cesspools, pits dug into the ground into which flowed the contents of the lavatories. The night-soil men earned three times the weekly wage of a skilled worker, but despite the good money there was little competition for their job, for emptying the stinking sludge of several dozen cesspools into buckets and transporting them by cart to outlying fields was seen as a vile way to make a living.

Resisting the temptation to put his hand over his nose and hurry past, as any sensitive person would, the policeman was mindful of his duty. He strode purposefully towards the cart to ascertain that these were not some ruffians with criminal intent but honest citizens doing their disgusting job under cover of darkness as all night-soil men did.

Just as this conscientious officer of the law drew level with them, however, the driver gave an almost

imperceptible nod to the boy ambling alongside. Immediately he stooped to pick up a large pile of dog droppings from the pavement and put them into the box on the side of the cart, for as well as removing London's sewage the night-soil men made extra money selling dog dirt to the leather industry.

The pure finder, as the boy was called, was clumsy and in depositing the dog droppings in the box he accidentally tipped one of the buckets. Its reeking contents spilled on to the pavement, splashing the policeman's trousers and boots.

With a muttered oath he backed away.

'Sorry, guv,' said the boy in a contrite voice. But in trying to push the bucket upright he somehow managed to spill yet more filth on to the policeman's clothes.

The poor man was now faced with a dilemma — should he stop to investigate the night-soil men or hurry back to the police station to rid himself of the disgusting stench? Throwing duty to the winds, he chose the latter and with another muttered oath strode away in high dudgeon.

When the policeman had disappeared from view the driver and his companion exchanged grins and with a whispered 'Well done, Jem', they drew up in front of an elegant four-storey mansion, its area and ground-floor windows heavily barred.

The driver sprang lightly from his seat and put his arm around the boy's shoulders. 'You know what to do, Jem?' he whispered, his mouth continually pulled to one side in a nervous tic, as the boy took off his sou'wester and oilskins.

'Yeh, Uncle Rudd. I got to squeeze through them,' he pointed to the railings that protected the front of the house, 'get in through the pantry window, creep up the stairs and open the door to let you in.'

'Off you go then. And plaguy quick. That crusher'll change his trucks and trotter cases and be back on the beat in a few minutes, so we got no time to waste.'

Getting through the railings was as easy as sliding down a greased pole. But the pantry window was more of a challenge. However he pushed, pulled, wriggled and squirmed, Jem could not get through the small opening.

'Oh crimes!' he muttered in despair. He had to get in. He had to! This was the biggest job his uncle had ever done – the Star of India, a fabulous necklace set with ten exquisite sapphires the size of pigeon's eggs, each worth a king's ransom. Many

had tried to steal it, but all had been caught and transported to Australia for their crime. But Rudd was a top cracksman. His nimble fingers could pick the lock of any safe. If anyone could steal the dazzling jewels, thought Jem, it was his brilliant uncle. And who was his accomplice? Who was the little snakesman who had squeezed through the pantry window and opened the front door for him? Jem Perkinski!

He would be the toast of London's underworld.

At first Rudd had wanted one of Jem's brothers to help him – 'Billy's so small he could get through a drainpipe,' he said.

'But Billy'll make a hash of it, he always does,' Jem protested. 'The little varmint spoils all our dodges.'

'Well then, Ned, cos he's a lot skinnier than you.'

'Nah!' Jem recoiled in horror. That Ned was a year younger than him but already two inches taller was hard to bear – but Ned helping Rudd to do a burglary, the burglary of the century, Ned strutting around, calling himself a master criminal . . . ? Never!

'He's not up to snuff like me, Uncle Rudd. I'm the sharpest bloke in the family . . . Well, apart from you.'

'All right. But remember – you got to be quiet,

cos there are servants sleepin' in the kitchen and it's right next to the butler's pantry,' said his uncle, who had made it his business to find out about the house. 'And if they hear you . . .'

'They won't. I'll be quieter than a mouse in socks,' said Jem confidently.

But first he had to get through the window.

'I'm goin' to,' he growled, 'even if I have to cut my arms and legs off.' And he launched himself at it again with steely determination, struggling and straining until his eyes almost popped out of their sockets and his body screamed in agony. But just as he was about to give up he suddenly shot through like a ball out of a cannon and landed with a resounding thud on the pantry floor.

'Ouch!' he cried — and immediately slapped a hand over his mouth. But it was too late. He could hear sounds coming from the kitchen, women's voices raised in alarm. A light in the passage . . .

Jem leaped to his feet, looking desperately for somewhere to hide. Beneath the desk? Under the chair? Behind the cabinet? No, no, they'd see him. The door began to open and he shot behind it, flattening himself against the wall, his heart pounding so hard he was sure they would hear.

Through the crack he could just make out a young woman, her face illuminated by an oil lamp.

'Well, go on, Milly,' said someone behind her.

'Don't push me, Minny. What if there's a burglar in here? What if he's got a cosh or a knife or . . . ?'

'Don't be soft, Milly. There's no one in here, you can see that. Look – that pesky butler's left the window open again. Him and his cigars. Her Ladyship should hear about it.'

'I reckon a cat must've got in . . .'

'And done somethin' on the floor,' exclaimed Minny, pinching her nose. 'Lawks, what a stink,' she said, catching wind of Jem, who in splashing the constable's clothes with urine and excrement had liberally doused his own.

'Smells like a dozen cats've done somethin' on the floor if you ask me,' gasped Milly. 'We'd best clear it quick or Mrs Maltby'll blame us for not doin' our job proper.'

'Yeh, but where is it, Milly? Damned if I can see any.'

'Well, look.'

'I am.'

Jem knew he had to act, and act quickly or he would be caught. Leaping out of his hiding place, he pushed Minny as hard as he could. With a cry of alarm she catapulted into Milly, who dropped the lamp. Instantly the glass shattered and a stream of oil snaked across the floor and burst into glittering flames.

'Fire! Fire!' screamed Milly.

'Thief! Thief!' yelled Minny.

Jem ran. Along the passage, up the stairs, across the entrance hall, barging into tables, falling over chairs, sending ornaments crashing to the floor.

There were anxious voices throughout the house now – 'What's happening? Who's screaming?' And lights. Oil lamps and candles everywhere.

Jem tore at the locks and bolts on the front door, breaking his fingernails and tearing his skin in his desperation to get out.

'You! You there!' A man ran down the stairs. 'Stop, I say! Stop!'

At last the door was open and Jem hurtled down the steps just in time to see Rudd whip up the horse and gallop away.

'Wait! Wait for me!' he cried, running after the cart. And as it slowed to turn the corner he made a flying leap and landed splat! in one of the buckets of sludge.

'Faster, damn you! Faster!' Rudd urged the horse, for suddenly policemen started to appear from all directions, running down side streets, shouting to each other and springing their rattles.

On careered the cart, lurching from side to side, tearing around corners at breakneck speed, the buckets swaying, spraying their filthy contents over everything and everybody.

'We got to stop, Uncle Rudd!' Jem yelled at him.

'Stop? You barmy or somethin'?'

'But we're leavin' a trail behind us. Long as we keep goin', the crushers'll follow us.'

'The nipper's right,' said Rudd's companion, glancing over his shoulder. 'Even if they can't see us, they can smell us. And the nag's done up anyway. We'd best cut'n run.'

Rudd pulled the steaming horse to a halt and all three jumped down. The two men took off at the double.

Jem was a fast runner. He'd had a lot of practice, running away from shopkeepers whose goods he'd tried to steal or men and women whose pockets he'd tried to pick or policemen who were trying to arrest him. But his boots were so full of sludge he could only squelch along, slipping and sliding on the rough cobblestones. His uncle and the other man were soon out of sight, while behind him Jem could hear the policemen pounding closer and closer. If they caught him . . . No! No! Nobody was ever going to catch Jem Perkinski!

He bent down, untied the bits of frayed string that held his boots together, took the boots off, held them in his hands for a moment as if they were old friends he was loath to say goodbye to and threw them in the gutter. Then, putting his head down and tucking his clenched fists under his chin, he set off for Devil's Acre, going like the wind.

Ma would warm his backside when she found out he'd thrown his boots away, Jem knew. But he didn't care. Better to be given a right walloper than end up in clink, he thought as he raced along. And anyway, he'd soon steal another pair – or take Ned's.

He had the stitch so badly when he got home he could barely stumble up the steps of the caravan. Just as he was about to bang on the door it was thrown open by his mother. She stood over him, hands on hips, the kind of expression on her face that would have made God tremble.

'No need to ask where you've been,' she said, casting an irate eye over his dripping jacket and trousers. 'You look like a dung heap and you stink like one. You've been down the sewers again, haven't you? I thought I told you never to . . .' She raised a hand to cuff him.

'I wasn't down the sewers, Ma,' Jem said, stepping out of reach. 'I was in one of them carts that collects muck from cesspools.'

'Oh yeh? And what were you doin' in there? Havin' a swim?'

'Nah, me and Uncle Rudd were on a job.'

'My brother?' Ma looked mystified. 'What the devil were you doin' with him?'

'We were . . .' Jem lowered his voice, for their neighbours in the surrounding tenements had remarkably good ears when it came to hearing things they shouldn't. 'We were goin' to nab the Star of India,' he whispered.

'*The Star of India?*'

'Yeh. It's a—'

'I know what it is, Jem.'

'But we didn't get it.'

'Well, there's a surprise,' said his mother witheringly.

'We came a mucker.' Jem decided not to tell her it was his fault. 'And we had to make a run for it and . . .'

'You nearly got caught and you lost your boots too,' Ma said, glaring at his bare feet. 'And what happened to your Uncle Rudd?'

'Oh, he got away, Ma.'

'Pity,' she growled. 'I wish the crushers'd copped him, the varmint.'

Jem was shocked. His uncle was a master criminal, the pride of the Perkinskis. There wasn't a thief in London who didn't admire and envy him. The police were desperate to catch him, but time and time again he got away, taking with him a selection of gold, silver and jewels from the city's most illustrious houses, for Rudd Jupp was a refined burglar who only preyed on the upper classes.

'I mean it, Jem,' snapped his mother. 'He'd no right to take you with him on a job like that. D'you know what'd happen if you'd been copped?'

'They'd put me in clink, Ma.'

'Nah, they wouldn't. They'd send you to Australie in a leaky old tub alongside a thousand other prisoners, all crammed in the hold in the dark with chains on your legs so's you couldn't move. And they'd beat you every day for nothin' and give you biscuits full of maggots to eat. And you'd get thinner and thinner till there was nothin' left of you and they'd chuck you overboard. And don't think it'd be any better if you lived, cos when you got to Australie that's when your troubles'd really start. You'd have to stay there for years'n years and never see me nor Pa nor Gran nor Kate nor Ned nor Billy

never again . . . And I know what I'm talkin' about,' she added, seeing the look of doubt on Jem's face, 'cos Mrs Rivers told me.' She nodded at an upper window in one of the tumbledown buildings that surrounded the courtyard. 'Her son was boated to Australie for ten years for nickin' a scarf off a toff. Told us all about it when he got back. Terrible it was, wicked . . . Oh, Jem,' her voice broke, 'why'd you go and do such a sappy thing?'

'I was just tryin' to help, Ma, what with Pa too poorly to work and no money comin' in – not proper money. Uncle Rudd said he'd sell the Star of India and give me half . . . well, a bit. We'd have been rich, Ma, filthy rich. You'd never've had to work again, none of us would.'

Ma's face softened. 'You're a good lad, Jem. But I want you to promise you won't see Uncle Rudd again, never speak to him, never even think of him. D'you understand?'

Jem nodded.

'Show me your hands.'

'But, Ma . . .'

'I know you're crossin' your fingers behind your back.'

Reluctantly Jem uncrossed his fingers and showed his mother his hands.

'Right, now you can't break your promise. And go and clean all that muck off.' She pointed to a barrel in a far corner of the yard, its greenish water thick with rotting twigs and leaves and the odd dead bird, mouse and cockroach. 'Oh and Jem,' she called him back and whispered in his ear, 'don't say nothin' to Ned and Billy about this. I don't want them gettin' ideas. Them two are daft enough as it is.'

2

Detective Inspector Craddock had been with the Metropolitan Police since the Detective Branch was formed in 1842. A portly man with a stern eye and an undeniable air of authority, he had been responsible for so many arrests and subsequent convictions that half of London cursed him while the other half praised him. But the one criminal he longed to capture, the cracksman he yearned to put behind bars, was Rudd Jupp.

Just as the Star of India was the prize every thief coveted, so Rudd Jupp was the trophy Inspector Craddock craved. The man filled his waking thoughts and invaded his dreams, taunting him – 'Catch me! Catch me if you can!' But Craddock could not. More slippery than an eel, wilier than any serpent, the canny thief always slid out of the inspector's grasp.

Although he would have been drawn and quartered before he admitted it, Craddock had a grudging

admiration for Rudd Jupp. He was impressed by the ingenuity of the robberies, the meticulous planning, the sense of timing, the attention to detail. Rudd was a worthy rival and arresting him would be the pinnacle of Craddock's career, but first . . . he sighed and drummed his desk irritably with his fingers . . . first he had to catch the wretch.

'It was him that tried to steal the Star of India, no doubt about it,' he said to his detective sergeant. 'Nobody else would have dreamed up a clever dodge like that. He would have succeeded too, if the boy he used hadn't spoiled it. Panicked, apparently. Woke the whole house. Would have burned it down if a couple of kitchen maids hadn't been quick with buckets of water.'

'Did anyone get a good look at him, sir?'

'The boy? No. But I'll wager it was one of the young Perkinskis, Rudd's nephews. Pests!' he growled. 'If I had my way I'd ship the lot of them to Australia.'

3

At five o'clock on a summer's morning Devil's Acre was already buzzing. Men, women and children tumbled out of the dilapidated houses, their faces pale and drawn after a sleepless night on a hard floor in a filthy room shared with a dozen or more others and a legion of rats. Scratching themselves vigorously, for there were more fleas, lice and bedbugs in their threadbare mattresses than straw, they waited their turn for a quick sluice under a tap at the corner of the street. But since more often than not the water had run out, they went off to their day's work hungry, weary and unwashed.

In one corner of a courtyard in this horrendous slum stood two caravans, one bright and shiny new, in which Gran Perkinski lived, and the other an old wreck which was home to her son and his family. There was always a great deal of noise coming from the latter, what with Jem and Ned squabbling, Billy whining, Pa bellowing and Ma scolding, but on this

humid morning the usual commotion had reached a deafening volume.

'He's pinched them, he has, and they're mine,' yelled Ned in an aggrieved tone, pointing to the boots on his brother's feet.

'Course I haven't,' Jem shouted back. 'They're mine.'

'Yours? They don't even fit you. They're much too small.'

'They're mine, I tell you,' insisted Jem, scrunching up his toes. 'You must've lost yours.'

'How could I, you stupe? I had them on my feet when I went to sleep. You must've took them off me.'

'Hold your jaw, the pair of you,' Ma upbraided them. 'Jem, take them boots off and give them back to Ned . . . Go on, stop argufyin' or I'll give you a good jacketin'. You can wear Pa's boots. He won't be needin' them for a while, more's the pity,' she said, looking sadly at her husband who was stretched on the floor clutching his stomach and moaning.

'But I can't wear Pa's boots,' protested Jem. 'They're much too big.'

'Then you'll have to go barefoot, won't you? Now eat your breakfast quick,' said Ma, putting a small bowl of oatmeal broth and a tiny piece of bread in front of each of her sons, 'cos I want you to cut along to Mother Murray's baby farm and get one for me. There's nothin' like a dear little brat to open people's hearts and purses.'

'Why can't you have one of your own, Ma?' said Jem, scoffing Ned's piece of bread when he wasn't looking. 'Then it wouldn't cost us nothin'.'

'No, thanks. I don't want to get lumpy again. I got quite enough with you lot,' said Ma tartly.

'How long'll I say we need it for, Ma?'

'Till your pa's better.'

'And how long'll that be?'

'How do I know, you ninny? Here, take this.' She reached into the bodice of her ragged dress and pulled out a coin. 'And make sure the kid's all right. Last time I got one from Mother Murray it was cross-eyed. Put people off givin', I can tell you.'

'And Jem,' his father called after him weakly, 'don't bring back a squally one neither. There's enough shindy round here without a brat grizzlin' its head off.'

Mother Murray was a jovial woman with a face like a scraped beetroot and a belly the size of a rain barrel. She lived in a small house close to the River Thames and to get there the three boys had to walk through streets so narrow a donkey and cart could barely pass through. But they teemed with people, all of them shabbily dressed, some barefoot, a seething mass of humanity, pushing, shouting, arguing and laughing in an endless riot of noise and confusion.

Mother Murray looked after the babies of women who had no time to care for them themselves. Given the choice, she preferred to trade only in very small babies because she could keep them nice and quiet with a generous dose of Godfrey's Cordial — a mixture of opium, a strong drug which made them sleep, and molasses, which soothed their little stomachs.

At any one time there would be upward of a dozen cardboard boxes on the floor of her kitchen, each containing a tiny, naked body wrapped in a dirty piece of cloth, sleeping the sleep of the drugged.

For a sum of money, large or small depending on how much she could squeeze out of her customers, Mother Murray also hired out babies to people like Ma Perkinski, who used them as useful props for begging on the street.

She greeted Jem, Ned and Billy with her usual cheerful grin and showed them into the kitchen,

where Mr Murray, a whey-faced, bleary-eyed man, sat smoking a pipe before the fire.

'How do?' He nodded at them. 'How's your father then? Still at the Fancy, is he?'

Jem shook his head. 'Nah, he can't fight. He's too poorly.'

'What's up with him?'

'Got a pain in his tripes, so we're real short of the ready, what with Pa not workin' and Kate gone.'

'Your sister? What's happened to her?'

'Took up with a waterman. They got a room in a paddin' ken down Shadwell way.'

'But I thought she wanted to be a singer?'

'She did till she met Henry. She's real spoony on him.'

'So you'll be wantin' one of my littl'uns then,' said Mother Murray. 'Come over here and tell me which one.'

Jem walked along the line of baskets, peering into them. 'They all look the same to me,' he shrugged.

'I like that one,' said Billy, pointing to the only baby with its eyes open.

'All right, we'll take it. How much for the week?' Jem asked.

'Sixpence,' said Mother Murray.

'I'll give you threepence.'

'Here, this isn't Petticoat Lane market, you know,' she huffed. 'I'm not sellin' old clothes.'

'Threepence,' said Jem, quite unfazed by her indignation.

'Fivepence.'

'Fourpence . . . and them.' Jem pointed to a pair of old, well-worn boots by the door that looked to be just about his size.

'Nah, you can't have them. They're my son's.'

'So why isn't he in them?'

'Cos he's workin', so he's wearing his goin'-out boots.'

'So I can have his other pair, can't I?'

'Nah, you can't.'

'Why not?'

'Cos they're his stayin'-in boots.'

'But . . .'

'Lor's sake, Flossie, let him have them,' said Mr Murray irritably. 'Fourpence and the brat.'

'Strike me lucky,' said his wife, clinching the transaction. And lifting the baby out of its makeshift bed, she made to put it in Jem's arms.

'Nah!' he exclaimed, pushing it away. 'Ned'll hold it.'

'I won't!' protested Ned. 'It'll leak all over me.'

'What a palaver over a drop of water,' said Mother Murray, picking up an old newspaper and wrapping it round the baby's bottom. 'Here, that'll keep her dry.'

'*Her?*' Jem frowned. 'Nah, we just got rid of Kate. We don't want another "her", thanks.'

'That's all I got. They're all girls this week.' Mother Murray held out the baby. 'Take it or leave it.'

'Oh, all right,' Jem sighed, picking up his new boots and walking away. 'Take it, Ned.'

'We goin' home now, Jem?' said Ned, tucking the baby under his arm.

'Nah, I reckon we should go up Piccadilly first, see if we can get a bit of the ready.'

'Yeh,' cried Billy. 'And we can look in that big shop too, the one with all the grub in the window.'

The 'big shop' that Billy was so eager to see was Fortnum & Mason, a high-class grocer on the corner of Piccadilly and Duke Street that supplied Queen Victoria and her court with gourmet delicacies.

Piccadilly was one of London's busiest thoroughfares, but on that sunny morning in June it was even busier than usual. In addition to the never-ending stream of horse-drawn barouches, broughams, phaetons, hansoms, growlers and omnibuses, the street was jammed from Regent's Circus to the door of Fortnum & Mason with carriages bearing elegantly dressed men and women, all waiting with varying degrees of impatience.

'What's up?' Jem asked a frock-coated salesman as footmen in the livery of the great houses staggered out of the shop under the weight of large wicker baskets. 'What're they doin'?'

'Goodness me, child, I have no time to answer your questions,' snapped the man. 'Be off with you!'

But Jem was not so easily deterred.

'What's happenin'?' he asked, running after a footman. 'What you got in there?'

'It's a luncheon hamper,' said the man.

'Eh?'

'It's full of,' the footman lowered his voice, 'grub for the toffs. They're all off to the Derby.'

'What's a Derby?' asked Billy.

'A horse race,' said Jem.

'Where is it?'

'Derby's . . . er . . . Derby's just the other side of the park.'

'Course it isn't,' the footman snorted. 'And the

Derby isn't run in Derby neither. It's run in Epsom, which is—'

'Clarence!' A cut-glass voice interrupted him. 'What do you think you are doing?'

'I'm sorry, M'Lady. I was just—'

'Wasting time gossiping with ragamuffins. Hurry up, man!'

'Yes, M'Lady.'

The footman loaded the hamper and sprang on to the footplate, motioning Jem and his brothers away with a jerk of his head.

Jem snatched Mother Murray's baby out of Ned's arms. 'Spare a coin for this poor little kid, M'Ladyness,' he said, thrusting it at the crusty old aristocrat in the carriage. 'She fell off the back of a cart and would've been run over by a omnibus if I hadn't thrown myself under it just in time.'

'Move on!' the old woman ordered her coach-man. And she stared stonily ahead as it pulled away.

Jem immediately ran up to the next carriage, in which sat two young men, clearly swells in their loud check trousers and flash waistcoats, their hair gleaming with Macassar oil.

'I thay, Charles,' said one of the men with an affected lisp, 'what nag are you bettin' on today?'

'Runnin' Rein,' said the other. 'He's tipped for an easy win, Percy.'

'And where did you get that tip?'

'From the horse's mouth, so to speak.'

'Well, I reckon you got it from the wrong end, Charlie. Runnin' Rein couldn't beat a one-eyed three-legged cat. If you want to make money, Lythander's the nag for you. I've heard thay that—'

'Spare a coin or two, guv,' Jem shouted. 'Not for us, for her.'

As if on cue the baby obligingly woke from its drug-induced stupor and began to whimper.

'Oh, and why should I thpare a coin for that brat?' said Percy.

'Cos she's got cholera.'

'*Cholera?* How dare you hawk a child around the streets in that condition,' exclaimed the other man. 'You should be arrested, the lot of you.' And getting to his feet he looked around for a policeman.

'Come on, Jem, plaguy quick, before a crusher catches us,' urged Ned, tugging nervously at his sleeve, for they could have been arrested and whipped for begging.

'Don't be a stupe,' said Jem, pushing him away. 'Every toff in London's here today. We're bound to get the ready off one of them sooner or later. What about them two?' he nodded at a man and woman in a phaeton. 'They look dirty rich.'

The baby was now fully awake and hungry, a fact it announced to the world by opening its mouth and letting out a series of ear-piercing shrieks.

''Scuse me! 'Scuse me!' Jem shouted above the din. 'Could you spare a coin or two so's I can buy her some vittals?' He jiggled the baby so that she cried all the harder. 'She's starvin'. She hasn't eaten nothin' but worms since the day she was born. She – Oh!' Jem stopped short as the man in the phaeton turned round.

'I believe we have met before,' he said, staring at the boys intently.

'It's quite likely, my dear,' murmured his wife. 'These children spend their whole lives on the street.'

'No, no, Parthenope, I am quite convinced I have made the acquaintance of these young fellows. I just cannot recall where.'

'It was when we were in the Strand Workhouse, guv,' piped up Ned. 'You came round with a load of toffs and—'

'Hold your jaw, you block'ead!' Jem hissed at him. 'He'll put us back in again.'

'The Strand Workhouse. Of course, now I remember.' The man nodded. 'You must be Jed.'

'Jem,' muttered the boy.

'And you are . . . ?'

'Ned.'

'Jem and Ned.' The man smiled. 'I recall the occasion quite clearly now. My dear –' he turned to his wife – 'this is the young fellow I told you about, the one who recited that amusing verse for the benefit of the Workhouse Visiting Society. Now, how did it go? Let me think,' he said, stroking his chin. 'Ah, yes . . . "Thirty days hath September . . ."'

'Nah, it's *dirty* days,' Jem interrupted him.

'"Dirty days . . ." Of course. Would you be so kind as to recite it for Lady Eden? I'm sure she would enjoy it as much as I did.'

'I've got a better one if you want to hear it. My gran learned it me. It's about an old crone that's just snuffed it.'

Lady Eden clearly hadn't understood.

'An elderly lady who has just died,' her husband explained.

'But that is hardly amusing, Edmund,' she said.

'We shall see, my dear. Pray, continue,' he said to Jem.

'Right you are, Your Honour,' said Jem, perking

up, for he knew there was a good chance of money changing hands if he performed well. 'Ned –' he turned to his brother – 'take that brat somewhere else, will you? She's deafenin' me.'

'Why don't you take her?' retorted Ned hotly.

'Cos I got to stay here and do the poem, haven't I?'

'I could do it as well as you.'

'But they didn't ask you, did they? They asked me. So hook it!'

Grumbling and muttering under his breath, Ned moved further down the street with the screaming baby while Jem recited:

'Here lies a poor woman who was always tired.
She lived in a house where help wasn't hired.
Her last words on earth were, "Dear friends, I am goin'
To where there's no cookin' nor washin' nor sewin'.
Everythin' there is exact to my wishes,
Cos where they don't eat there's no washin' of dishes.
I'll be where loud anthems will always be ringin'
But havin' no voice I'll be quit of the singin'.

Don't mourn for me now, don't mourn for me
    never,
Cos I'm goin' to do nothin' for ever and ever."'

'Splendid,' laughed Lady Eden, clapping her gloved hands.

'Can I come back now?' Ned called. 'The brat's shut up.' He pointed at the baby, who must have realized there was no chance of any food coming her way and fallen asleep again.

'What is your sister's name?' said Lady Eden, leaning forward to look at the baby.

'Kate,' said Billy.

'Nah, it isn't, M'Ladyness,' said Jem. 'Kate's my big sister. This one's called . . . er . . . Elsie.'

'And how old is she?'

'About a year or two.'

'A year or two? What nonsense! I would say she is barely a month old.'

'Yeh, well, I got so many brothers and sisters I can't rightly remember how old they are.'

'How many do you have?'

'A dozen, two dozen – I lost count.'

'How on earth do their parents support so many children?' Lady Eden murmured in an aside to her

husband. 'Tell me,' she leaned towards Jem, raising her voice, 'what does your father do?'

'Nothin'.'

Lady Eden exchanged a meaningful look with her husband. 'Like all of them, I'm afraid,' she sighed. 'He's feckless.'

'Nah, he's not a feckless,' said Ned. 'He's a prize fighter, only he can't do it no more on account of he's poorly.'

'How very unfortunate. What is wrong with him?'

'He's got the molly grubs.'

'And what is that?'

'Every time he eats somethin' he gets a pain in his tripes . . . here.' Jem pointed to his stomach for Lady Eden clearly had no idea what tripes were. 'And then he chucks his grub all over the caravan.'

Lady Eden blanched and put a hand over her mouth.

'Your father is clearly in need of a doctor,' said her husband.

'Nah, Gran's givin' him some of her medicine. 'Sides, we haven't got the ready for no quacks. We haven't got the ready for nothin'. That's why we're all starvin', Your Highness.'

'I am not Your Highness, Jem,' said the man.

'That title is reserved for a royal prince or princess. My name is Sir Edmund and I am a baronet. And here –' he put a crown into Jem's outstretched hand – 'I trust this will help.'

'Lor', thanks, Your Baronetness,' beamed Jem. And he swept off his wideawake and bowed low.

Ned had no hat to take off but he bowed anyway and swept off Billy's cap so that the little boy's dirty blond curls tumbled around his face.

'Bow to them,' he whispered, giving Billy an encouraging kick.

'What a beautiful child,' exclaimed Lady Eden.

'Where?' said Jem, looking up and down the street.

'Your brother.'

'What? Ned?' said Jem in disbelief.

'The little one.'

'Oh – oh, Billy.'

'He's quite enchanting,' said Lady Eden, gazing at the little boy. 'Just look at those big, blue eyes, Edmund, and his eyelashes – they're so long and silky. And that sweet little rosebud mouth. How old are you, Billy?'

'Goin' on six.'

'And where do you live?'

'Devil's Acre.'

'Devil's Acre?' Lady Eden looked enquiringly at her husband.

'A low-class neighbourhood close by Westminster Abbey,' he said sotto voce.

Lady Eden was about to ask another question but at that moment the footman returned with their lunch hamper.

'Well, we must be on our way,' said Sir Edmund.

'Wish I was goin' with you,' said Billy, eyeing the hamper hungrily.

'Yes,' said Lady Eden, looking at him thoughtfully. 'Yes, so do I.'

4

'A crown,' said Ma, turning the coin over and over in her hand. 'A whole crown. That's jammy. That's very jammy.' Her tired face relaxed into a rare smile. 'You must find them coves and see if you can get some more off them. Where do they live?'

'Don't know,' said Jem.

'You should've run after their carriage, you mug.'

'They weren't goin' home, Ma. They were goin' to a horse race.'

'A horse race? Huh! Wastin' good money on mullock like that,' she exclaimed in disgust. 'Well, you get up to Piccadilly and keep your eyes open. We don't want to lose a couple of fat gulls like them.'

But the Perkinskis did not lose Sir Edmund and Lady Eden, for the very next day their phaeton appeared in Devil's Acre, drawn by two jet-black horses, their coats burnished to a lustrous sheen.

As the mares picked their way daintily around the piles of rubbish and dung, the shabby residents of the infamous slum tumbled out of their tenement houses and ran alongside, gawping at the handsome man and woman in their fine clothes and the two footmen behind them in gold-braided livery.

'Lawks a mercy,' muttered Ma, as the phaeton drew up alongside the caravan, 'it must be the Queen. What's that old duck doin' here?'

One of the footmen began to get down, pausing for a moment to find somewhere to put his leather slipper that wasn't inches deep in mud and slime. But it was quite hopeless and with a despairing shrug he squelched to the door of the carriage and opened it for Sir Edmund.

Fortunately the baronet was not so squeamish, or perhaps too well mannered to show his distaste, for with a murmured aside to his wife – 'Please stay here, my dear. I shall not be a moment' – he stepped down without hesitation and offered his hand to Ma Perkinski.

'Good morning, madam,' he said, with a little inclination of the head.

Ma stepped back, blinking in surprise. No one had ever called her madam before. And as for bowing to

her . . . Quite overcome, she bobbed a curtsy and said, 'Mornin' to you, guv.'

'My name is Sir Edmund. And this is my wife, Lady Eden.'

'It's the bloke and his missus I told you about,' Jem whispered to his mother. 'The one that gave us the crown.'

'Oh, nice of you to come,' said Ma, bobbing another curtsy.

'We are here on a rather delicate matter,' said Sir Edmund. The baronet glanced at the crowd of men, women and children who now surrounded them and were listening avidly to every word. 'Could we, perhaps, retire to somewhere a little more private?' he said, nodding at the caravan.

'Nah, you can't go in there, guv.' Ma shook her head. 'Bert's just had one of his nasty turns. It's all over the floor.'

'How very unfortunate,' Sir Edmund said sympathetically. 'I understand from Jem that your husband has been unwell for some time.'

'Too much booze, if you ask me,' muttered someone in the crowd.

'No one did ask you, Old Mother Perry,' snapped Ma, 'so keep your trap shut, you interferin' old hay-bag!'

'And I understand,' Sir Edmund hurried on, 'that you have many children to support.'

Ma frowned. 'Nah, I haven't, guv. I got f—'

Jem, who was standing behind Sir Edmund, shook his head at his mother furiously.

'F-far more than I can handle,' she said.

'Nah, she hasn't,' scoffed Old Mother Perry.

'Yeh, she has, you lyin' old crone,' said someone else, for the old woman was thoroughly disliked by all her neighbours. 'If Liza says she's got dozens of kids, then she has.'

'Yeh, dozens,' said a man. 'It's like a whole army, guv.'

The crowd joined in, beginning to enjoy the game and hoping that they might be able to scrounge something off this wealthy couple as well.

Sir Edmund looked around the yard. 'Your children are not here at the moment. All the other . . . dozens?'

'Nah, they're all out tryin' to earn a bit of the ready cos they haven't had nothin' to eat for so long, poor little darlin's,' Ma sighed, wiping a tear from her eye.

The crowd murmured appreciatively, impressed by her heart-rending performance.

'Well, I'll come straight to the point, madam,'

said Sir Edmund. 'Lady Eden and I have seven daughters, beautiful girls who are the delight of our lives. However, we had always rather hoped for a son.'

'Oh yeh?' said Ma. 'Well, I reckon one'll come along sooner or later. They always do – worse luck.'

The women in the crowd nodded in agreement. Too many sons had come along for their liking. Too many daughters too.

'Until that happy moment,' continued Sir Edmund, 'we should like to adopt a son, one of your sons.' He pointed at Billy.

Ma stepped back, visibly shaken. 'Billy?' she said, aghast.

Billy didn't know what adopted meant, but from his mother's expression it looked like it might be something nasty and, bursting into tears, he ran to her, burying his face in her skirts and crying, 'Nah! Nah, don't want to.'

'Here, guv,' said one of the women in the crowd, pushing a boy forward, 'you can have one of mine.'

'Nah, take mine,' said another woman. 'He's much better lookin' than hers.'

'Nah, take mine, guv. He's a lot smarter.'

In a trice all the mothers were pressing their sons on Sir Edmund and one even offered all six of her boys – 'And if you give me a quid you can have my old man too,' she cackled.

'I realize this must be distressing for you, madam,' said Sir Edmund, trying to make himself heard over the hubbub, 'but I assure you we would raise Billy as one of our own and do our utmost to ensure that he has a happy and fulfilling life. But should he decide he no longer desires to stay with us, the contract would in no way be binding.'

'Eh?'

'Billy could come back whenever he wanted to,' explained Lady Eden from the phaeton.

'Nah. Nah, I couldn't . . .' began Ma.

'Go on, my tulip, give it a go,' one of the mothers urged her. 'It's one less mouth to feed. And what with Kate gone and your Bert taken so queer . . .'

'I will not press you for an answer now, madam,' said Sir Edmund. 'I shall return at this time tomorrow, if I may, to hear your decision.'

And with another inclination of the head to Ma Perkinski, he got into his carriage and was driven away.

Ma, Pa, Gran and the boys sat up late that night discussing Sir Edmund's offer.

Pa lay on his back looking grim-faced and Ma

could hardly speak without crying, but everyone, except Billy, agreed that it would be better for him if he were to live with Sir Edmund and his family.

'You'll be the son of a baronet,' said Pa.

'Don't want to be the son of a barnet,' wept Billy.

'You'll be edercated proper,' said Ma.

'Don't want to be edercated proper.'

'You'll grow up to be a gen'leman,' said Gran.

'And live in a big house,' said Ned.

'And sleep in a warm bed,' said Pa.

'And wear nice togs,' said Ma.

'And never be bitten by bugs and fleas and lice,' said Gran.

'And never have to scrounge or 'arf-inch money,' said Ned.

'Nah! Nah! Nah!' cried Billy. 'Don't want to go!'

'And you'll never be hungry again,' said Jem.

The little boy stopped protesting and stared at his brother.

'You'll eat as much as you like,' continued Jem. 'You'll eat hot eels and fried fish and mutton patties and plum cake and jam tarts and sherbets till your belly's fat as a pig's. You'll eat so much grub you won't be able to stand up proper. You'll eat pork pies by the hundred, pork pies big as houses. You'll eat so many pork pies you'll begin to look like one – all fat

and gristle on the inside and crusty on the top. But I can see why you don't want to leave us, Billy, cos you're only a little kid. So, to show what a decent kind of cove I am, I'll go in your place. I don't mind stuffin' my belly with grub till it bursts, if it will help Ma and Pa.'

There was a short pause while Billy drew in his breath, filling his lungs to capacity, before screaming, 'Nah! Nah! Nah! Don't let Jem go, Ma. Don't let him! I want to! I want to!'

5

The Edens lived in an imposing house on Stratton Street, just a stone's throw from Green Park. On one side lived a cabinet minister and on the other a Hungarian prince.

The cabinet minister lived quietly with his wife, the daughter of a duke, and their ten children, but the Hungarian prince was much given to lavish entertainment to which all the titled émigrés of London were invited. At least once a week his residence was lit up like a lighthouse and men with fearsome black beards and women in low-cut dresses could be seen dancing the csardas with un-British abandon. But as the walls of Victorian mansions were thick, Sir Edmund and Lady Eden slept peacefully in their half-tester beds with the family crest embroidered on the back curtains, oblivious to the revels.

Billy was conveyed to this illustrious abode in the Edens' carriage. Very wisely, Sir Edmund had

brought a light blanket with which to cover the small boy, as a protection not so much from the air, since it was a warm summer's day, as from the prying eyes of his neighbours, who would have been shocked to the very centre of their snobbish being to see a grubby, barefoot urchin entering Sir Edmund's house – and by the *front* door.

As the carriage drew up one of the footmen jumped down and opened the door for Sir Edmund while the other reached in to pick up Billy.

'Pack off!' the boy cried, pushing the man away.

'Billy,' said Sir Edmund in a gentle but firm voice, 'in this instance I should be most obliged if you would permit Ralph to carry you.'

'Oh, all right,' said the little boy grudgingly. But he buried his head in the blanket lest someone he knew happened to be passing, for the thought that people in Devil's Acre might hear that he had been carried up the steps like a baby filled him with shame.

'Ah, Pole,' the baronet said as the butler opened the door, 'ask Miss Jermyn to—'

'There's no need to disturb the governess, Edmund,' said Lady Eden, coming out of her morning room to greet him. 'I can see to Billy.' And bending down she put her hands on each side of the little boy's face, kissed him on the forehead and said, 'Welcome to your new home, my dear. I do hope you will be very happy here.'

'Got any grub?' said Billy, looking past her for sight of some food.

'Grub? OK . . . yes . . . of course. But first you must be bathed and dressed.'

'Bathed?' Billy narrowed his eyes. 'You mean – in *water*?'

'Just so.'

'Nah, water makes you poorly. Gran reckons Pa was took ill cos he got wet – and I *am* dressed.' He threw off the blanket to show his brothers' cast-offs – a pair of ragged trousers of Jem's, turned up and up and up, and a shirt full of rips and tears that had once belonged to Ned.

'You must dress like a little gentleman now, Billy,' said Lady Eden, taking him by the hand and leading him up a very grand staircase. 'And little gentlemen must be clean.'

'Why?'

Lady Eden looked momentarily flustered. Clearly nobody had ever asked her that before; nor had she given it any thought.

'Because . . .' she said, 'because it is not nice to be dirty.'

Billy, who had never been anything but, shrugged. 'Who're them old trouts?' He pointed at the oil paintings of men and women, gorgeously attired, that covered every inch of the walls.

'Those ladies and gentlemen are Sir Edmund's ancestors.'

'His what?'

'His parents and grandparents and great-grand-parents.'

'Ugly lot, aren't they? Crimes, look at that one,' Billy exclaimed, stopping in front of an elderly woman with a stern expression, her mouth tightly pursed. 'What a prune-faced old crone.'

'Billy,' Lady Eden bent down and whispered urgently in his ear, 'we do not use words like that in this house.'

'What words?'

'The ones you just used. Ah, here is Dolly.' She smiled as a young woman ran lightly down the stairs towards her. 'Dolly is going to look after you. Dolly, this is Billy.'

'Pleased to meet you, I'm sure,' said the nurse-maid, stifling a giggle.

'Take Billy to the nursery and give him a bath and bring him down in time for tea, please, Dolly. He can wear some of Alice's garments, but tomorrow I shall

45

buy him a wardrobe. Go with Dolly, Billy,' said Lady Eden, releasing his hand.

'What's she goin' to buy me?' he asked the nursemaid as she led him up to the nursery on the top floor. 'What's a wardrobe?'

'A lot of nice new clothes.'

'Not grub then?'

'No, not grub,' Dolly laughed. And when she laughed Billy saw that some of her teeth were missing and one or two at the back were black just like his mother's, and thinking about his mother made him sad and he began to whimper.

'What's up, my treasure?' said Dolly, looking at him anxiously.

'My ma . . .' he began.

'Oh, you're bound to miss her, my pet, but you'll be happy here, you'll see,' said the maid, wiping away his tears with a corner of her apron. 'The master and Lady Eden are real decent people and their daughters are nice too, 'cept for Georgiana. She gives herself airs – quite the little madam she is. Mrs Maltby's a good-hearted party but the new governess, Miss Jermyn, is a right old crab and as for the new butler, Mr Pole . . .' She shivered and wrapped her arms tightly around her ribs as if to protect herself from something threatening. 'He scares me to death, that man. One minute he's not there and the next he's right behind you, breathing down your neck. He's not normal. If you ask me—'

'I don't know who you're talkin' about,' complained Billy, whose head was beginning to buzz with all the names.

'Oh, sorry, my angel, I'm such a chatterbasket. One of the orderlies where I used to live said, "You know your trouble, my girl. You let your tongue run away with you. It'll get you into mischief one day."'

'When'm I goin' to get some grub?' insisted Billy.

'When you've had a bath, my pet, and put on nice, clean clothes. Now, do you want to use the chapel of ease?'

'Eh?'

'The water closet. It's where you . . .' Dolly blushed. 'Where you . . . you know.'

'Oh, the bog,' said Billy. 'Yeh, I do.' And letting go of the nursemaid's hand he started back down the stairs.

'Where're you going?' she called after him, leaning over the banisters.

'The yard.'

'You can't go in the yard,' cried Dolly, catching up with him and grabbing his arm. 'We've got a –' she lowered her voice – 'a "bog" in the house.' And

holding Billy tightly, she led him back up to the nursery floor and opened a door. 'There,' she said, pointing to the lavatory, a mustard-coloured stoneware pan with no seat.

'Lor'!' Billy stared in amazement. He had never seen anything like it. His idea of a lavatory was a smelly cesspool that was forever overflowing because nobody in the slums where he lived could afford to pay the night-soil men to clean it. 'But . . . but where do I do it?'

'In there.'

Billy peered down the hole. 'Nah,' he said. 'I'll fall in.'

'Of course you won't. Go on, get on with it. And when you've finished you can use some of them.' She pointed to several dozen pages cut from newspapers and magazines and threaded on a string by the side of the lavatory.

'What for?' said Billy, mystified.

'They're for wipin' your . . .' Dolly patted her bottom.

'Why?'

'Oh, for goodness sake!' exclaimed the nursemaid, beginning to lose patience with him.

'All right, all right,' pouted the little boy. 'But I

think it's sappy. You could sell all that paper and make a penny or two.'

Having survived the dangers of the Edens' newfangled sewage system, Billy was then plunged into a bath. Initially this incensed him and he tried to fight his way out, splashing water everywhere and drenching Dolly, but after a while he had to admit that taking a bath in the Edens' house was not so very terrible after all.

For a start the water was warm. It should have been cold, because everyone knew that taking a cold bath was good for the health, but Dolly had sneaked up a few pans of boiling water from the kitchen – 'Cos I can clean you better in a warm bath,' she said. And though she rubbed him vigorously she was by no means rough and she used a soap that smelled of lavender. But just as Billy was beginning to enjoy himself Dolly had to spoil it by pouring a bucket of water over his head and washing his hair.

'Nah, don't!' he cried. 'It'll all drop out. I'll be bare as a bird's bum.'

'What nonsense,' she laughed, going at it even more vigorously. 'I've got to get all them nits and lice out. If the mistress sees one, just one on your head, she'll scream blue murder.'

Billy had to endure several more minutes of this torture until Dolly pronounced herself satisfied and, lifting him out of the now very grey water, she wrapped him in a towel and carried him into a small room furnished with an iron bedstead, a cupboard with a basin and jug on it and a rail across one corner on which to hang his clothes.

'This is the sickroom,' she explained as she rubbed him dry. 'The girls sleep in the night nursery. If you'd been a girl we'd've put you in with them, but seeing as how you're a boy it wouldn't've been proper, so you're going in here. Now, stand up and we'll get you dressed.'

'Where are my togs?' said Billy, looking around for his dirty trousers and ragged shirt.

'Burned,' said Dolly peremptorily.

'What, all of them?'

'Boots, cap, the lot. This is what you're going to wear now.' She pointed at the bed, where a little girl's dress and pantaloons were laid out.

'Nah!' Billy looked at them, aghast. 'Nah, I won't! I won't!' he cried. And before Dolly could catch him he wrenched open the door and hurtled down the stairs stark naked.

6

'Wonder what Billy's doin'?' said Jem as he and Ned walked along the Strand looking for wealthy old women with pockets to pick or generous hearts. 'Seems funny without him, doesn't it?'

'Yeh.' Ned nodded. 'You kind of get used to hearin' him goin' on and on all the time cos he's too hot or too cold or he's got the wiffle-woffles or his trotters ache or his belly's empty.'

'Let's go and see him.'

'Nah, we can't. We got to earn some of the ready. Ma says if we don't get nothin', we don't get no supper.'

'But Ma's got that whole crown the toff gave us.'

'Nah, it's gone.'

'Gone where?'

'She put it on Lysander.'

'Who's he?'

'The horse that bloke said'd win the Derby.'

'What bloke?'

'Them couple of swells we met in Piccadilly.'

'And did it?'

'Did it what?'

'The horse – Lysander – did it win?'

'Nah, it came last.'

'Oh Lor'!' exclaimed Jem. 'That's your fault.'

'Nah, it isn't. I was nowhere near it.'

'You shouldn't have told Ma about it. Now she's wasted a whole crown.'

'Yeh, but supposin' it'd won?'

'Supposin'? Supposin'?' Jem raged. 'Supposin' won't fill our bellies tonight, will it, you knocker-faced block'ead!'

7

In his headlong flight down the stairs Billy hadn't noticed a sombrely dressed woman in grey coming up and he careened into her, tumbling on to his back with a cry of surprise. With a steely expression she hauled him up by his arm and carried him to the nursery floor, where she dropped him at Dolly's feet as if he was a sack of coal.

'What exactly is this child doing, running around the house in a state of nature?' she demanded in a frosty voice.

'Sorry, Miss Jermyn,' said the nursemaid. 'I'd just given him his bath and I was trying to get him dressed, but he said he didn't like the clothes the mistress had put out for him and he didn't want to wear them.

'*Didn't like? Didn't want?* How dare he say what he doesn't like and doesn't want? Such ingratitude. If I were Sir Edmund I would put him straight back on the street where he belongs. Although,' Miss Jermyn sniffed, 'I would never have removed him from it in the first place.'

'But you know what the master's like,' Dolly said. 'He's got a heart of gold. Always trying to help them that's not so fortunate. He'd give them the shirt off his back, he's that kind.'

'Giving them the shirt off his back is one thing, bringing them back here is quite another. As if we don't have enough to do without having riff-raff like that to look after,' grumbled Miss Jermyn.

'I don't want the old man's shirt,' Billy pouted. 'But if he gives me money I'll take it and go,' he added obligingly.

'You'll stay right where you are,' said Miss Jermyn. 'This is Sir Edmund's house and we all do what he says.'

'And who're you? His gran?'

'I am the children's governess,' said the woman, flushing with indignation. 'Has the boy eaten?' she asked Dolly.

'Not yet. Her Ladyship wants me to take him down to the drawing room for tea.'

'Good heavens!' Miss Jermyn rolled her eyes in horror at the prospect. 'A pig in the drawing room? Whatever next?' She bent down and smelled Billy's breath. 'Just as I thought,' she said. 'Worms.'

'I haven't eaten no worms,' Billy protested.

'You *have* worms, child,' snapped Miss Jermyn. 'They are in your abdomen. Give him a dose of syrup of figs twice a day, Dolly.' And she stalked away.

'Come on, Master Billy. The sooner you're dressed the sooner you can go down and have some tea,' said Dolly, for she had quickly realized the way to the little boy's mind was through his mouth.

'Tea?' Billy's face fell. 'I don't like tea. Pa and Ma drink it sometimes, when they've got enough of the ready, but I don't—'

'Tea isn't just a drink, you goosecap,' said Dolly. 'It's food too.'

'What, like kippers and whelks and pork pies?' said Billy hopefully.

'Don't be soft.' Dolly shook her head. 'The quality don't eat things like that. You'll have bread and butter and strawberry jam and muffins and—'

'Muffins?' cried Billy. He had seen the muffin men walking the streets in the afternoons, going from door to door selling the delicious buns all warm from the oven.

'Toasted?' he said.

Dolly nodded. 'Cut in half, toasted and oozing with lovely butter. And after the muffins, it's nearly

always chocolate cake, cos that's the master's favourite.'

'Come on!' Billy grabbed her hand and pulled her towards the door. 'Plaguy quick, before he scorfs the lot.'

'You can't go to the drawing room –' Dolly lowered her voice to whisper the indelicate word – 'uncovered. You've got to look proper.' And she held up a dress with pearl buttons, short puff sleeves and a lace collar and cuffs.

Billy looked at it with disgust. 'That's girls' stuff,' he said scornfully.

'Boys wear the same clothes as girls until they're big enough to go into necessities,' said Miss Jermyn, coming into the room. 'At least, they do in polite society – not that you'd know anything about that,' she sniffed disdainfully.

'What're nesties?' demanded Billy.

'Necessities are –' Miss Jermyn lowered her voice – 'trousers.'

'Don't worry, we'll make a gentleman of him yet, Miss Jermyn,' said Dolly, putting a pair of frilly pantaloons on him while the governess pulled white socks up to his knees and buttoned little leather shoes on his feet.

'I look sappy,' wailed Billy. 'I'm not goin'.'

'Bread and butter and strawberry jam,' Dolly whispered in his ear. 'And muffins and chocolate cake.'

As if by magic Billy stopped struggling. He held his head still while the nursemaid brushed his hair, exclaiming with delight about his 'beautiful gold curls', and he even allowed Miss Jermyn to tie a satin sash around his waist.

'What a little angel,' sighed Dolly, gazing at him fondly.

'Angel indeed!' sniffed Miss Jermyn. And taking his hand she led him out of the room, across the landing and down two flights of stairs to the drawing room on the first floor. 'And remember,' she said, pausing in front of the door, 'you must be on your *very* best behaviour.'

Billy nodded. He hadn't the faintest idea what behaviour was, but he was quite willing to be on it if it meant he'd get chocolate cake.

'Why, young fellow, you're looking splendid,' said Sir Edmund as Miss Jermyn pushed him into the drawing room. 'I hope everything has gone well so far.'

'Nah, it hasn't,' retorted Billy. 'Dolly tried to push me down the bog and made me sit in water till

my skin went all crinkly and then put these crummy togs on me – and I'm hungry. Where's the chocolate cake?'

'We'll take tea in a while, Billy, but first I'd like you to meet my daughters,' said Sir Edmund, smiling at the seven girls standing in line behind him, all in white dresses with tight bodices and bell-shaped skirts just short enough to show their long, frilly drawers. 'This is Georgiana,' he said, drawing the tallest of them forward.

Georgiana at fifteen was the eldest and prettiest of Sir Edmund's daughters, her glossy chestnut hair gathered in ringlets on either side of her heart-shaped face with its violet eyes and perfectly straight nose. Unfortunately her mouth spoiled the whole effect, a mouth by turns sulky, scornful or imperious, but rarely amiable. The corners of this mouth turned decidedly down now.

'I'm pleased to meet you,' she said, although it was quite obvious she was not, and she put out her hand.

Billy frowned. 'I haven't got nothin',' he said. 'I've not got no money, if that's what you're after.'

The younger girls all started giggling and it was only a reproving look from their father that made them stop.

'Georgiana doesn't want anything from you, Billy,' he explained. 'She just wants to shake your hand.'

'What for?'

'Because it's a polite way to greet people, especially when meeting them for the first time.'

'Why?'

'Oh, never mind. These are Leopoldina, Theodora, Henrietta, Thomasina and Edwardina,' he said, introducing his other daughters. 'They have been looking forward to meeting you, Billy. And this,' he said as the door flew open and another girl ran in, 'is my youngest daughter, Alice. Always late, I'm afraid. What is your excuse today, my love?'

Unlike her sisters, Alice was not a beauty. She was not even pretty. But there was a sparkle in her eyes and a warmth in her smile that set her apart from, and some would have said above, the others, and she was clearly her father's favourite.

'Oh, Papa, I'm so sorry, I was just—'

'Drawing and painting, of course,' said her father, tapping the sketchbook under her arm. 'Never mind, I forgive you, just this once,' he added, pretending to be stern. 'Alice, this is Billy.'

'Have I got to shake hands with her?' said Billy in alarm.

'Not if you don't want to,' Alice laughed. And leaning forward she gave him a kiss.

In normal circumstances Billy would have pushed her roughly away, rubbing furiously at the wet spot on his cheek and protesting that he didn't want any girl mucking about with him and if she tried it again he'd get Jem or Ned to wallop her. But nothing in his life was normal any more and Jem and Ned weren't there. Nevertheless he felt a mild reproach was in order, if only to show Alice that he was not a boy to be kissed whenever the fancy took her, and he was just wrinkling his nose with disgust and opening his mouth to say, 'Ugh!' when the door opened and the butler came in.

'Ah, here's Pole with our tea,' said Sir Edmund.

Norris Pole was a tall, skeletal man with a face carved out of the whitest marble. Within this austere mask the mouth and eyes were mere slits and the eyebrows as pale as straw. As he glided across the floor the temperature in the room seemed to plummet as if an icy wind had suddenly sprung up despite the warmth of the summer's day. The Eden girls shuddered involuntarily and even the haughty Georgiana frowned and stared into her lap as if she was half afraid of the man.

Pole was followed by two footmen, the first

carrying a tray of fine bone-china cups, saucers and plates and gleaming silver cutlery and the other a three-tiered cake stand and a dish of hot buttered muffins. They were barely half way across the room when Billy shot off his chair, snatched a slice of bread, rammed it in his mouth and grabbed a muffin in one hand and a piece of gingerbread in the other.

The butler stared stonily ahead, the footmen blinked in astonishment and Georgiana exclaimed, 'Oh, Mama!' as Billy swallowed the bread, replaced it in his mouth with the muffin and reached out for another one. 'He is so ill-mannered.'

'And so would you be, Georgiana, if you lived in the appalling conditions this poor little fellow has been obliged to endure all his life,' Sir Edmund admonished her.

Georgiana bit her lip, but her expression was one of anger rather than shame.

'Billy, it isn't nice to eat like that, my dear,' said Lady Eden, taking him by the arm and pulling him away from the footman's tray with some difficulty, for the little boy was intent on stuffing his pockets as well as his mouth. 'You should eat one thing at a time – and *slowly*.'

'But I'm hungry,' he whined, spraying her with a mouthful of gingerbread.

'I know you are, my dear, but you'll make your-self sick in a minute. Now I think you should sit down quietly and have a slice of bread and butter. No –' she kept a firm grasp on his shoulder – 'Ralph will bring it to you.' She nodded at the footman, who put a thin slice on a plate, cut it into quarters and gave it to him.

'Say, "thank you",' said Lady Eden.

'Thanks, guv,' said Billy. But before Lady Eden could stop him he had swallowed one piece and filled his mouth with the second.

'Oh dear,' she sighed.

'You see, Mama,' sniffed Georgiana, 'he is quite impossible.'

'Billy, you must chew your food,' Alice said, sitting beside him. 'Chew it with these,' she tapped her very white, very straight teeth. 'Like this.' She picked up a piece of bread, bit off a tiny corner and chewed it very slowly and deliberately.

'Why?' said Billy.

'Because . . .' Alice paused to think. 'Because if you don't you won't get any more.'

'Oh. Oh, right.' Billy nodded. At last somebody had explained it to him in words he understood.

Moving with the speed of a snail on crutches, he lowered his hand over the remaining piece of bread

and butter on his plate, grasped it between his thumb and first finger as Alice had done, brought it to his mouth, inserted his teeth into it — two at the top and three at the bottom, all the others having been knocked out — and proceeded to chew, his jaw moving up and down, up and down for what seemed an eternity, while Sir Edmund and Lady Eden and their daughters watched him as if mesmerized.

'Well done, Billy,' Lady Eden murmured. 'I think you should swallow now.'

'I could chew some more if you want,' said Billy obligingly, his mouth full.

'No, my dear, that's quite enough.'

'Can I have a bit of chocolate cake then?' He pointed to the table.

'No, you may not,' said Lady Eden. 'I think you have had a pleasant sufficiency.' And she nodded at the footman to remove his plate.

Billy was about to erupt into a volcanic tantrum when the door opened and an elderly woman came in followed by a footman carrying a small terrier on a brocade cushion. Immediately everyone in the room, with the exception of Billy, rose to their feet.

'Lady FitzHubert,' announced the parlour maid.

'Good afternoon, Great-aunt Hildegarde,' chanted the girls in unison, bobbing a curtsy.

'Their skirts are too short, Parthenope,' snapped the woman, who was dressed entirely in black, a woollen shawl around her thin shoulders, her silver hair drawn back in a tight bun under her lace and taffeta bonnet. 'A few inches less and I should be able to see their knees. Really!' she huffed at Lady Eden in disgust.

'It is an unexpected pleasure to see you, Aunt,' said Lady Eden through gritted teeth.

'I am not here for my pleasure nor yours, Parthenope. I have been given to understand by servants who listen to gossip –' she glanced at her footman who blinked nervously and shuffled from foot to foot – 'that some villain attempted to steal your sapphire necklace. Is that correct?'

'Yes, Aunt, it is. But fortunately two of our maids disturbed him in the act.'

'And he was apprehended, I assume?'

'No, he escaped.'

'Escaped?'

'He was just a small boy and—'

'A *small boy*?' Lady FitzHubert's eyebrows shot up. 'Are you telling me, Parthenope, that the police were not able to capture a *small boy*?'

'I understand there were others, Aunt. Two men. They fled from the scene in a . . . in a . . .' Lady Eden flushed. Unwilling to offend the elderly lady's ears with vulgar words, she sought for some genteel way of describing the vehicle that Rudd and Jem and his accomplice had escaped in, but before anything appropriate came to mind Alice said, 'In a night-soil cart, Great-aunt. The barrels were full and as the horses galloped away the barrels tipped over and covered everyone with—'

'How are you, dear Aunt?' cut in Sir Edmund, before his daughter could say something excruciating. 'I confess you are looking in excellent health.'

'And more's the pity, you're thinking, no doubt. So you will have to wait a while before you inherit my money, Edmund.'

'Aunt Hildegarde, I assure you I have no desire to—'

'Stuff and nonsense! There is not a man or woman on this earth who does not covet money, as much as they can lay their hands on. And you are no exception.'

Sir Edmund sighed. His aunt was one of life's burdens that he tried to bear bravely. She and her husband, Lord Hubert FitzHubert, were renowned throughout London society for their immense

wealth, which included a diamond tiara that rivalled Queen Victoria's. They were equally famed for their meanness. They ate frugally, dressed in the same clothes they had worn for years, never entertained, never gave gifts, scrutinized and contested every tradesman's bill and treated their servants so shabbily that they came and went in a flash.

It was uncanny that such a miserly man should have met and wed such a tight-fisted woman. A marriage of true minds, everyone agreed. The only bone of contention between them was the dog. Lady FitzHubert loved it. Lord FitzHubert loathed it.

'And how is Uncle Hubert?' enquired Sir Edmund.

'He is also in excellent health, so you can expect nothing from that quarter either.'

Sir Edward turned away, biting his lip. He was a very rich man and had no need of his aunt's money, but the old lady, like many a miser, believed everyone, including her nephew, was as avaricious as she.

'And young Cecil?'

'A weakling, I regret.' Lady FitzHubert frowned. 'And foolish as well.'

Cecil was the only child of Sir Hubert's cousin Thomas and his wife, Anne. In the unlikely event of their premature death Thomas and Anne had asked

Sir Hubert if he would consent to be Cecil's guardian. Since both parents were young and in good health Sir Hubert had agreed to their request, but neither he nor they had allowed for the cholera epidemic of 1831, which took the lives of thousands of people throughout the country, including Thomas and Anne.

And so it was that Cecil had appeared on the FitzHuberts' doorstep looking for shelter. Sir Hubert had been horrified by the unwelcome intrusion. Nevertheless, he was a man of his word. He brought up young Cecil in the way his parents would have wanted and sent him to Eton, an expense that broke his heart.

Unlike his parents, Cecil was of a delicate and nervous disposition and to add to his misfortunes he had developed a pronounced stammer, which had thus far prevented him from finding any form of employment. But he was a very intelligent young man and Sir Hubert had assigned him the task of putting his library in order. As this involved sorting and cataloguing many thousands of books, Cecil spent all his days in the dark, dusty room, his steel-rimmed glasses perched on the end of his nose as he turned page after yellowing page.

Most young men would have been driven mad

by such a confined lifestyle, but Cecil was grateful for a home and glad to be of service to Sir Hubert. He also knew his presence in the gloomy house was not welcome and so he was relieved to find a corner of it where he could hide himself.

'I fear he will be a financial burden on us to the end of our days,' said Lady FitzHubert, curling her lip in disgust at the prospect.

'Will you take tea, Aunt?' said Sir Edmund, who felt nothing but pity for the young man in such a miserable situation.

'I never take tea, Edmund. It is a gluttonous habit. Three meals a day are quite sufficient. But Sir Lancelot has such a tiny interior –' she gazed fondly at the little dog, which had hopped off the cushion and was now running around the room, sniffing everything and snarling at anyone foolish enough to try to stroke him – 'he needs to eat more often. Perhaps a little bread and butter, sliced very thinly, and a sliver of chocolate cake as a treat.'

From the look of Sir Lancelot's very round belly it was obvious he was given frequent treats and Billy, who had been sitting quietly up until that moment, watched with mounting horror as a footman put the bread and cake on a plate for him.

'Nah!' he cried. 'Nah, you're not givin' that grub

to a varminty old fleabag!' And leaping to his feet he grabbed the plate the footman was just bending down to put on the floor and began to ram the food into his mouth.

There was a horrified silence, broken only by Sir Lancelot. Enraged that Billy had taken his treat, he launched himself at the little boy, biting his ankles. Billy retaliated, pushing him roughly away, which sent the dog howling to its mistress.

'I'm so sorry, so sorry, Aunt,' said Sir Edmund as Lady Eden grabbed Billy and pulled him back to his seat. 'Ralph, prepare another plate, please,' he said to the footman.

Lady FitzHubert was almost speechless with anger. 'Did you see . . . ?' she spluttered. 'Did you see what that . . . that boy did to Sir Lancelot? Did you hear what he said? How dare he!'

'I'm sure he is very sorry, Aunt,' said Lady Eden. 'He will, of course, apologize.'

She looked at Billy and waited. Everyone in the room looked at Billy and waited.

'Go on!' whispered Alice in his ear.

'Go on what?' he said, looking perplexed.

'Say you're sorry to Aunt Hildegarde.'

'But I'm not.'

'Billy, if you don't say you're sorry you will not get any more choc—'

'All right, all right.' Billy raised his voice. 'I'm sorry, Aunt Illgard.'

'I accept your apology, child. But kindly do not address me as your aunt. I am most certainly not your aunt. Parthenope,' she said, turning to Lady Eden, 'I assumed this boy was one of *your* relatives or a small friend of your daughters, but I see now that he most certainly is not. Would you kindly explain what a street urchin is doing in your drawing room?'

'We have adopted him, Aunt.'

Lady FitzHubert gasped and clutched at her bosom as if she feared she would faint. 'You mean you intend to raise him as one of your own?'

'Quite so, Aunt.'

Lady FitzHubert put a lorgnette to her eye and stared at Billy as if he was something that had just crept out of the woodwork on eight legs.

'Have you taken leave of your senses, nephew?' she demanded.

'On the contrary, Aunt. Billy is a very welcome addition to our family,' said Sir Edmund, waving the little boy forward.

'Have I got to shake her hand?' asked Billy, look-

ing doubtfully at the old woman's leathery hands in their black lace mittens.

'Certainly not,' she retorted. 'You may be bathed and dressed in the manner of a young gentleman, but I have no doubt that beneath the veneer you harbour one or more of the loathsome diseases with which your kind are always afflicted. Come closer, boy.' She put her lorgnette to her eye again and studied his face intently. 'Yes, yes,' she murmured, 'you have the face of an angel but the heart of a devil.'

'And you've got a face like a monkey's bum,' retorted Billy, sticking his tongue out at her.

'Mark my words, Edmund,' said Lady FitzHubert, pointedly ignoring the helping hand her nephew offered as she rose stiffly to her feet, 'this gutter urchin will bring you nothing but grief.'

8

Ma cried so much she could hardly eat her supper that night.

'I'll have it,' said Jem, eyeing it ravenously, for a bowl of watery soup with half a potato and a few carrots had done little to assuage his hunger pangs.

'Nah, you won't, you little guts. You're gettin' to be as bad as Billy . . . Oh, Billy, my Billy, I do miss him,' Ma wailed, bursting into tears again.

'Don't take on so, Liza,' said Pa. 'You'll wake that brat up,' he nodded at Mother Murray's baby, 'and I've had enough of her squallin'.'

'It's *his* fault Billy's gone.' Ma rounded on Jem angrily. 'He made him go. He said—'

'Jem did it for the best, Liza, you know that,' Pa admonished her.

'Bert's right, Liza,' said Gran. 'If Jem hadn't told Billy about the grub, he'd never have gone. He'd be here now, eatin' this –' she looked at the miserable contents of her chipped bowl – "stead of scorfin' a

nice bit of beefsteak oozin' with blood, bacon sizzlin' in fat, kidneys floatin' in cream, lumps of fried fish and—'

'Shut up, Gran,' Ned muttered as his stomach grunted and gurgled.

'And a plum duff with loads of plums in it and jam roly-poly and—'

'Gran!'

'The way I see it, Jem did Billy a big favour, makin' him go,' said Gran. 'At least one of us'll go to bed tonight with a full belly.'

Ma heaved a big sigh and dried her eyes on the hem of her skirt. 'You're right,' she said. 'Billy's struck lucky. I'm sorry, my pet.' She put an arm around Jem's shoulders and gave him a hug. 'I shouldn't've said what I did. From now on whenever I think of Billy I'll think of him eatin' somethin' golopshus like kippers and periwinkles and . . .'

'Pork pies,' sighed Jem, drooling at the thought.

'Yeh,' Ma grinned at him. 'Pork pies.'

9

Seated at the table in the day nursery with the five younger Eden girls, Billy ate a supper of hot milk and arrowroot biscuits under the stern eye of Miss Jermyn. Although he still wore a dress, much to his chagrin, the girls had changed into plainer clothes with long white aprons and sat bolt upright, eating and drinking in silence.

Alice, who had made a point of sitting next to Billy, whispered to him, 'You're my adopted brother now.'

'What's 'dopted?' he said.

'It means you won't live with your papa and mama any more.'

'Yeh, I will.'

'No, you won't. You'll stay here with us for ever and ever.'

'Miss Alice!' the governess said sharply. 'How many times must I tell you that young ladies do not chatter at the table.'

'I wasn't chattering, Miss Jermyn, I was talking. And Mama always talks at the table. She talks a lot. I heard her the other evening when the Duke of Wellington came to dinner.'

'Miss Alice, how dare you contradict me!'

The little girl bowed her head and murmured, 'Sorry, Miss Jermyn.'

'That old fogey's the spit of my Uncle Sid,' said Billy in his high-pitched voice. 'He's got a lot of black bristles here —' he patted the space above his lips — 'and some up his nose and in his ears. Just like her.'

'The hairs above the lip are called a moustache,' Alice said helpfully.

'Miss Alice!' The governess was quivering with rage.

'But I was just telling Billy the correct word, Miss Jermyn,' protested the little girl in an aggrieved voice. 'Papa said we should teach him to speak properly.'

'Dolly,' Miss Jermyn turned to the nursemaid who was standing by the door waiting to clear the table, 'take Master Billy to his room, please.'

'But I want another biscuit,' he said.

'Dolly!'

'Yes, miss. Come along, Master Billy,' said the

nursemaid, dragging him from his seat as he struggled and screamed.

'Girls?' Miss Jermyn raised her eyebrows at them.

'Goodnight, Billy,' they chanted in unison.

'And what do you say, Master Billy?'

'Want another biscuit! Want another biscuit!' he yelled all the way to his room.

'Listen to me, Master Billy,' said Dolly, closing the door behind her and taking him firmly by the shoulders, 'you won't get anything if you keep making that hullabaloo. Now stop it,' she said, dabbing his cheeks with a handkerchief as the tears welled up in his eyes. 'Little gentlemen don't cry.'

'I don't like it here,' sobbed Billy. 'I want to go home.'

'You can.'

'No, I can't. I can't never go home. Alice said so.'

'Well, Miss Alice was wrong.'

'You mean I can?'

'Yes.'

Billy stopped in mid-sob. 'When?'

'Right now, if you like. Of course, you'll miss breakfast, which is a pity, cos Her Ladyship said she wants you to grow big and strong so you're to have – I mean you were *going* to have porridge and eggs and bread and butter. And then there's roast beef and boiled potatoes and steamed pudding for dinner and I happen to know Cook's making a sponge cake filled with raspberry jam for tea. But I'd best go down now and tell Her Ladyship you're leaving.'

'Nah!' Billy yelped, clinging to her knees like a monkey to a branch. 'Nah, I want to stay! Want to stay!'

'Very well. But you must do what you're told, especially when Miss Jermyn tells you.' Dolly bent down and put her arms around him. 'She's a right old crab,' she said in a softer voice, 'but she's the governess and you and me have got to obey her or we'll be in trouble. Now come along, my treasure, let's get you into bed.'

'I don't want to go to bed.'

'You must. It's late.'

Billy had no idea how to tell the time, but he did know that when the sun went down it was night and when it came up it was day and it was definitely day now for the sunshine was still pouring through the window. He was about to explain this to the nursemaid when she said, 'The sooner you go to bed and fall asleep, the sooner it'll be breakfast.'

Since the logic of her argument heavily

outweighed his, Billy allowed her to remove his dress and pantaloons and put him in a long white nightshirt of finest linen and a matching bonnet.

'Jem always wears his hat in bed,' he said as Dolly tied the bonnet strings under his chin. 'He wears a wideawake.'

'That's very sensible of him.' She nodded approvingly. 'It must keep his head nice and warm.'

'Nah, he wears it so's his fleas can't jump about.'

'Well, there are no fleas here,' laughed Dolly. 'Now, kneel down and we'll say prayers.'

'What are prayers?'

'Prayers are . . . They're . . . Well, they're talking to God.'

'Who's God?'

'He's Our Father.'

'Nah, my pa's called Bert.'

'Not *your* father, *Our* Father – the father of everyone.'

'You mean we've got two?'

'That's right.'

'Where's the other one live?'

Dolly pointed at the ceiling. 'Now put your hands like this,' she said, pressing her palms together over her heart, 'and close your eyes – no, close them proper! Right, now say after me, "Our Father, which—"'

'Lor', is he a witch?' said Billy. 'My gran's a witch too. She can do magic spells that really work – well, some of them do sometimes. And she can make lucky charms out of bits of old tin and she can tell fortunes. If you crossed her palm with silver she'd tell you you were goin' to marry a tall, handsome stranger who's filthy rich . . . It's true,' he insisted as Dolly made to silence him, 'she tells all the bone-heads the same thing, I've heard her.'

'Be quiet,' Dolly frowned, 'we're supposed to be praying not chattering about your gran. "Our Father, which art in heaven—"'

'I thought you said he lived upstairs.'

'Don't be silly, he lives in heaven.'

Billy had never heard of a place called Heaven, but then there were lots of places in London he'd never heard of. It would a good idea to tell Jem and Ned about their other father though, he thought, so they could go over to Heaven and touch him for a bob or two.

'Hallowed be thy name – Master Billy, are you listening to me? Hallowed be thy name. Thy king-dom come, thy will be done on earth as it is in heaven. Give us this day our daily bread—'

Billy perked up. 'And pork pies,' he said eagerly.

'And forgive us our trespasses . . .'

'And a pork pie. Ask him if he's got any pork pies.'

'. . . As we forgive them that trespass against us. For thine is the kingdom the power and the glory for ever and ever amen,' Dolly rushed on before the little boy could say anything else blasphemous. And lifting him into bed she covered him with innumerable horse-hair blankets, despite the warmth of the evening. 'If you need to answer a call of nature in the night, the convenience is under the bed,' she said, reaching behind the valance and producing a pottery chamber pot decorated with the Eden family coat of arms. 'Now go to sleep, my pet,' she said, giving him a big hug and several kisses.

When she had gone Billy lay for a long time gazing out the window as the branches of a horse-chestnut tree in the garden swung up and down and back and forth in the breeze. There were a lot of good things about living with the Edens, he thought, like food, and plenty of it, and a warm bed and Dolly and Alice, and some bad things like baths and silly clothes and Miss Jermyn and Georgiana. And as for not using words like blimey and bum and

bog – Barmy. Plain barmy. Jem and Ned used them all the time.

In his mind's eye he imagined his brothers in the Strand at that moment, Jem telling far-fetched stories to try to prise money out of gullible people or stealing a pie or piece of fried fish off a stall and eating it quickly in a back alley before he and Ned were caught.

Billy's eyes filled with tears. 'Jem,' he sighed. 'Ned.' And then, 'Ma . . .'

At the thought of his mother he began to cry. But just when he was going at it in earnest another thought struck him – he could go home; he could go home right that minute if he wanted to. Dolly had said so.

This cheered him up so much that he snuggled down under the blankets, his head sinking into the soft goose-feather pillow, and after a while he came to a sensible decision: much as he wanted to see his mother and father again, and Gran and his brothers, he would not go back yet, not until his belly was really full and he stopped feeling hungry. That might take a day or two, he realized, or a week, or even a bit longer, but he would definitely go home eventually.

Having contented himself with that, he fell into

a deep sleep and dreamed he was going to have porridge with fresh, creamy milk and boiled eggs and
bread and butter for breakfast — and woke up in the
morning to discover it was true.

10

As well as telling fortunes and making magic spells, Gran considered herself skilled in the healing arts.

'I've been thinkin', Bert,' she said, looking at Pa thoughtfully as he lay on his back, groaning. 'I reckon leeches would make you better.'

'Nah,' said Pa. 'Fruit only makes me feel worse. 'Sides, we can't afford them.'

'I said leeches, not peaches. They're like worms, only fatter.'

'Like eels, you mean?' Pa perked up. Eels were his favourite food.

'You don't eat leeches, Bert, you put them on your body and they take away the badness.'

'You pullin' my leg?' chuckled Pa. 'How can a load of worms . . . ?'

'Leeches've got teeth, big'uns, and they bite you and suck the badness out of your blood.'

'Whoa!' cried Pa in alarm. 'I'm not havin' no worms suckin' my belly.'

'Ma Rivers says her youngest worked for a toff and he had ulcers on his legs and they put leeches on them and he got better. All over him they were, she said, drinkin' his blood like you and me'd knock back a pint of porter.'

Pa sat up abruptly. 'Now listen to me,' he said, wagging a stern finger at his mother. 'My belly is not a pub for leeches. If they want to drink blood they can find another bar.'

'Where d'you reckon we'll get some?' Ma asked Gran.

'Well, since they're like worms, it stands to reason they live in the ground.'

'I've never seen no worms in Devil's Acre.'

'That's cos there's no earth, Liza.'

Gran was right. There was not one bit of earth in Devil's Acre – it was all cobblestone roads and dusty pavements. But just a short walk from the dismal slum were elegant houses surrounding squares filled with trees, bushes and shrubs.

'We'll wait till it's dark, Liza,' said Gran. 'We don't want no one seein' us. Them toffs can get very snaggy if you so much as look at their stuff.'

'But they don't own the leeches and worms, Gran.'

'Nah, but they own the ground the leeches and worms live in.'

'What're you up to?' asked Jem, coming awake as his mother crept out of the caravan in the early hours of the morning, carrying the pot she used to cook gruel in.

'Never you mind,' she whispered, motioning him back to sleep.

She stole down the steps of the caravan and stood at the bottom waiting for Gran. Gran's caravan was in the far corner, but Ma made a point of not looking at it, pretending it didn't exist. It still irked her that Gran had asked for and received a brand-new caravan from a wealthy benefactor when all Ma had got was a bonnet with frills and ribbons. But what really vexed her was that Gran wouldn't allow the rest of her family in or near it – 'Cos they'll only make it dirty,' she said.

'As if she ever cared about dirt,' fumed Ma, as Gran tottered towards her, wrapping a threadbare shawl around her shoulders.

The two women stole through the streets, staying close together.

'Lucky it's cloudy so's no one can see us,' whispered Ma. 'Here we are,' she said, turning into a

large, tree-lined square. 'I'll wager there'll be plenty of the little darlin's in this ground,' she said, peering through the iron railings. 'But how're we goin' to get them?'

'Easy,' chuckled Gran. 'I'll just shin up this—'

'Nah, you won't!' protested Ma, dragging her back. 'A woman your age can't climb railings.' And hauling up her skirts, Ma clambered over the top, landing heavily in the middle of a flower bed. 'Crikey!' she exclaimed, peering into the under-growth, 'we don't need to do no diggin', Gran. There are dozens, hundreds of leeches here.' And bending down she quickly filled her pan.

'Let me see! Let me see!' Gran said eagerly as Ma clambered back. 'Oh nah, Liza.' Her face fell as she looked at the writhing bodies in the pan. 'Them're not leeches, you ninny. They're slugs.'

'Well, how was I to know?' grumbled Ma. 'It was dark in there, very dark, and they—'

'Oy! What do you think you're doing? That's private property.'

'Nah, don't cop us, guv,' Gran pleaded as a uniformed figure hurried towards them waving his truncheon. 'We were lookin' for leeches for my son that's been taken poorly, but all we could find was these pesky slugs.'

She held out the pan for him to see.

'Slugs! Ugh! Varminty things!' said the police-man. 'My brother's got a bit of land and he says they eat everything – his lettuces, his watercresses, his cabbages, his cauli—'

'So where can we get leeches?' said Gran, who was not interested in a tour of his brother's allot-ment.

'From a doctor, of course.'

'A quack?' Gran's said in dismay. 'But we don't have no money to *buy* them.'

'Then you won't get any, will you?' said the policeman gruffly. 'Now move along or I'll run you both in for damaging these gardens.'

When they got back to the caravan Pa was fast asleep, and since it was a hot night he had thrown aside the tatty strip of cloth that passed as a blanket, revealing his huge belly.

'What do you reckon?' Ma said, looking at the slugs doubtfully.

'It can't do no harm to give them a try, Liza,' said Gran. 'That crusher said they eat everything, so they might do a better job than leeches.'

'You're right,' agreed Ma. 'Quick as you can then. We don't want to wake Bert.'

'Wake him?' said Gran incredulously. 'Lawks a mercy, Liza, the way he's snorin' he wouldn't hear it if the whole of the Russian army came marchin' through here with hobnail boots on.'

Nevertheless the two women moved stealthily, covering Pa's belly with dozens of slimy slugs, for they knew if he woke up he would definitely not cooperate.

Now, slugs are greedy. Having thoroughly explored the vast expanse of Pa's abdomen they set off in search of food in more promising areas – Pa's navel, his groin, his armpits, his ears and his nostrils.

He woke at dawn with a strange tickling sensation in his mouth.

'What the devil . . . ?' he exclaimed, spitting out one of the more adventurous slugs, which had been gliding towards his tonsils, leaving a silvery path in its wake. 'Get the varminty things off me! Get them off!' he roared, scraping them from his body by the handful and hurling them at Ma and Gran.

'Now don't get snaggy, Bert,' said Gran, catching them and putting them back in the gruel pot.

'You feelin' better, my tulip?' said Ma, bending over him anxiously.

'Nah, I am not. And if you ever do that again, I'll . . . !'

'All right, all right, we were only doin' it for the best, Bert. We thought slugs'd be as good as leeches.'

'Seems a pity to waste them, Liza,' murmured Gran, looking in the gruel pot. 'Wonder what they taste like?'

'Golopshus, I'd say. There's a lot of meat on them.' Ma picked one up and gave it a good squeeze. 'And no bones.'

'They'd probably do Bert good,' Gran whispered in her ear.

'Yeh.' Ma nodded. 'I'll make him a nice, juicy stew.'

11

Jem and Ned woke at dawn, stretched their aching bodies after a night on the caravan floor, ate a Spartan breakfast of watery gruel and a piece of dry bread and set off for their day's work. While Ma took Mother Murray's baby and sat on the steps of the National Gallery, pleading with passers-by to give a few coins to a poor widow woman whose only child was dying of typhoid, Jem and Ned went to see Billy.

They were ambling along Arlington Street, past the elegant four- and five-storey mansions, when the door of one opened and a liveried and powdered footman came out leading a small over-fed terrier, followed by an elderly woman dressed entirely in black, a woollen shawl around her shoulders, her silver hair drawn back in a tight bun under a lace cap.

'Be very careful with Sir Lancelot, Maurice,' she cautioned the footman. 'Do not let him out of your sight.'

'I won't, M'Lady,' he replied.

'Mama would be heartbroken if she lost her little darling, wouldn't she?' cooed the woman, bending down with some difficulty to stroke the little dog, which immediately began to yap in an ear-piercing way. 'Off you go then, my precious,' she simpered, kissing the ball of hair tenderly. 'Mama will be waiting for you. Do not be long, Maurice,' she said to the footman. 'I do not want Sir Lancelot to catch a chill.'

'Very well, M'Lady,' said the footman. And he led the noisy little dog up the street while its mistress waved her handkerchief in fond farewell.

'Let's follow him,' Jem whispered to Ned.

'Why? I thought we were goin' to see Billy.'

'We can see him later, after we've done this job.'

'What job?'

'Nabbin' the dog.'

'Nah.' Ned pushed him away. 'Nah, I don't think we should do that.'

'Why not?'

'Cos that old woman's spoony on it.'

'That's why we're goin' to nab it, you stupe. I reckon she'll cough up anythin' to get it back.'

But Ned was still troubled. 'How're we goin' to nick it?' he said. 'That bloke's holdin' on to it like it's the Crown jewels.'

But luck was on their side, though not on the dog's that morning, for as soon as the footman went into Green Park a pretty young woman in a maid's uniform ran up to him.

It soon became apparent that the young couple knew each other well, for they strolled along hand in hand, gazing into each other's eyes. The dog, which had clearly been expecting a brisk walk rather than a leisurely stroll, began yapping hysterically and taking nips at the young woman's ankles.

'Oh, Maurice,' she cried, springing away, 'stop him. He's hurting me.'

Muttering angrily, the footman tied the dog to a tree, told it to, 'Shut up!' – a command it ignored – and walked away with his girlfriend, his arm around her waist, with never a backward glance.

'Anyone watchin' us?' said Jem, sauntering towards the dog, doing his best to look nonchalant.

Ned shook his head. Apart from a herd of cows that cropped the grass or stood chewing the cud, there was no other creature on two legs or four in Green Park at that early hour.

Quickly Jem untied the dog, stuffed it under his jacket and walked away.

'We'd best get it home plaguy quick, before them two come back and find it gone,' he said.

'Pa won't like it,' warned Ned. 'He says all dogs do is nick your grub.'

'Pa'll like this one when we get the reward . . . Don't start runnin',' Jem hissed as they turned into Piccadilly, 'or people'll know we're up to something – Ouch, now the pesky varmint's gone and bit me!' he exclaimed as Sir Lancelot, enraged at being conveyed in such an unseemly manner, sank his teeth into Jem's ribcage. 'Here, you carry it, Ned.'

'Nah.' Ned backed away. 'Nickin' it was your idea. You carry it.'

'Fair enough,' said Jem airily. 'I reckon we'll get a few quid from that sappy old haybag for it, but since it was my idea and you won't do nothin' to help I'll keep the money for myself.'

'Oh, all right,' Ned conceded sulkily. 'I'll carry it.'

12

The Eden girls ate what was considered to be a plain and wholesome breakfast for children of the middle and upper classes – porridge with salt and a little watered-down milk, followed by a thin slice of bread with a meagre scrape of butter. They watched, trying hard not to drool, as Billy tucked into porridge with creamy milk fresh from the cow that morning and boiled eggs newly laid by obliging hens on nearby farms, followed by bread and a generous helping of butter with raspberry jam.

'Why is Billy allowed to have such lovely things, Miss Jermyn?' asked Alice, looking longingly at the golden yolk of his egg.

'Because Master Billy is undernourished – that means he has not enjoyed the benefit of nutritious food to develop his body,' explained the governess, glaring at him as he wiped his mouth on his sleeve. 'In my opinion it is a mistake. Such children when they grow big and strong cause nothing but trouble,'

she said sniffily, 'but I must do as Her Ladyship requests . . . And where are you going, Master Billy?' she said as he got down from the table in the day nursery and headed for the door.

'Out.'

Ever since he could remember he had got up, eaten his breakfast, gone out on the streets and stayed there with Jem and Ned until they went back to the caravan at night. 'I'm goin' to see if I can make a bit of the ready. I might do wheels in the Square or gull some rich old fogey,' he said chattily while the Eden girls stared at him, their mouths agape, 'or nick someone's purse or—'

'Stealing is a sin, Master Billy,' thundered the governess. 'And sinners go to hell.'

Hell was another place Billy had never heard of.

'Is it near heaven?' he asked.

'It most certainly is not. Hell is down there.' She pointed to the floor. 'A place of everlasting torment, of agony, a fiery furnace of searing heat,' she said, warming to the subject.

'I think she means the kitchen,' Alice whispered in Billy's ear. 'It's always hot in there.'

'You must promise me, Master Billy, that you will never cheat or steal again, never even think about it,' said the governess sternly.

Billy was about to say, 'Don't be a stupe!' when he remembered Dolly's warning that he should obey the governess or he would be in trouble – and trouble could only mean that she would cut him off from his food supply. And it was only for a short time, he reasoned, just a few weeks until his belly was as fat as a pig's and then he'd be back on the street again with his brothers.

'All right.' He nodded.

The Eden girls let out a collective sigh of relief. A confrontation with Miss Jermyn was something to be avoided at all costs for she had a vicious temper and could, and frequently did, make all their lives a misery if one of them upset her.

'Go and sit over there with Alice.' The governess pointed to a small table in the corner while the other girls took their places around the big table. 'We shall begin our day with an art class,' she said as breakfast dishes were cleared away and replaced by slates and coloured crayons.

'Oh good,' Alice whispered in Billy's ear, 'I love drawing and painting, don't you?'

'I want you to pay particular attention to the petals of this flower,' said the governess, holding up a single rose in a blue vase. 'Notice how the edges curl gently as they open out, the delicate shading from pale pink to a deeper shade of – Master Billy, do not put the crayons in your mouth. They are not edible. Now, children, you may begin,' she said, putting the vase on the window sill.

Immediately all the girls picked up their crayons and, staring intently at the rose, began to draw it. Billy watched them, perplexed. He had seen street artists at work, men down on their knees drawing pictures on the pavement, usually of famous people like Queen Victoria or Prince Albert or the Duke of Wellington. Sometimes they drew funny pictures of clowns and monkeys and people gathered round, laughing. But the artists' intent was always serious – they wanted money, and the better their pictures the more money they made. So why, Billy wondered, were the Eden girls doing it? Nobody would see their pictures, nobody was going to give them any money – they didn't even need it.

The little boy sighed. The ways of the gentry were very odd, not to say downright ridiculous, and it seemed a sad waste of a summer's morning to be sitting on a hard chair in a dull nursery drawing a silly flower, but if it meant he'd get roast beef and boiled potatoes for dinner . . . He picked up a crayon, drew a pink blob and attached it by a wobbly black line to a blue blob, which was supposed to be the

vase. Not surprisingly, this masterpiece took no more than a minute to achieve.

He glanced at Alice. She was bent over her slate, her tongue pressed between her lips, her brow furrowed in concentration.

'Alice . . .' He nudged her. But she frowned and edged away.

Billy looked around, wondering how to fill the time until all the girls had finished. There was nothing to play with, since all the toys were locked in a cupboard, and nothing but watery landscapes to look at on the whitewashed walls. He was just about to nudge Alice again when his eye came to rest on Miss Jermyn, who was sitting at a desk by the window, writing. He would draw her, he decided. She would like that. He might even get another biscuit for it at supper. And rubbing out the rose on his slate with his sleeve he began to draw the governess's profile.

13

Horace Stephens was a screever. Born into a poor but law-abiding family who valued respectability above all other virtues, he had joined a firm of solicitors when he left school and worked for some years as a clerk. Unfortunately he did not share his family's veneration for respectability and having forged a client's will in his own favour he was arrested and sentenced to five years' hard labour.

With a prison sentence and no references, he had little hope of finding work of the legitimate kind, and so in recent years he could be found on the top floor of a seedy lodging house in Westminster, busily writing for the wrong side of the law. For a price he would write anything, in a beautiful copperplate hand. For begging letters he charged between sixpence and ninepence. For bogus certificates, petitions, letters of reference, et cetera, the tariff was one to three shillings, depending on the length and difficulty of the document.

Since the majority of men and women living in London's slums could neither read nor write, Horace Stephens's services were much in demand and he was a wealthy man, or would have been if he had not downed a bottle of gin and innumerable tankards of porter every day.

'I imagine you require a letter to the distressed owner of a missing dog,' he said, wincing as Jem and Ned came into his rooms with Sir Lancelot barking himself hoarse.

Jem nodded. 'Nicked it from a toff who lives just off Piccadilly,' he said. 'Sappy about it, they are. I reckon they'll give anythin' to get it back.'

'Hmm . . .' Stephens looked at the dog thoughtfully. 'In the circumstances, I recommend you ask for two pounds.'

'Right you are.' Jem grinned.

'And the letter will cost you one shilling.'

'A shillin'? You only charged Ma a penny for that sign she put on her tray.'

'I did that as a favour, since your father is kind enough to convey me to my lodgings from the Dog and Bacon when I am feeling unwell.'

'Yeh, well, the next time you're too boozy to walk home I'll tell Pa not to carry you,' said Jem

defiantly. 'Sixpence. I'll give you sixpence – when I get the ready from them toffs.'

With an angry gesture the screever took a sheet of paper, dipped his quill pen into an inkwell and said, 'To whom shall I address the letter? The name, boy, the name!'

'I don't know.' Jem shrugged.

'Then I had better address it to Your Lordship. If he is a lord he'll be satisfied, and if he isn't he'll be flattered.'

'Why don't you send it to his missus?' asked Ned. 'She's the one who's sweet on the dog.'

'Because the master of the house is the one who holds the purse strings,' said the screever. 'A woman has no money of her own. "Your Lordship,"' he wrote, saying the words aloud, '"it is with the deepest regret that I inform you that your beloved pet . . ." What's the dog's name?'

'Sir Somethin',' said Jem.

'Sir Larkalot,' said Ned, who had a good ear for names.

'. . . "that your beloved pet Sir Lancelot is in the possession of ruthless criminals. For the modest sum of two pounds I am willing to persuade these scoundrels to release the dog. Be so good as to leave the money . . ." Where do you want him to leave it?'

'In the bushes in Green Park,' said Jem.

The screever shook his head. 'It must be a place where you won't get caught by the police or the man's servants.'

'Well . . . er . . . Oh, I know. Tell him to leave it at Uncle Arthur's stall in the market. He sells taters.'

'"Be so good as to leave the money at Arthur Perkinski's potato stall in Covent Garden market,"' wrote the screever, '"after which I assure Your Lordship that your cherished pet will be restored safely into your keeping. Should you attempt to apprehend me, however, I regret that Sir Lancelot will meet an untimely and painful end. Your most humble and obedient servant, Constance Mugsmith."'

'Constance Mugsmith?' frowned Ned. 'Who's she?'

'It's my little joke, gentlemen,' said the screever, folding the letter into four and sealing it with wax. 'The shortened version of the name is Cons Mugs.'

'Jammy!' cried Jem. And he and Ned fell about laughing.

14

It has to be said that Miss Jermyn was not an attractive woman. Her skin was sallow, her eyebrows met in the middle and her nose . . . it was the kind of nose that sets out determinedly from the face but realizes, after an inch or two, that it is going in quite the wrong direction and promptly turns sharply downwards, screeching to a halt within a whisker – or, in Miss Jermyn's case, many whiskers – of the owner's top lip. It was, in short, a nose to be reckoned with.

Billy, inspired by his subject, put a great deal more effort into Miss Jermyn's nose than he had her rose and he was just adding a few more bristles to her moustache when she said, 'You may stop there, children. I should like to see what you have done. Miss Theodora, please.'

One by one the girls went up and presented their work for the governess's inspection.

'Hmm, the colours are rather too bright, Miss Henrietta . . . The vase is quite the wrong shape,

Miss Thomasina . . . The stem is much too thick, Miss Edwardina . . .'

While the governess commented on her sisters' pictures, Alice finished her own. Well satisfied, she sat back waiting her turn and glanced at Billy's slate.

Her eyes opened wide and her mouth fell open.

'Oh, Billy!' she gasped. 'Oh, Billy, why did you do that?'

Before he could answer, the governess called in an imperious voice, 'Master Billy, bring your work here, please.'

Billy was upset. He had done a magnificent like-ness of the governess, in his opinion, as good as any street artist could have done, but Alice was gabbling frantically in his ear that he would be punished for it. He slid down in his chair, his lower lip beginning to tremble.

'Come along, Master Billy,' snapped the gov-erness. 'You are keeping me waiting.'

'Here, take mine,' said Alice, thrusting her slate into his hand and pushing him forward.

Miss Jermyn's face fell when she saw it. Clearly disappointed that he had done so well, she pursed her lips and said grudgingly, 'It is better than I would have expected. Miss Alice, please bring me

yours now. Miss Alice!' she barked as the little girl
hesitated.

There was nothing for Alice to show her but
Billy's picture and picking it up she crossed the
room, her eyes glued to the floor, and put it on Miss
Jermyn's desk.

The woman leaned forward to look at it.

Her mouth opened. And closed. And opened
again. But no sound came out.

Alice's sisters stared at her accusingly. What terrible thing had she done to upset the governess so
much that she looked as if she was about to explode?

'I have never been so insulted in my whole life,'
she exclaimed, finally regaining her powers of
speech. 'The outrage! The outrage! Your mama and
papa shall hear of this.'

15

There was probably no dog in London more spoilt than Sir Lancelot. Apart from a short walk morning and evening, he spent his entire life on a satin cushion at Lady FitzHubert's feet, filling his rapidly expanding stomach with all manner of delicacies from smoked salmon to sponge cakes. He lived in a gilded cage and nothing, it seemed, would ever release him from the monotony of it . . . And then he was kidnapped.

At first Devil's Acre was rather a shock to his system. Where was his cushion with his name embroidered on it in letters of gold? Where the tasty titbits constantly fed him by his doting mistress? But within minutes of his arrival in the squalid courtyard in Westminster where the Perkinskis lived surrounded by piles of garbage and manure he began to feel happier than he had ever been before.

For a start there were other dogs – mangy,

starving creatures, who hadn't the strength to put up a fight when Sir Lancelot challenged them, and in no time at all he had seen them off and established himself as not just the top dog but the only dog in Devil's Acre.

And then there were the cats. He had seen them, dozens of them, when the footman took him for walks. They sat on walls or window sills, jeering at him as he went by. How he longed to get at them, to wipe the insolent grins off their smug faces. But always the wretched leash held him back, that and a stern voice saying, 'No, Sir Lancelot. No! Bad dog!' As if chasing a cat could ever be bad.

But in Devil's Acre it was different. He terrorized cats, chasing them over walls and through drainpipes. Some, the older ones, fierce toms that stalked around as if they owned the place, put up a fight, hissing and slashing at him with their claws. But Sir Lancelot wasn't named after the bravest knight of the Round Table for nothing. With commendable dedication he routed every tabby and tortoiseshell.

And then there were the rats and mice . . .

'Will somebody stop that blasted cur!' bellowed Pa. 'It's makin' enough of a shindy to wake the dead.

Why did you have to bring it back here?' He rounded on Jem angrily.

'I keep tellin' you, Pa, we're goin' to get a lot of the ready from his owner. They'll pay anythin' to get him back.'

'And I'd pay anythin' to get rid of him . . . Oy! Get off, you little devil!' he yelled as Sir Lancelot sank his sharp teeth into Pa's ankle.

The ransom letter was delivered to the house on Arlington Street under cover of darkness and the two brothers hurried back to the caravan, where they spent a restless night – Jem excited, Ned terrified.

'They'll put us in clink or ship us to Australie if they catch us,' he whispered time and again. 'We shouldn't have 'arf-inched that dog. We shouldn't have—'

'I keep tellin' you we won't get caught,' said Jem. 'All we got to do is—'

'Cheese it!' snapped Pa. 'What with that brat squallin' and the varminty dog barkin' and you two chatterin', I might as well go and kip in Trafalgar Square. I reckon it'd be a lot quieter.'

*

Although the sun came up early in June, Jem and Ned were out of bed and on the way to Covent Garden well before dawn. The market was still quiet when they arrived, although a few costermongers were already there, including Uncle Arthur.

Jem told him of his plan to collect the ransom, and Uncle Arthur listened attentively. 'You'll help us, won't you?' pleaded Jem.

'Course I will,' said Uncle Arthur, clearly offended that they would doubt it. 'You're my brother's kids. What kind of a bloke would I be if I didn't help my own flesh and blood, eh? How much're you touchin' this toff for his dog?'

'Two quid.'

'That's the ticket!' Uncle Arthur grinned. 'So just give me one.'

'*One quid?*' cried Jem, aghast. 'But, Uncle Arthur—'

'Nah, nah, I don't care what you say, I won't take more, I'm not a greedy man. Now go and stand there, behind them.' He pointed to a pile of porters' baskets. 'And don't come out till I tell you.'

'D'you think we'll have to wait long?' asked Ned, crouching down behind the baskets.

'Nah, the old crone'll be screamin' her head off for her little darlin',' chuckled Jem. 'I reckon someone'll be here any minute to cough up the ready and get it back.'

But he was wrong. It was almost mid-morning and the market was full of traders and customers when Jem nudged Ned and said, 'There he is!' as a footman came in and looked around. 'And he's got it! He's got the ready!' he exulted, seeing the letter in the footman's hand.

'He's seen Uncle Arthur's stall,' said Ned excitedly. 'He's goin' over to it.'

'He's puttin' the letter on the stall. He's – Oy, now what?' Jem exclaimed as a dozen or more market boys appeared, surrounding the stall and clamouring for potatoes. The footman, who was caught in the middle of the hubbub, looked taken aback, but regaining his composure he pushed aside the screaming urchins and walked away.

As soon as the man was out of sight Uncle Arthur gave each of the children the smallest, mouldiest potato he could find and told them to, 'Hook it!' Then he signalled to Jem and Ned.

'That's rum,' he said as they approached. 'That's real rum, that is.'

'What is?' said Jem.

'I thought there'd be a trap. I thought the crushers'd come. That's why I got all them kids here, so's

I could slip one of them this –' he pulled from his pocket the letter the footman had left and gave it to Jem – 'if the crushers tried to cop me. But they didn't. That's rum.'

'It's cos they didn't want nothin' to happen to the dog,' explained Jem.

'Nah.' Uncle Arthur shook his head. 'Toffs don't think like that. Their money's more important to them than any dog.'

'Open it, Jem,' Ned urged him. 'Open it plaguy quick.'

'Nah, Pa said he wanted to open it.'

'You off your chump?' Ned was aghast. 'Soon as Pa sees all that money he'll—'

'I got to, Ned. I promised him.'

'Right. Well, just remember you owe me a quid,' said Uncle Arthur, looking very put out that he wasn't getting his payment there and then. 'And it'll go up by a penny a day, so the sooner you cough up the better.'

Jem nodded and cut up a side street, where he ducked into a doorway and, glancing over his shoulder to make sure nobody was watching, opened the letter.

'Oy!' cried Ned. 'I thought you said you'd promised Pa . . .'

'Don't be a mug,' Jem retorted. 'If I'd opened it in front of Uncle Arthur he'd have pinched the lot. But you can run back and give him his quid and then we'll split the rest between us,' he said, breaking the wax seal on the letter and opening it.

'But we'll give Pa some, won't we?' said Ned anxiously.

'Course we will, we'll give him . . . Oh!' Jem's face fell.

'What? What's wrong?'

'There's no money in here – just a bit of paper with writin' on it.'

'What does it say?' asked Ned eagerly, peering over his brother's shoulder at the copperplate writing.

'It says two quid is not near enough for a dog like Sir Larkalot so they're givin' us a couple of hundred and a gold watch for Pa and a crate of pork pies for Billy . . . How do I know what it says, you knocker-faced block'ead!' exclaimed Jem irritably. 'I can't read, can I?'

'All right, all right, no need to get snappish,' muttered Ned.

'Come on, let's go and see old Horace,' said Jem.

And away they went, running as fast as they could to the lodging house where the screever lived.

'We've got it! We've got it!' they cried, bursting into his room.

Horace Stephens took the letter and looked at the crest.

'Very impressive,' he said. 'An ancient family of some renown. Rich too. Rich as Croesus.'

'Never mind about him,' cried Jem. 'What does it say?'

While the two boys waited with mounting excitement the screever began to read.

He smiled. Then he chuckled. Then he laughed. Then he put down the letter and rocked back and forth, convulsed.

'What does it say?' shouted Jem, beside himself now. 'What does it say?'

The screever took a grubby handkerchief from his pocket, dabbed at his eyes, blew his nose and, with a great effort, pulled himself together.

'It says: "Madam. I was pleased beyond measure to receive your letter and to learn from its contents that my wife's dog had been stolen. I cannot begin to describe the utter misery that insufferable animal has inflicted on me with its incessant barking. My house has reverberated to the noise day and night for the past three years. Please accept my grateful thanks. I would have given you some token of my appreciation but common sense advised against it. Your most humble and obedient servant, Hubert FitzHubert."'

16

Billy was well pleased with all the food he was given at the Edens. And why would he not be, when his stomach was always full? Breakfast was splendid, lunch was superb and tea – all those muffins and scones and cakes. There was no word to describe how wonderful tea was. But there was still something he craved, something better than all the pies and puddings and pastries, something that made his mouth water whenever he thought about it – and he thought about it all the time. A pork pie.

He had asked for one repeatedly. Lady Eden simply smiled and shook her head while her daughters looked at him, baffled. They had never eaten a pork pie and seemed to have no desire to.

'It is something unspeakable that the lower classes eat,' Georgiana had informed her sisters. 'Ladies and gentlemen eat more refined foods.'

Billy had asked Norris Pole for a pork pie – 'I don't mind givin' up a bit of bread'n butter or a bit

of cake instead,' he had pleaded with him. But the butler had simply ignored him, staring straight ahead with his usual glacial expression. And when Billy had asked one of the footmen, who smiled and was about to say something, Pole had silenced him with a look that would have turned the sun into a snowball.

Billy had tried approaching his father – not Pa Perkinski in Devil's Acre but the other one, who lived in Heaven. Every night when Dolly had gone, giving him a hug and closing the door softly behind her, he got out of bed and knelt on the floor with his eyes closed and the palms of his hands pressed together, just as she had taught him, and earnestly prayed, 'Our Father Richard in Heaven, give us this day our daily pork pie.'

But nothing happened. Every day Billy rushed down to the drawing room at teatime and waited eagerly for the butler and footmen to arrive with dishes laden with all manner of delicacies. But there was never a pork pie. Not a crumb.

Surely, he thought, surely there was one some-where in that vast house.

'Where does our grub come from?' he asked Dolly.

'Well, meat comes from cows and pigs and . . .'

'Nah, I mean here, in this place.'

'Oh . . . oh, the kitchen.'

'Old Jermyn said that's where hell is and it's stinkin' hot.'

'Don't be a ninny,' Dolly laughed. 'The kitchen's hot cos Mrs Maltby does so much baking and boiling and roasting.'

'Does she live down there?'

'No, she's got a room in the attic above us, but she spends all her days in the kitchen. A real hard worker she is, up at six o'clock and . . . Oh, look, there she is.' Dolly drew him to the nursery window, from where a short, stout woman could be seen walking away down the street. 'She's very nice, except when things go wrong, like Minny burning a hole in the kettle or leaving the eyes in the potatoes. Then she can get very snappish.'

'Could I see the kitchen?'

'Why?'

'Cos . . . cos I've never seen one, not a proper one.'

Dolly looked doubtful for a moment. Then she said, 'Well, I don't see why not. We could do it now, while Mrs Maltby's out. And it's Mr Pole's afternoon off so we won't bump into him neither. We just have

to pray that Miss Jermyn doesn't see us, cos she'll make a fuss and report me to Lady Eden.'

'All right.' Billy fell to his knees and closing his eyes clasped his hands together and began, 'Our Father . . .'

'No, no, don't be a ninny,' Dolly giggled, pulling him to his feet. 'I didn't mean a proper prayer, just a . . . Oh, never mind. Come on.' And taking his hand she led him down two flights of stairs to the main hall of the house. By a stroke of luck – or maybe God was watching over them after all – Miss Jermyn did not appear, nor did any of the Eden family or the other servants.

'Through here,' whispered Dolly, pushing open a green baize door.

Immediately everything changed. Gone was the embossed wallpaper in shades of green and purple, the patterned carpets, the heavy furniture and plush curtains, the paintings and mirrors and ornaments, for this was where the servants lived and worked and all was plain and gloomy.

Billy followed Dolly along a corridor and down a flight of steps.

'This is the kitchen, Master Billy,' she said quietly, opening the door to a huge room with a large wooden table in the middle and a cooking range to one side. On the shelves and hooks that covered every wall were dozens of pots and pans and fish kettles and baking trays and bains-marie and mixing bowls and spoons, all polished and shining.

'Mrs Maltby keeps a very clean kitchen,' Dolly whispered in Billy's ear. 'Very precise, she is.'

'What's that?' Billy pointed to a much smaller room leading off the kitchen with two big, deep sinks in it and a vast array of mops, brooms, brushes, burnishers, scrubbers, polish and soap.

'That's the scullery. And over there's the larder.'

'What's a larder?'

'Where all the food's kept.'

'Grub!' cried Billy and pulling free of Dolly's hand, he ran towards it.

'No!' she cried, quite forgetting she was supposed to be quiet. 'No, you're not allowed in there, Master Billy. No one is except Mrs Maltby and Mr Pole.'

'But I want a pork p—'

'Shh! Stow it, you little goosecap,' said Dolly, putting a hand over his mouth and looking nervously over her shoulder. 'If anyone hears us I'll be in trouble.' And ignoring his whining, she hurried him back upstairs to the nursery floor.

17

Slug stew had done nothing for Pa's stomach. In fact, it had made it a great deal worse.

'I'm dyin',' he groaned, rolling from side to side on the caravan floor. 'I reckon you've done for me this time.'

'I've been thinkin', Bert,' said Gran.

'Oh Lor', more trouble.'

'I think you should put—'

'I've told you a hundred times, Gran, NO MORE SLUGS! I'm not eatin' them and I'm not havin' them creepin' all over me neither. One of them even got up my—'

'Not slugs, Bert. I'm not sayin' slugs. I think you need a poultice.'

'And what's that when it's at home?'

'It's a kind of paste of bread and water and you put it on your belly and it draws out the badness.'

'Sounds like a waste of good grub, if you ask me,' grumbled Jem.

'Well, nobody did,' snapped Ma. 'And if it'll make your Pa well again, then we should try it. Ned, get that end of loaf out of the bin.'

'But that's our breakfast, Ma.'

'You can eat it afterwards.'

'What? After it's been on Pa's belly?'

'Oh?' said Pa indignantly. 'Somethin' wrong with my belly, is there?'

'Just stop argufyin', the lot of you,' said Gran. 'Jem, go and get some sticks for a fire. And, Ned, you fill the gruel pot with water and bring it to me when it boils.'

'You ever made a poultice before, Gran?' asked Pa, looking nervous.

'Course I have, dozens of times,' said Gran, who had no idea what a poultice looked like but had overheard a woman in the market describing one to one of her customers. 'Don't you worry, Bert,' she reassured him.

Jem couldn't find any sticks, since anything in the courtyard that wasn't actually nailed, glued or bolted down was stolen by the residents, so he ripped a plank from the roof of the pigsty and made a fire of it, fanning the flames until the wood was white hot. Ned in the meantime had found some dirty water at the bottom of a rotting rain barrel and after skimming off the green scum and dead insects he poured it into the gruel pot, which he suspended over the fire.

As the two boys squatted on their haunches waiting for the water to boil there was an ear-piercing shriek from one of the nearby tenements and the next moment Sir Lancelot appeared with a piece of meat in his mouth, followed closely by Old Mother Perry brandishing a knife.

'Stole my supper, he has,' she yelled. 'That varminty cur's stole my bit of liver. You wait till I get hold of him, I'll . . . !' Fortunately for Sir Lancelot he was saved from a bloody end because his would-be murderer slipped on a pile of slimy cabbage leaves and landed head first in a dung heap.

'Come on, Ned, plaguy quick,' Jem said, hurrying up the steps of the caravan with the pot of boiled water, 'or she'll top us too when she gets out of there.'

'But what about the dog?' said Ned anxiously.

'She'll never catch him,' said Jem. For having eaten Old Mother Perry's dinner, Sir Lancelot was now running round and round the courtyard like a clockwork toy gone mad, yapping his head off and snapping at anyone or anything that got in his way.

'Pesky nuisance,' muttered Ned.

'Yeh,' agreed Jem. 'I reckon he's more trouble than Billy. We'll have to get rid of him.'

'What, Billy?'

'Nah, you stupe. The dog.'

When they went into the caravan Gran had already broken the bread into small pieces and, slapping Jem's hand away as he tried to steal one, she put them into the pot and stirred them into a thick paste.

'That looks very hot to me,' growled Pa.

'It's got to be, Bert, hotter the better. That's how it draws the badness out. Now hold still while I—'

'Ouch! Argh! Aye!' shrieked Pa as the old woman spread the red-hot paste over his abdomen with a wooden spoon. 'It's burnin' my skin off! It's burned a hole in my belly!'

'That's good, Bert,' beamed Gran. 'The badness'll come out of the hole in a minute – you see.'

But, of course, it did not. The badness, whatever it was, stayed in. All Pa got was a scorched belly. And to make matters worse Gran didn't know that she should have put a layer of linen or some other material between Pa's skin and the poultice so that it could be lifted off easily.

Now, Pa made up for the lack of hairs on his head by growing them in abundance everywhere else, especially on his chest and belly. They were like a thick, curly carpet. As good as any Axminster or Wilton. And as the hot paste cooled and dried it stuck mercilessly to this hairy carpet.

'Feelin' better, my dove?' asked Ma, bending over him anxiously.

'Nah, I am not. Get this muck off my belly – NOW!'

But the poultice had dried so hard it was like a stiff board.

'D'you reckon it's ready to come off?' asked Ma, tapping it.

'Yeh, course it is,' said Gran, who had no idea. And the two women each took a corner and tugged.

Pa yelled so loudly all the residents of Devil's Acre came running, eager to see who was being murdered, and Uncle Arthur swore he heard Pa bellowing from as far away as Covent Garden.

'Stop!' he pleaded, for in trying to rip off the wretched poultice Ma and Gran were also ripping out every hair on Pa's chest and belly – and some of his skin too. 'Stop! You're killin' me.'

'Go and get some more water, Ned,' said Gran. 'We'll have to wash it off.'

'There's none left in the barrel, Gran. I used the last drop.'

'Oh crimes,' groaned Ma. 'Now what're we goin' to do?'

'Birds like bread, Ma,' said Jem.

'What?'

'If Pa was to lie on his back in the yard, all the birds'd come down and—'

'I am not havin' nothin' peckin' at my belly!' thundered Pa. 'I'm not a confounded bird table!'

18

Billy was convinced there were pork pies in the larder. It stood to reason. No self-respecting household would be without them. Even if the Edens didn't eat them, or wouldn't admit to eating them because they thought it was a common thing to do, Mrs Maltby looked like the kind of woman who would. She certainly didn't get those big hips and numerous wobbly chins from eating potato peelings, he thought. And then there were the maids, chubby most of them, definitely secret eaters of pork pies.

Billy's plan of action was simple. He would wait until dark, when everybody in the house was fast asleep, and creep down to the larder and take a pork pie or three. There might be a bit of fuss in the morning when the cook or the butler found out, but he would have eaten the evidence by then, every crumb, so no one would know it was him — and, anyway, the Edens were enormously rich; they could buy plenty more. In fact, provided he was careful he could go down every night and take a couple . . . He heaved a sigh of deep contentment.

And so went the little boy's thoughts that warm summer evening as he lay in bed waiting for darkness. The trouble was that, although he was used to working on the streets of London with his two brothers until all hours of the night, he had grown accustomed to going to bed at seven o'clock in his new home. And try as he might, he couldn't stay awake.

Finally he hit upon an excellent idea and taking the brush that Dolly used on his hair he put it in the middle of his bed and lay on it. After that, of course, it was impossible to sleep, for every time he nodded off and turned over the bristles pierced his skin and he woke with an ouch!

At last darkness fell and the house was silent. Stealing from his bed, Billy opened his door as quietly as he could and crept down the stairs in bare feet, pausing every so often to listen. The only sounds he could hear were clocks ticking, especially the big old grandfather that stood in the entrance hall.

He pushed open the green baize door that divided the servants' quarters from the rest of the

house and was about to run along the corridor, his heart pounding with excitement, his mouth watering at the thought of all those delicious pork pies waiting for him, when he saw two people at the far end, clearly a man and a woman, their features dimly outlined by the light of the moon.

Billy froze. If they were to turn and see him he would be caught and punished. But fortunately they were so busy cuddling and kissing each other they weren't aware of the little boy standing by the door, watching. Stealthily he opened it and slipped back upstairs.

19

That same night, under cover of darkness, Jem and Ned dumped a yapping terrier on Sir Hubert FitzHubert's doorstep and ran away.

'And good riddance,' muttered Jem.

But next morning, as they turned into Arlington Street on their way to see Billy, Jem grabbed Ned's arm and said, 'Look! Look! There's that pesky dog again.'

A different footman was walking Sir Lancelot that morning, Maurice having been dismissed for gross negligence. He was followed closely by a carriage in which sat Lady FitzHubert issuing a torrent of instructions in stentorian tones – 'Do not permit anyone to approach Sir Lancelot, Luke . . . Hold tightly to his lead . . . Keep away from the areas; a villain could be hiding there, lying in wait . . . On no account go into Green Park.'

Jem narrowed his eyes, assessing the situation.

'When I point at you, run away plaguy quick,' he whispered to his brother. 'I'll meet you at Billy's.'

'What d'you mean, "run away"? What're you goin' to do? Why should I?' protested Ned. But Jem had gone, haring along the street until he caught up with the carriage.

'Your Ladyness,' he cried, 'I know who nicked your dog.'

Lady FitzHubert put her lorgnette to her eye and peered at him suspiciously.

'I said, I know who nicked your mutt,' said Jem, staying well out of range of the terrier's snapping jaws.

Lady FitzHubert rapped smartly on the roof of the carriage with her ebony cane and the driver eased the horses to a halt.

'Who?' she demanded, leaning out of the window. 'Tell me who committed such a dastardly deed?'

'A right toerag by name of Bobby Grimes. He's 'arf-inched hundreds of dogs. Ugly customer he is. If the owner won't cough up the ready, he tops their dog and chucks it in the sewers for the rats to eat.'

Lady FitzHubert recoiled in horror.

'Thank the good Lord Sir Lancelot was returned safely to us,' she said fervently.

'Yeh, you were dead lucky this time. But next time – Oh Lor'!' Jem exclaimed, feigning surprise at seeing Ned squatting on a kerbstone at the far end of the street looking at him with a very puzzled expression. 'There's the article himself. There's Bobby Grimes.' He pointed at Ned. 'And from the look of him he's just waitin' for the chance to nab your poor little dog again.'

'After him, Luke!' Lady FitzHubert barked at her footman. 'After him! Quick, man, or he'll get away!' she cried as Ned, seeing Jem's signal, leaped to his feet and took off.

'Catch him!' screamed Lady FitzHubert, brandishing her cane. 'Catch him, Luke!'

'Oh, he will, Your Ladyness. Bobby Grimes can't run for toffee,' said Jem, knowing full well his brother would lead the footman a merry dance down alleyways, over rooftops, into courtyards and through holes in the wall where no grown man could follow. 'And here's your mutt, safe and sound, thanks to me,' he added, grabbing it by the scruff of the neck and putting it into Lady FitzHubert's arms before it could sink its teeth into him.

'You are a good boy,' she said, hugging the dog closely to her, 'an honest, upright child, unlike so many of your class. And it is my pleasure to give you . . .'

Jem held out his hand. With a house and carriage like that, he thought, running his eye over the handsome phaeton, the old woman should be good for at least a crown, if not two.

'. . . my deepest gratitude.'

'Your *what*?' said Jem.

'My thanks,' she said, rapping the roof. 'It is my firm belief that virtue is its own reward.'

And away went the horses at a smart pace.

20

Jem knew that Billy's new home was in Stratton Street, but what he did not know until he turned the corner and saw the house was that it was the same one he had burgled, or tried to, with Uncle Rudd.

'Oh crimes!' he muttered, backing against a wall and looking nervously to left and right as if he half expected a posse of policemen to bear down on him shouting, 'Stop, thief!' and spinning their rattles. 'What if someone recognizes me? What if one of them maids saw me? Nah, they didn't. They couldn't have. No one got a good look at my mug . . . Did they?'

The worrying thoughts whirled round and round in his head until he felt quite dizzy. Should he go or should he stay? He'd promised his mother he would keep an eye on Billy, but what if someone *had* recognized him on the night of the robbery, a servant looking out of a window, for example, or the footman that had shouted at him from the stair-case . . . ?

Oh well, he decided finally, he'd just have to risk it. And pulling his shoulders back and sticking his chest out he sauntered across the road as if he hadn't a care in the world, mounted the steps to the impressive front door and rang the bell. Moments later it was opened by Pole, his face an impenetrable mask.

'Good morning,' he said, without moving a muscle.

Jem was so intrigued he peered round the butler to see if someone behind him had spoken.

'Good morning,' said Pole again.

'I've come to see my brother Billy.'

'This entrance is for the sole use of the gentry. Tradesmen and others of your class use the area entrance,' said Pole in a voice devoid of expression. And he closed the door.

'Crimes, he's a queer cove and no kid. Looks like somethin' you find in a cemetery,' muttered Jem. And he ran down the area steps and banged loudly on the kitchen door.

It was immediately opened by Pole.

'Yes?' he said.

'Oh Lor', not you again,' grumbled Jem. 'They should have nailed down your coffin.'

The man stared impassively ahead, his eyes almost invisible under their marble lids.

'I want to see Billy,' said Jem.

'Master Billy is not at home to visitors.'

'What's that supposed to mean?'

'It means Master Billy is not at home to visitors,' said Pole, shutting the door.

Jem was about to pound it again when Ned ran up, looking hot and tired.

'How much did you get out of the old crone?' he asked eagerly, for he had twigged Jem's little ploy.

'Her deepest gratitude,' said Jem.

'Her *what*?'

'She didn't give me nothin'.'

'Lor', you mean you made that varminty bloke chase me all over London and all you got was nothin'?'

'I said she didn't give me nothin', not I didn't *get* nothin',' grinned Jem. And he held up Sir Lancelot's lead, a very fine leather one with brass studs.

'Lor'!' cried Ned. 'Let's take it home plaguy quick before the crushers catch you with it.'

'Nah, they'll never catch me. 'Sides, I want to see Billy and find out if he's – Hey up!' He pointed to

a man standing on the corner. 'Look who's over there.'

'Where?'

'There. It's Sam. Sam!' cried Jem, running across the road to greet his cousin. 'What're you doin' here?'

'Waitin' to see Dolly,' said the young man.

'Who's that?'

'My girl,' said Sam proudly. 'She works over there,' he nodded at the Edens' house, 'as a nurse-maid. But when we've got enough of the ready we're goin' to get spliced.'

'But —' Jem looked perplexed — 'you've got enough of the ready. You make loads nickin' and sellin' horses.'

'I did,' Sam corrected him. 'But I don't no more. I'm straight now.'

Jem stared at his cousin, too stunned to speak. No Perkinski worthy of the name would ever admit to such a thing, and to hear Sam, one of the best horse thieves in the business, saying that he had given up a life of crime shocked the boy to the very centre of his being.

'It's true,' said the young man, laughing at Jem's expression. 'Dolly's a nice piece of goods, but she says she won't marry me 'less I get a honest occupation, so I'm workin' as a groom for a toff in Berkeley Square. I come here to see her when I can. But what're you two doin' in these parts? And where's Billy? He's always snivellin' along behind you.'

'He lives with the same toffs your Dolly works for,' explained Jem. 'They've – what's the word, Ned?'

'Adapted.'

'Yeh, that's right. They've adapted Billy.'

'Blimey!' Sam exclaimed. 'Dolly told me they'd adopted a kid called Billy but I didn't know it was your Billy. He's fallen on his feet and no flies.'

'But they won't let us see him no more.'

'Why?'

'They said he's not at home, which is soft, cos he's not in our home and if he isn't in theirs, where is he?'

'*They* said that? What, Sir Edmund and his lady?'

'Nah, not them, the old codger that opens the door.'

'Oh, the Ghost.'

'That his name?'

'Course not. His name's Norris Pole but I call him the Ghost. Ever touched his hand, have you? Well, don't. It's like an icicle. Matches his face. I reckon

 *137*

there's not a drop of blood in his body. It must've all been sucked out by vampires.'

'Does he let you see Dolly?' said Jem.

'No, he does not,' retorted Sam. 'But when he's busy, like cleanin' the silver or workin' in the wine cellar, she gives me a signal and I nip over. There she is now, bless her.' He pointed to a window where the nursemaid was waving a white handkerchief at him. 'Come on,' he said, running across the road and down the steps. 'The coast's clear.'

Dolly was already at the kitchen door waiting for him and they wrapped their arms around each other.

'There they go, canoodlin',' said Jem in disgust as the couple cuddled and kissed.

'I've warned Dolly,' said a round-faced woman wearing a voluminous apron, her greying hair pulled back under a white cap. 'I've told her time and time again, servants are not allowed followers. If someone was to see her now –' she nodded at the nursemaid who was whispering sweet nothings in Sam's ear – 'she'd get the sack.'

'I don't know why they do it, straight I don't,' said Jem. 'I wouldn't let no varminty girl kiss me.' And he shuddered at the thought.

'Oh, and who might you be?'

'Jem Perkinski. And this article's my brother Ned. And we've come to see our brother Billy, only the Ghost won't let us.'

'The Ghost?' said Dolly, pulling away from Sam's embrace. 'Who's that?'

'What I call Norris Pole,' said Sam.

Dolly laughed out loud. 'That's a good name for him, isn't it, Mrs Maltby?' she said.

'Keep your voice down, girl,' the cook admonished her. 'I reckon he hears everything we say even when he's asleep. Now listen –' she turned to Jem and Ned – 'you can't see Master Billy cos he's doing his lessons.'

The nursemaid nodded. 'Every morning, right after breakfast till lunchtime.'

'Lessons?' cried Jem, aghast. 'Oh Lor', the poor little nipper.'

'He's a very lucky little nipper, you ask me,' huffed the cook. 'Living like a lord he is. But he's got to have lessons so's he can read and write and speak properly.'

Jem frowned. He could see no earthly reason why anyone would waste time and energy learning to read and write and speak properly, but Mrs Maltby was clearly the kind of woman who didn't take kindly to being contradicted.

'So when can we see him?' he said.

'Come back tomorrow, early afternoon,' said Dolly. 'Wait for my signal and I'll bring Master Billy down.'

'Right you are.' Jem grinned.

'You'd better be going now,' said the cook. 'You too, Sam. Mr Pole's in the cellar, but he'll be up in a minute and if he catches you here . . .'

'I'm on my way, Mrs Maltby,' said Sam. 'And I'll see you tonight, sweetheart,' he said to Dolly, giving her a last, lingering kiss.

'Tonight?' cried the cook in alarm. 'You can't come here tonight, Sam Perkinski.'

'I can in my dreams, Mrs Maltby,' chuckled Sam, winking at Dolly. 'I can in my dreams.' And he ran lightly up the area steps, whistling a jaunty little tune.

'I don't trust him,' said the cook darkly, watching him go.

Dolly flew to his defence. 'My Sam's a good man.'

'So he may be. But I wouldn't trust him not to do something foolish. He's too devil-may-care for my liking. Now come in, my girl, and quick about it. There's work to be done. And you two . . .' She waved Jem and Ned away.

But neither boy moved, for as the cook turned

they had caught sight of the kitchen table laden with loaves, pies, cakes and all manner of mouth-watering dishes she had made that morning.

'Lor'!' sighed Jem, who had never seen a more magnificent sight, not even in the window of Fortnum & Mason. 'Don't that look golopshus.'

'And don't it smell golopshus,' sighed Ned, sniffing the air like an eager bloodhound.

'Are you hungry?' said Dolly.

The two boys nodded.

'Give them a bite to eat, Mrs Maltby,' she pleaded.

'I can't be feeding every street urchin in London,' huffed the cook.

'But their little brother's getting his stomach filled, so it's only fair they should get something too.'

'And our pa's so poorly he can't work,' said Jem. 'And our sister Kate's gone.'

'Gone? You mean she's . . .' The cook faltered, unable to say the awful word.

'Yeh.' Jem nodded, wiping an imaginary tear from his eye. 'So we don't get no money from her no more neither.'

'You poor little souls,' sighed Mrs Maltby, quite overcome by the double tragedy that had hit the

Perkinski family. 'Wait a minute,' she said. And a moment later she reappeared with a large paper parcel.

'Don't let anyone know,' she said, handing it to them. 'If Mr Pole was to find out, he'd get me sacked. But if you keep quiet about it,' she added, lowering her voice to a whisper, 'I might be able to find a bit more for you tomorrow.'

21

'Very nice,' said Pa, examining Sir Lancelot's lead. 'A good bit of leather. Should bring us a shillin' or two, which is more than that pesky kid did,' he added sourly, for Ma had earned nothing with the baby she'd borrowed, probably because it never stopped bawling at the top of its lungs, forcing people to cross to the other side of the road to avoid it. And so, at Pa's insistence, she had returned it to Mother Murray's baby farm early.

'Did she give you your money back?' Jem asked.

'Money back from that old trout?' Ma gave a hollow laugh. 'Mother Murray's never given nobody nothin' – except a thick ear for darin' to ask.'

'Ma, the woman that does the cookin' for the Edens, an article by the name of Maltby, said we could go back and see Billy tomorrow and she'd give us some more grub long as we keep quiet about it,' Jem said as they tucked into the pigeon pie and seed cake Mrs Maltby had given him.

'You comin' with us, Ma?' said Ned, looking at her in a puzzled way, because every time somebody mentioned Billy his mother went very quiet or started talking about something else.

'Nah.' She put down her piece of pie as if she'd suddenly lost her appetite. 'I'd only blub and that'd upset him and he'd want to come home and . . .' She gulped back tears. 'Pa's right, Billy's goin' to have a much better life with them toffs. Long as he's happy . . . Listen to me, Jem,' she said, clutching his arm, 'you'll tell me if he's not happy, won't you?'

'Yeh, Ma.' Jem nodded. 'Course I will.'

22

Under the hypercritical eye of Miss Jermyn and the gentler but equally determined eye of Lady Eden, Billy was slowly and painfully learning how to behave like a young gentleman.

Breakfast and lunch were eaten in the day nursery – light meals for the Eden girls, more substantial ones for Billy. Tea was taken in the drawing room and, if Sir Edmund and Lady Eden were not entertaining or being entertained at some other establishment, all the children joined them for an early supper in the very grand dining room on the first floor, with its Turkish carpet, deep crimson curtains and matching wallpaper and glittering candelabra.

It was here that Billy's newly acquired table manners were put to the test. He was learning to eat with a knife, fork and spoon instead of with his fingers, to finish one mouthful before shovelling in the next, to drink soup without sounding like a

sinkful of water disappearing down the plughole, to wipe his mouth on his napkin instead of on his sleeve or the tablecloth, to remove fruit pips from his mouth in a discreet way rather than spitting them at Georgiana and to resist the temptation to fidget, pick his nose, scratch his bottom, belch — or worse.

After supper the family retired to the drawing room. While Sir Edmund read the *Illustrated London News* his wife, like many middle and upper-class women, embroidered. During the course of her lifetime she had embroidered a multitude of usually useful but sometimes useless items — tablecloths, place mats, doilies, napkins, cushions, antimacassars, footstools, aprons, slippers, spectacle cases and pincushions. In short she had embroidered everything except the canary — but she had embroidered a cover for its cage.

'What's that on your finger?' Billy had asked the first time he saw Lady Eden embroidering. 'You got somethin' wrong with it?'

'Not at all, Billy,' she smiled, 'but I would have if I didn't wear this. It's called a thimble.' She held it up the tiny gold cup studded with jewels for him to see. 'It protects my fingertip from being pierced by the needle as I push it through my embroidery.'

Billy reached for it eagerly.

'Pray be careful, Mama,' Georgiana cautioned her. 'Children of the lower orders are taught to pocket small, valuable items without their owners noticing.'

'Georgiana,' Sir Edmund snapped shut the *Illustrated London News* and addressed his daughter in an unusually abrupt tone. 'I find your attitude distasteful. Just because Billy did not have the good fortune you have had to be born into a life of privilege, that does not mean that he is automatically a criminal. Indeed, I might say there are as many rogues and scoundrels in our own class, with considerably less reason to steal than many of the poor wretches who lie starving in the gutter.'

'Yes, Papa. I'm very sorry I displeased you, Papa,' said Georgiana, bowing her head. Nevertheless she kept a close eye on Billy as he twirled the pretty thimble on his finger and uttered an audible sigh of relief when he returned it to her mother.

Before they retired for the night, the girls amused themselves in their various ways. Georgiana played the piano, Leopoldina the violin and Theodora sang. Henrietta was making a scrapbook in which she had pasted pressed flowers, poems, drawings, letterheads, visiting cards and autographs. Thomasina and

Edwardina played draughts or cribbage and Alice played with her toy theatre, pushing cardboard figures on stage from the wings and declaiming their lines so loudly that Theodora protested nobody could hear her singing – which was probably all to the good.

Billy begged in vain for someone to play marbles or pegtops or fivestones with him – street games with which, of course, the Eden girls were not familiar.

'You should teach Billy some of your games, my darlings,' said their mother, 'like "Oranges and Lemons" or "Here We Go Round the Mulberry Bush".'

'Or "Ring a Ring of Roses",' said Edwardina eagerly. 'That's my favourite.'

'How d'you play it?' said Billy, perking up.

'We all join hands and dance around singing, "Ring a ring of roses, a pocket full of posies, A-tishoo! A-tishoo! We all fall down."'

'Why d'you fall down?'

'Because . . . because we do.'

'And then what happens?'

'We all get up.'

'That's a load of tosh,' scoffed Billy.

'What's "tosh"?' said Henrietta.

'Another of Billy's rude words,' said Georgiana tartly. 'He doesn't seem to know any polite ones.'

'We could play hunt the thimble,' suggested Theodora.

'Why should we hunt it when she's got it?' said Billy, pointing at Lady Eden, who was busily sewing.

'No, no, you don't understand, Billy. Someone hides a thimble and we all have to go and look for it.'

'And what happens when we find it?'

'Nothing.'

'That's tosh too,' said Billy. And he yawned, opening his mouth so wide they could practically see his tonsils.

'Cover your mouth when you yawn, dear,' said Lady Eden.

'Why?'

'Because that's what little gentlemen do.'

Billy sighed. Being a little gentleman was a very tedious business. If it wasn't for the grub, he thought, he'd much rather be a little boy.

23

Ma was all for tugging the remainder of the bread poultice off Pa's belly – 'cos you can't go round for the rest of your life with half a loaf stuck to it' – but Pa wouldn't let her anywhere near it. He'd already lost a pile of hairs and a considerable amount of skin too.

'It'll come off in its own time,' he said, pushing her hands away. And it did, but not before most of it had turned so green and mouldy that even the mice turned their noses up at the shower of crumbs that fell from Pa whenever he moved.

'Bert, I've got another idea,' said Gran.

Pa let out a groan of anguish. 'Keep her away from me . . . Please!'

'Nah, this is a proper cure. And it really works. It's called the Royal Touch. Doesn't matter what's wrong with you – boils, warts, a pain in the tripes – when the Queen touches you you get better.'

'Oh, well, that's easy then, isn't it?' scoffed Pa. 'Jem, just nip over to Buckin'am Palace and tell Her Maj I'll be there in a bit so's she can touch my belly . . . Nah, on second thoughts, ask her to pop round and have supper with us. After all, we've got loads of grub,' he said, indicating the few remaining patches that still stubbornly stuck to his belly.

'All right, Bert, no need to get snappish,' huffed Gran. 'I was only tryin' to be helpful.'

24

June the twentieth was the anniversary of the Queen's accession to the throne, an event she marked with a grand ball at Buckingham Palace. As Sir Edmund was Victoria's cousin, seven times removed, and Prince Albert considered him, 'the most honourable and philanthropic gentleman in the land' – after himself – he and Lady Eden were invited to attend the celebrations.

'Shall you wear the Star of India, Mama?' asked Edwardina at tea in the drawing room.

'Of course, my darling.' Lady Eden nodded.

'What's the Star of Inja?' asked Billy, reaching out for the largest piece of fruit cake on the plate offered by the footman, although he had been warned time and time again that it was not a polite thing to do.

'It is a sapphire necklace,' said Lady Eden, 'so called because if you hold each stone up to the light you can see a beautiful six-pointed star on its surface. It was given to our family many years ago by a

grateful maharaja – an Indian prince,' Lady Eden explained before Billy could ask, 'who lived in Kashmir.'

'It is absolutely priceless. Is that not so, Mama?' said Leopoldina. 'Even if someone were to sell their house and all their furniture and all their clothes and all their jewels they still would not have enough money to buy your necklace, not even one stone of it.'

'So it's worth nickin' then,' said Billy, picking the raisins out of his cake and chewing them thoughtfully.

'What does "nickin'" mean?' asked Theodora.

'It means stealing,' explained Thomasina, who had begun to learn some of Billy's expressions. 'A lot of people have tried to nick it,' she said to the little boy, 'but Papa keeps it in a strong box in his study. He says it's safer there than in the Bank of England because—'

'Thomasina, please do not chatter in the drawing room,' her mother reproved her.

'I am sorry, Mama,' said the girl, looking abashed.

'I'll wager my Uncle Rudd could open your pa's strong box and nick them sparks,' said Billy. 'He's the best, he is. He's so fly he could—'

'Billy, do not speak with food in your mouth,' Lady Eden interrupted him.

'I haven't got no grub in my mouth,' he pouted. 'D'you want that, Alice?' He pointed to the slice of cake, untouched, on her plate.

The little girl shook her head.

'Are you not hungry, my darling?' asked Lady Eden.

'No, Mama.'

'You are very quiet. Are you unwell?'

'I have rather a headache, Mama, and a pain here . . .' Alice indicated her stomach with a delicate gesture.

'Come here, child . . . Oh, my goodness,' cried Lady Eden, putting her hand on Alice's forehead, 'you have a fever. Pole –' she turned to the butler – 'send Miss Jermyn to me at once and instruct Dolly to prepare the sickroom.'

'She goin' to eat that piece of cake or not?' Billy asked as Alice was led away.

'Oh really!' exclaimed Georgiana. 'Is that all you think about – stealing and eating?'

Billy nodded. What else was life for?

25

'You look like a little prince,' enthused Dolly, pinching Billy's cheeks to make them glow.

'Nah, I don't, I look like a half-baked dummy,' he grumbled, scowling at himself in the mirror. 'And I'm not goin' down to see Jem'n Ned lookin' like this.'

'Of course you are.'

'Nah, I'm not.'

Billy was looking forward to seeing his two brothers again, if only to tell them how much grub he was getting, but the clothes he was made to wear horrified him. And it was Queen Victoria's fault. The young monarch had bought a castle in the Cairngorms and developed a passion for all things Scottish, especially the tartan. And when Prince Albert and his son put on Highland dress, every woman in the land who could afford it kitted out their hapless sons in similar fashion.

Billy also fell victim to the Queen's whim.

Protesting violently, he was dressed in a kilt, a short jacket with silver buttons and white collar, tartan socks to the knees and a tartan scarf over his right shoulder.

Billy knew exactly what his brothers would say when they saw him — and they did.

'Lawks a mercy,' squealed Jem in a silly voice, 'it can't be Billy, not in a skirt. It must be Betty.'

'Hello, Betty,' simpered Ned, bending down to tweak Billy's golden curls, clean and shining now thanks to the nursemaid's enthusiastic scrubbing, 'what a thweet little girl you are.' And he almost peed himself laughing.

'You shut your trap!' yelled Billy, enraged, and he hurled himself at Ned, punching, kicking, gouging and scratching. Ned was so surprised he fell back spreadeagled across the steps, trying in vain to fend off the blows that Billy rained on him with clenched fists.

'Oy, stop that, you varmint!' cried Jem, making a grab for him. But Billy spun round and gave him a sharp nip on the ankle.

'Crimes!' cried Jem, hobbling away. 'He's gone looney tic.'

'What's all the noise?' demanded Mrs Maltby,

appearing in the kitchen doorway. 'Billy, get up this minute. Get up, I say!'

Billy ignored the cook and set about Ned again.

'I'll stop him, Mrs Maltby,' Dolly said. And bending down she whispered in the little boy's ear, 'No more muffins, no more scones, no more chocolate cake . . .'

Immediately Billy sprang up.

'Such behaviour!' huffed Mrs Maltby. 'You say you're sorry to your brothers, specially when they've come all this way to see you.'

'Begging your pardon, Mrs Maltby, but I think it's Jem and Ned that should say sorry to Billy,' said Dolly. 'They were very rude to him. They laughed at his clothes.'

'Did they indeed?' said the cook, giving the boys a steely eye. 'Well, let me tell you this, you rascals, if you make fun of Billy again you won't see him any more – and you won't get any more grub from me neither.'

'Yeh, all right, sorry, Mrs Maltby,' muttered Jem, looking suitably cowed, for although he felt not the slightest remorse for laughing at Billy, he was deeply grieved at the thought of never again sinking his teeth into one of the cook's delectable pies and pastries.

'Blimey!' exclaimed Ned when they were out of earshot. 'I've never seen Billy like that before. He was like one of them mad dogs you see fightin' rats. What's got into him?'

'Pork pies,' said Jem. 'Didn't you notice how big he's got? I reckon in a week or two he'll be bigger than both of us, bigger than Pa even. It's cos of pork pies.' He nodded sagely. 'I'll wager he eats them all the time.'

'Lor',' sighed Ned, clutching his empty stomach, 'I wish I lived with them toffs and ate pork pies all day.'

'Me too,' said Jem. 'I wonder if they'd adapt us.'

26

'Bert,' said Gran, 'I've been thinkin' . . .'

'That sounds like trouble,' growled Pa.

'I've got an idea . . .'

'If it's anythin' like the last one . . .'

'Nah, this one really works. My gypsy gran learned me it.'

'So it's a load of hocus-pocus then.'

'Gypsy cures always work,' said Gran indignantly. 'All you got to do is take some pills . . .'

'Gran, I keep tellin' you, I won't . . .'

'They can cure anythin': cross eyes, knock knees, webbed feet . . .'

'Gran, I'm warnin' you . . . !'

'And they're easy to make.'

'Oh yeh? Just a bit of flour and water, I suppose, like that varminty poultice.'

'Nah. They're made of spiders' webs.'

'*What?*'

'The pigsty's full of them, Bert. Great big'uns. All we got to do is get a handful and . . .'

'Nah, you daft old haybag! How many more times . . . ? Nah!'

'All right, no need to get obstropolous,' huffed Gran. 'It was just a suggestion. Now, how about some snake oil?'

27

The pleasurable prospect of the grand ball at Buckingham Palace that evening was overshadowed for Sir Edmund and Lady Eden by the sudden illness of Alice. The little girl woke in the morning with a high temperature and a pain in her belly.

'Cholera,' the servants whispered, huddling together in frightened groups.

The ghastly disease stalked the land like a vicious predator and struck terror in the hearts of everyone, from the poorest slum-dweller to the richest landowner, for there was no treatment, no cure, and the unfortunate man, woman or child who woke at sunrise with uncontrollable diarrhoea, fever and vomiting was, more often than not, dead by sunset.

'My aunt died of it,' said Pearl, the chief house-maid. 'Her skin turned blue and she kept having terrible fits. Even after she was dead she was still having fits, jumping about like a flea in a pepper pot she was.'

'They made my brother gargle with gin and bromide,' said Minny, the scullery maid, 'but it didn't do him no good.'

'I've heard you should take eucalyptus on a lump of sugar,' said Jim, the bootboy.

'No, camphorated oil on the chest covered by a piece of flannel's the best,' said Milly, the kitchen maid.

'Well, if you ask me—'

'Nobody did you ask you,' snapped Pole, suddenly appearing in their midst like an evil genie. 'Get on with your work, all of you.'

The doctor, a lugubrious-looking man in the sombre attire of an undertaker, arrived within the hour, examined Alice, and said she should be kept in a darkened room and fed a mixture of salts and senna pods every hour – 'And a bread poultice on the abdomen if the pain worsens.'

Lady Eden was distraught. 'I can't leave her, Edmund,' she said.

'My dear, you must. The Queen's invitation is a command and as loyal subjects we have no choice but to obey.'

'But Her Majesty has children. She will under-stand.'

'Her Majesty is a monarch first and foremost, Parthenope, and does her duty, as you must do yours. And there is nothing you can do here, my dear. Alice is in good hands.'

As a special treat the children were allowed to visit their mother's bedroom that evening when she had dressed for the ball.

'Oh, Mama, that is quite the most beautiful gown I have ever seen,' exclaimed Edwardina as she and her sisters clustered around Lady Eden, running their fingers over the knots of rosebuds caught up in ribbons over her ivory satin skirt. 'You will look prettier than the Queen herself. Don't you agree, Billy?' Edwardina turned to him, her eyes shining.

But Billy wasn't listening. He was staring as if mesmerized at the sapphire necklace around Lady Eden's throat.

'Lor'!' he said. 'Them sparks are bigger than chicken's eggs.'

'Not quite, my dear,' laughed Lady Eden. 'And please don't keep saying "Lor!"'

'You'd best not let my Uncle Rudd see them,' Billy warned her solemnly. 'He's the sharpest cracksman in London. He could pinch the beak off your face and you'd never know it. I reckon my uncle'd have them sparks off you before you could say, "Blimey".'

'Mama,' said Edwardina. 'What does "blim—?"'

'Children, I must go or I shall be late,' said Lady Eden, hurrying her daughters out of the room before Billy could add yet another vulgar word to their rapidly expanding vocabulary.

Queen Victoria liked to stay up into the early hours of the morning dancing and chattering and as none of her guests was permitted to leave before she did, no matter how old or sick or tired they were, Sir Edmund and Lady Eden did not return to their house in Mayfair until the sun was beginning to tinge the sky with a rosy hue.

'How is my daughter?' Lady Eden asked anxiously as her maid helped her to undress and put on a nightgown and negligee.

'I understand Miss Alice is a little better, M'Lady,' said Mademoiselle Victorine, folding her mistress's clothes and storing them in trays and boxes.

'I must go to her. Victorine, be so good as to prepare a glass of hot milk for me.'

'Yes, M'Lady,' said the maid. And she went down

to the kitchens while Lady Eden climbed the stairs to the sick room. The nursemaid, who was slouched in a chair by the bed, her head lolling on her chest, woke with a start when Lady Eden entered.

'I'm sorry, M'Lady, I haven't been asleep for long, just a few minutes,' she said, looking flustered, 'but I was so tired, I couldn't keep my eyes open. I—'

'Do not concern yourself, Dolly. It's natural you should be tired,' said Lady Eden. 'How is Alice?' She bent over her daughter, stroking her sweaty forehead.

'She's been sleeping peaceful, M'Lady.'

'God be praised,' said Lady Eden fervently.

Alice woke when she heard the voices and opened her eyes.

'Oh, Mama,' she sighed, 'I did so want to see you in your ball gown and jewels.'

'And so you shall, dearest. When you are well I shall put them on just for you. Dolly, you may leave us,' Lady Eden said to the nursemaid. 'I shall sit with Alice for a while.'

'Very well, M'Lady.' And stifling a yawn Dolly stumbled sleepily away.

Since Alice was putting the sickroom to its rightful use Billy had been moved into Dolly's bedroom, a tiny room sparsely furnished. Dolly was obliged to

share the narrow, iron bedstead with Billy, but neither she nor the little boy objected to this arrangement. On the contrary, they were both delighted. Billy missed the companionship of his mother, father and brothers, all of whom were used to curl up together in a convivial heap on the floor of their caravan. And Dolly, who had never known a family of her own, drew comfort from Billy, stretching out her hand to caress his cheek as he slept as if he was the little brother she'd always longed for.

Dolly was getting into bed as stealthily as she could so as not to wake Billy when he cried out in his sleep, 'Nah! Nah! Hook it! Hook it!' and began thrashing his arms wildly as if to ward off some evil.

'Master Billy!' Dolly shook him. 'Master Billy, wake up!'

'What? What's happenin'?' he said, looking confused.

'You were having a nightmare, my tulip. You were telling someone to hook it.'

'That bloke – that bloke, the Ghost,' Billy babbled. 'He was after me.'

'But he's never hurt you, has he?'

'Nah, but he doesn't like me. I heard him say to that old haybag.'

'Who?'

'You know, the guv'nor.'

'The governess, you mean.'

'Yeh. The Ghost said to her, "I reckon that little brat's goin' to be a damned nuisance."'

'What?' Dolly stared at him in disbelief.

'I said the Ghost said . . .'

'When did you hear him say that?'

'When I was runnin' down the stairs to the bog. Miss Jermyn grabbed me and old Pole was comin' up and he whispered to her . . .'

Dolly pushed him away and looked at him hard.

'Master Billy, you're telling fibs – whackers,' she said.

'Nah, I'm not.'

'But,' Dolly frowned, 'Mr Pole never talks to Miss Jermyn.'

'Don't be soft. I saw them . . .' Billy hesitated. It would be a mistake to tell Dolly about his pork-pie adventure in the night or she might tell Lady Eden and he would be sent back to Devil's Acre before his was belly was well and truly full – which might take some time, he thought. But he had recognized the couple in the servants' quarters, for the moonlight had been flooding through a rear window, capturing the Ghost's white face. And as for Miss Jermyn –

how could anyone mistake her grotesque snout? 'They're spoony on each other,' he said.

'Billy, if you keep telling whackers, I'll . . .'

Incensed that Dolly refused to believe him, he cried, 'It's true. It is. I saw them canoodlin'.'

'*What?*'

'They were kissin' and—'

'I know what canoodling means, Master Billy, but I don't believe you. Mr Pole and Miss Jermyn don't even like each other. And even if they did they know it's strictly against the rules for servants in the same house to have a relationship. If they're caught they get the sack and – Oh, my goodness, whatever's that?' said the nursemaid as a loud scream echoed around the house, followed by another and another. 'It's Her Ladyship. Something must've happened to Alice. Oh no!' she cried, scrambling over Billy in her haste to get out. 'Oh no, please God, not Alice.'

28

Lady Eden's screams had woken the whole house. The Eden girls crowded on to the landing, peering over the banisters, while the servants rushed out of their bedrooms or the kitchen looking bewildered.

'I must insist that nobody leave this house for any reason whatsoever until the police have arrived,' Sir Edmund said to Pole.

'Very well, sir.' The butler made a faint inclination of the head. 'I shall see to it.'

'What has happened?' Theodora leaned over the banisters and hissed to Mademoiselle Victorine, who was wringing her hands and muttering distractedly to herself.

'*La parure . . . La parure . . .*' The Frenchwoman's command of the English language had an unfortunate tendency to desert her in times of stress. '*Quelqu'un a volé la belle parure de Madame.*'

'What? What is she saying?' The girls crowded around Theodora, who spoke French tolerably well.

'Someone has stolen Mama's sapphire necklace.'

'Oh no!'

'It must have been Mademoiselle Victorine herself.' Henrietta dropped her voice to a barely audible whisper. 'She has no jewels of her own, not even a ring. Look at her now.' She nodded at the lady's maid, who was pacing up and down the landing in a nervous frenzy. 'She knows when the police come they will arrest her.'

'No.' Thomasina shook her head. 'I do not believe it was Mademoiselle. I think it was Maurice.'

'The new footman?' said Leopoldina. 'Why do you think it was him?'

'Because I overheard the Duchess of Coventry telling Mama that footmen are never to be trusted, especially the handsome ones.'

'In my opinion,' said Georgiana loftily, 'it is not one of the servants. It is almost certainly the villain Billy warned Mama about, his Uncle Rudd.' She spat out the name as if it were poison. 'In fact, I should not be at all surprised if Billy himself were not involved. He is probably an—'

'Children!' Miss Jermyn's shrill voice made them start. 'Go to your room at once. So indelicate, standing here in your night attire in full view of the male

servants,' she scolded. 'Your mama shall hear of this.'

'What were you going to say about Billy?' Theodora asked Georgiana as the sisters hurried back to their beds. 'He is probably an . . . ?'

'Accomplice.'

'What does that mean?'

'An accomplice is a person who helps another to commit a crime. It is perfectly obvious to me that since Billy was already in our house all he had to do was open a door or window . . .'

'. . . and let the burglar in!'

'Precisely.'

'What a horrible thing to do when Papa and Mama have been so kind to him,' said Edwardina.

'Indeed,' nodded Georgiana. 'But I knew all along that he was wicked. People of his class always are.'

29

As soon as he heard about the robbery Detective Inspector Craddock had no doubt who had done it. Rudd Jupp had succeeded at last. 'Curse the man!' he raged as he mounted the steps of the Edens' house the morning after the robbery. 'He's beaten me.'

If only . . . He sighed. If only the constable who had encountered Rudd and his accomplices in the night-soil cart had done his duty, Rudd would have been in prison by then — if not on the way to Australia. If only the constable hadn't rushed back to the station to change his foul-smelling clothes, Rudd would not have been free to finally get his greedy hands on the Star of India.

The wretched constable had been sacked, sent packing in disgrace, and rightly so, but that was small comfort for Craddock.

In answer to his knock the door was opened by the butler.

Now Craddock was a tough, no-nonsense police-man and had met some peculiar characters in the course of his career but rarely one as unnerving as the wraith that stood before him. Before he could stop himself he took a step back, but quickly regained his composure and said, 'I am Detective Inspector Craddock of Scotland Yard.'

'Sir Edmund and Lady Eden await you,' said Pole in his sepulchral voice and he indicated that Craddock should follow him.

'I'd be obliged if you would tell me how you dis-covered the loss of your necklace, Your Ladyship,' Craddock said as he sat with her and Sir Edmund in the morning room.

'When I returned from the palace, Inspector, I went to my room and my maid helped me to dis-robe and then I went to the sickroom. My daughter was feverish. She . . .'

'She was alone?'

'Indeed not!' Lady Eden said indignantly. 'I left her in the charge of the nursemaid, Dolly.'

Craddock looked abashed. He came from a modest background. He and his wife had only one maid, who was obliged to do everything from light-ing the fires and scrubbing the doorstep to sweeping carpets, polishing the brass and cooking dinner. The ways of the rich with their regiment of servants were a mystery to him.

'I dismissed Dolly and then recalled that I had asked Victorine, my maid, to fetch me some hot milk. I therefore went down to my room and it was then that I noticed my necklace was not where I had left it.'

'And where had you left it, M'Lady?'

'On my dressing table.'

Craddock stared at her open-mouthed.

'I know, I know, it was very foolish of me.' It was Lady Eden's turn to look embarrassed.

'Where is the necklace normally kept?'

'In the safe in Sir Edmund's study. I intended to tell the butler to put it there but . . . Oh dear, in my haste to get to Alice it slipped my mind.'

'Quite understandable in the circumstances,' said Sir Edmund, coming to her rescue.

'And the maid Victorine was in your room when you went down, M'Lady?' said Craddock.

'No, she was not. As I walked down the stairs I saw her coming up with the glass of milk.'

'So your maid was in the kitchen heating the milk while you were in the sickroom,' murmured Craddock, more to himself than to Sir Edmund or Lady Eden. 'And the other one, the nursemaid,

Dolly, where did she go after you told her to leave the sickroom?'

'To her bed, I assume. Since she had been up most of the night with Alice she was extremely tired.'

'And she sleeps where? In the kitchen?'

It was where the maid in his own home slept, but Craddock could tell from the slight tightening of Lady Eden's mouth that he had made yet another faux pas.

'Dolly has a room of her own on the nursery floor, next to the governess and the children.'

'May I ask how many servants you have?'

'Eighteen – no, seventeen at the moment. Signor Agnelli, the children's dancing master, returned to Salerno last week for the wedding of his sister.'

'And they all sleep in the house?'

'Yes, except for the coachman and grooms, of course. They sleep over the stable, in the mews.'

'And do you have any reason to suspect any of them of the theft of your jewels, M'Lady?'

'Certainly not.'

'Inspector,' said Sir Edmund, 'all our servants came to us with impeccable characters and have always given us stalwart service.'

*

 *175*

'It is not my place to contradict His Lordship, Inspector, but since this is a criminal investigation I feel it my duty to inform you that I am privy to knowledge of the servants in this household that His Lordship is not,' said Pole as he and Inspector Craddock sat in the butler's pantry.

Craddock nodded, edging his chair away as if to give himself more space to stretch his legs whereas, in fact, he was trying to get as far from Pole as possible.

'Go on, sir,' he said.

'While it is true that all the servants, myself included, have received impeccable character references from previous employers, there is one who has not.'

It was impossible for Craddock to know if the butler was looking directly at him or not from those narrow slits, but he had the feeling that a pair of cold, calculating eyes were boring into him and he shivered involuntarily.

'Chill in here,' he said, feeling foolish, for it was a warm summer's morning and the air in the small room was decidedly stuffy. 'And that one, Mr Pole, the servant who does not have an impeccable character is . . . ?'

'Dolly Medway, the children's nursemaid. I have

been displeased with her ever since I joined His Lordship's employ and on many occasions she has given me reason to castigate her. Alas, to no avail. She is incorrigible. When I tell you that the young woman was born and bred in the Strand Workhouse, Inspector, I am sure you will understand. Since her tenderest years Dolly has had the misfortune of associating with the dregs of society – men, women and children devoid of morals, unscrupulous, scheming predators. The workhouse is a cesspit and it is from this abomination that Sir Edmund, out of Christian charity, plucked Dolly.'

'I see,' said Craddock thoughtfully.

'Inevitably she has allied herself to one as base as herself, a young man by the name of Sam Perkinski . . .'

'Perkinski?' Craddock leaned forward intently.

'Bizarre as it may sound, that is the young man's name. He claims to be descended from gypsies.' Pole's expression came as close to a sneer as his rigid features would allow. 'In fact he comes from a family of beggars, pickpockets and swindlers and is himself a well-known horse thief.'

'Yes, yes, I am aware of that.'

The Perkinskis . . . Craddock sat back, rubbing his chin thoughtfully. He had always thought of them

as opportunists rather than hardened criminals — but they were related to Rudd Jupp through the mother. And Rudd Jupp would have led the Angel Gabriel astray.

'In recent months Sam Perkinski joined the Earl of Lampton's staff as a groom. I wonder if the earl is aware that his horses are in danger?' Pole mused, his thin lips twisting almost imperceptibly into a smirk. 'I have done my utmost to keep this young couple apart. I have forbidden Sam Perkinski to approach this house, but he is wicked and Dolly is wilful and I understand they have agreed to marry —' Pole paused — '*when they have the money,*' he said, emphasizing every word lest the detective fail to grasp its meaning.

'And Sir Edmund doesn't know about this?'

'His Lordship has more weighty matters with which to concern himself. It is the duty of the butler to resolve such problems himself.'

'For goodness sake, man,' Craddock burst out, irritated by Pole's frigid manner, 'don't you think His Lordship should have been told that a villain was pressing his attentions on one of the servants?'

'It is the duty of the butler to resolve such problems himself,' repeated Pole in a monotone.

Craddock leaned back in his chair, folded his arms and stared at the floor. He disliked Pole. There was no humanity, no soul behind the rigid mask and yet he had to admit the man had helped him considerably. There would have to be a full investigation into the theft of Lady Eden's necklace, of course. No self-respecting detective would allow his judgement to be swayed by the words of a butler, even the butler of a highly respected establishment. But since there was no evidence of forcible entry, he could only conclude that someone had opened a door or window and let the burglar in.

All he had to do, decided Craddock, getting to his feet, was question all the servants and eliminate each from his list of suspects until he was left with Dolly and Sam.

And the arch-villain himself, Rudd Jupp.

30

Jem and Ned leaned against a lamp-post on the corner of Stratton Street, waiting for Dolly's signal. But though they stood there for an hour or more, nobody appeared at an upper window waving a handkerchief. In fact, the house seemed strangely quiet, with none of the usual comings and goings.

'Sam's not here neither,' said Jem. 'That's rum.'

'Perhaps he doesn't want to see Dolly no more.'

'Don't be a stupe. It's a case of spoons with them.'

'So where is he then?'

'How do I know? Maybe he's got to wash the horses or give them their grub.' Grub. Jem's stomach began to gurgle at the thought of Mrs Maltby's crusty loaves and sponge cakes, for, true to her word, she always gave them tasty leftovers from the Edens' table. 'Come on,' he said, 'let's go over and get some.'

'Nah!' Ned clutched his brother's arm, pulling

him back. 'We got to wait till Dolly says the coast's clear. If we don't, the Ghost'll nab us.'

'I'm not scared of him,' retorted Jem. And shaking himself free he ran across the road, down the area steps and knocked on the door.

After a moment or so it was opened a crack and Mrs Maltby's face appeared. But it was not the usual, cheery face the boys were used to. In fact, from the look of her red-rimmed eyes the cook had been crying.

'What's up?' Jem frowned.

'Trouble. Terrible trouble,' she said. 'Her Ladyship's most precious necklace was stolen last night and . . . and –' she dabbed at her eyes, quite overcome with emotion – 'they've arrested Dolly.'

'Crikey!' exclaimed Jem.

'And Sam.'

'Blimey!'

'But Sam's straight now,' protested Ned. 'He wouldn't do it.'

'Neither would Dolly. She's a good girl, always has been. Mr Pole's had it in for her ever since he came here, says she's riff-raff from the workhouse. But it isn't true. She's honest and loyal. And she loves Her Ladyship, worships her. She wouldn't do anything to hurt her.' Mrs Maltby blew her nose and wiped her eyes, but the tears only flowed the faster.

'Mrs Maltby, can we see Billy?' said Ned.

She shook her head. 'Sir Edmund's taken Her Ladyship away for a bit; they've gone to their house in the country with Miss Alice. They've left Mr Pole in charge —' she pulled a face — 'and you know what that means.'

'"*Master Billy is not at home*,"' said Jem, mimicking the butler's sepulchral voice.

'He's hard-hearted, that man,' sighed Mrs Maltby. 'Matter of fact, I don't think he's got one. There's just a lump of ice in his chest where his heart should be.'

'So can't we see Billy no more?' said Ned in a small voice.

'You've got to wait till Sir Edmund gets back. He'll put it right.'

'And when's that?'

The cook shook her head. 'I don't know.'

Jem and Ned raced back to Devil's Acre to tell their parents the bad news.

'What'll they do to Sam, Pa?' panted Ned. 'What'll they do to him and Dolly?'

'I can't say about the girl, son, but it looks bad for Sam. He's been in clink twice before.'

'They'll put him away for the rest of his life,' said Ma.

'Or send him to Australie,' said Gran.

'Nah, they won't,' said Jem with his usual bravado.

'You goin' to stop them, are you?' said Pa, with a quizzical look in his eye.

'Yeh, I am.'

'And how you goin' to do that?'

'There's a jammy way out of this.'

'Oh, and what's that?'

'I can't tell you yet, Pa' said Jem. Because he had no idea what it was himself.

31

Billy was confused and angry when Pearl, the chief housemaid, came to wash and undress and put him to bed that evening.

'I'm only doing it till Her Ladyship hires a new nursemaid,' she explained.

'Why? Where's Dolly?' said Billy, pushing her away. 'I want Dolly.'

'She's gone, Master Billy.'

'Gone where?'

'Just gone.'

'But—'

'Now be a good boy, Master Billy,' Pearl pleaded with him, tucking the bed sheet in so tightly he could hardly breathe. 'Her Ladyship'll get a nice new nursemaid for you when she gets back.'

'Don't want a new nursemaid,' protested Billy. 'I want Dolly. Where is she? Where . . . ?'

But Pearl had gone.

*

The following morning the Eden girls were sitting at the breakfast table in the day nursery waiting for Miss Jermyn when Billy arrived looking decidedly dishevelled. His face and hands were unwashed, his blond curls in a tangle, his pantaloons on back to front and his shoes unbuckled. It was evident that he had fought a long, hard battle with Pearl – and won.

'Billy,' exclaimed Theodora, 'you can't come to the table looking like that! Miss Jermyn will be furious.'

'Don't care,' said Billy peevishly. 'I don't like Pearl. I want Dolly. Where is she?'

'You mean you don't know?' said Thomasina. 'Well –' she leaned towards him eagerly, relishing her role as bearer of bad news – 'she has been arrested for the theft of Mama's necklace.'

'*And* her lover,' said Henrietta. 'Her lover was arrested too.'

'Henrietta, such vulgar language,' Georgiana reprimanded her. 'Dolly's "intended" was also arrested, Billy. The police are of the opinion they were in collusion.'

Billy frowned.

'The crushers think Dolly and Sam were in on the scam,' Thomasina explained to Billy in words he could understand.

 *185*

'Thomasina, really!' huffed Georgiana.

'Who's Sam?' Billy frowned.

'Dolly's lover,' said Henrietta with a wicked look in her eye.

'Dolly's *intended*,' Georgiana snapped, glaring at her. 'An undesirable man from the lower classes by the name of Sam Perkinski.'

'Sam Perkinski? He's my cousin,' exclaimed Billy. 'But he couldn't've nicked your ma's sparks, cos he's not a fly bloke.'

'What is "a fly bloke"?' asked Henrietta.

'It means someone who is very clever and cunning . . .' began Thomasina.

'And it is an extremely coarse expression,' Georgiana cut her short. 'I suggest you cover your ears, Henrietta. Indeed, we should all cover our ears,' she said, putting her hands over hers and nodding approval when her sisters followed suit.

Billy sighed. Sometimes, he thought, Georgiana was even dafter than Gran.

'Good morning, children,' said Miss Jermyn, coming into the room and taking her place at the head of the table.

'Good morning, Miss Jermyn,' chorused the girls, quickly lowering their hands.

'Have you news of Alice, Miss Jermyn?' asked Georgiana.

'Not as yet.'

'Poor Alice, I do hope she will be all right,' said Henrietta.

The sisters looked at each other anxiously.

'Blimey!' Billy spluttered through a mouthful of porridge. 'The crushers haven't copped Alice as well, have they?'

'Language, Master Billy!' frowned the governess. 'And do not speak with your mouth full.'

'But Alice—'

'Do not be so foolish. Of course they have not arrested Miss Alice. Miss Henrietta was referring to her sister's delicate state of health.'

'Mama and Papa have taken Alice to our house in Tooting,' Thomasina whispered to Billy. 'They are hoping the country air will bring the bloom back to her cheeks,' said the little girl, echoing her father's words.

Billy's face fell. With Dolly and Alice gone, his future looked bleak. There was no one to talk to, no one to give him a hug, no one to play with. 'Can I go too?' he said.

'No, you may not,' said Miss Jermyn, delicately removing a crumb from her moustache with the

edge of her napkin. 'You will stay here and do your lessons and learn to be a little—'

'Nah!' Billy's resentment boiled over. 'I don't want to be a little gen'leman. I hate bleedin' gen'lemen.' And in his rage he swept his bowl of porridge off the table and tipped over the milk jug.

With loud shrieks the Eden girls sprang up, dabbing at their skirts, while Pearl hurried away to get a cloth.

'Master Billy, go to your room,' said the governess in a frosty voice.

'Nah!"

'I said, "GO TO YOUR ROOM"'

'Nah, I won't!'

'Pearl, take Master Billy to his room this instant, wash his mouth out with soap and water and lock the door when you leave.'

Billy fought tooth and nail to prevent Pearl getting anywhere near his mouth with a bar of soap, but he was secretly pleased to be confined to his room for it meant no lessons. But it also meant no food.

The lunch hour came and went and though he cried, 'Let me out! I'm starvin'! I'm dyin'!', kicking the door with all his might, it was to no avail.

At teatime the door was finally unlocked and the

governess came in carrying a glass of water and a plate on which was one thin slice of dry bread. Billy lunged at it, cramming the bread in his mouth and swallowing it without chewing.

'I'm goin',' he shouted as Miss Jermyn turned away in disgust. 'I'm goin' home. I'm goin' right now.'

'You can't go home.'

'I can. Dolly said so. Dolly said I could—'

'Dolly is not here. She is in the police station and will soon be in prison where she deserves to be, the ungrateful wretch,' said Miss Jermyn with grim satisfaction.

'But that bloke Edmund said—'

'*Sir* Edmund, if you please. And he is not here either. In his absence Mr Pole is in charge. And I can assure you he will not allow you to leave without Sir Edmund's permission.'

Billy's shoulders slumped. That meant he would have to stay till the Edens came back, and who knew how long that might be – a day, a week, a month? His parents would forget him, they might even find another boy to take his place, one from Mother Murray's baby farm . . . He was about to burst into bitter tears when a cunning thought wormed its way into his brain.

'If you don't let me go home I'll tell everyone about you and the Ghost,' he said with a sly smile.

'The Ghost?' Miss Jermyn raised her eyes enquiringly. 'There is no ghost in this establishment to my knowledge.'

'Yeh, there is. It's old Pole, the butler.'

'And what precisely will you tell everyone about Mr Pole and me?' said the governess, her mouth twisting into a sardonic smile.

'I'll tell them I saw you and him canoodlin' in the passage by the pantry.'

Billy grinned as Miss Jermyn's face drained of all colour. Even her lips went white with fear.

'Dolly said servants get the sack if they're caught canoodlin'. She said—'

'Lies!' the governess screeched. 'Lies! All lies! How dare you accuse Mr Pole and me of such outrageous behaviour?'

'But it's true. I did see you, I did. The Ghost had his arms around you and you were kissin' and—'

'You are a wicked, wicked child. I knew it from the first moment I saw you.' Miss Jermyn clutched at her heart, panting.

'Is everything all right, miss?' said Pearl, poking her head round the door. 'I heard a lot of noise.'

'Get my smelling salts, girl,' said the governess,

staggering from the room. 'Quickly, please. I feel quite overcome.'

Billy now had two choices —try to escape or stay until Sir Edmund and Lady Eden returned. Escape would not be easy with a houseful of servants watching him night and day, but staying would be worse, if he was to be imprisoned in his room and get nothing but dry bread and water. Even his brothers fared better than that.

There were only three ways out of the room — the door, the chimney and the window. The door was locked – Billy had tried it just in case Pearl had forgotten. The chimney was out of the question. Although he could have climbed up it and escaped over the rooftops, he still had nightmarish memories of his experience as a chimney sweep.

He ran to the window and looked down. It was a long, long drop to the gravel path below and if he jumped the chances were he'd break every bone in his body.

There was no way out.

He was on the verge of tears when he heard voices, and leaning out of the window as far as he could he saw people in the garden next door, men and women seated around a table, sipping tea and chatting animatedly. Billy's heart leaped. All he had to do was get their attention. And screaming was something he was good at.

Filling his lungs he started to yell, 'Hel—!' but the rest of the word was muffled by an icy hand clamped around his throat.

Billy was so shocked he froze. Then he started to struggle, lashing out with his fists and elbows and kicking as hard as he could. But it was all in vain. The more he struggled the tighter the vice-like grip on his throat, until his breathing slowed, his heart missed a beat and his eyes glazed over.

Just when he thought his lungs would burst, the cruel hand released him and he slumped to the floor, panting.

'A little gentleman does not shout at windows,' a steely voice hissed in his ear. 'If a little gentleman is caught shouting at windows again he will regret it. Do you understand my meaning?'

Billy tried to speak, but no sound came out so he nodded. He looked up, expecting to see the spectral face of Pole glaring down at him, but no one was there. Puzzled, he got to his feet and half ran, half staggered to the door and turned the handle. It was still locked. The man had come and gone without a sound.

At that moment the key turned in the lock and the door began to open.

Billy sprang away.

'I w-wasn't doin' nothin', guv. I wasn't. Honest!' he babbled. But it wasn't the butler who came in but Pearl.

'You're a lucky boy,' she said. 'Miss Jermyn says you can have supper in the nursery with the young ladies. But you must be quiet. Miss Jermyn says if you talk you'll be sent straight back to your room. You're not to say a word, not one word, d'you hear?'

The governess was absent from the table that evening.

'She's been taken unwell, miss,' Pearl explained in answer to Thomasina's persistent questioning. 'She's had an attack of the vapours because someone –' she cast an accusing look at Billy – 'upset her.'

All the girls chatted happily, relieved to be free of Miss Jermyn's oppressive presence, but Billy did not join in.

'What did you do to upset her?' Thomasina whispered in his ear. 'Did you say something rude?'

Billy shook his head.

'Why aren't you eating?' Thomasina frowned. 'You have bread and butter and a hard-boiled egg,' she said, looking enviously at his plate. 'Are you not hungry?'

Of course he was hungry, very hungry, and he longed to tell her that he wanted to eat but every time he tried to swallow he could feel Pole's fingers digging into his throat.

32

Gran got up in the early hours of the morning, crossed the yard to the caravan where Pa lay on his back snoring and shook him awake

'Eh? What?' he exclaimed, coming to with a start.

'Shh!' Gran put a warning finger to her lips and pointed at Ma and the boys, who were asleep. 'Bert, I just had a dream about poor Billy. Some crushers copped him and put him in a cart and took him to the lock-up and—'

'Hold your jaw, woman!' growled Pa. 'You're talkin' a load of tosh.'

'I'm not, Bert. It's true, I tell you. I saw it with my own eyes.'

'It's just another of your varminty dreams.'

'Billy's in danger. He is!' The old woman's voice rose shrilly, waking Ma. 'You've got to get him out of that place before it's too late.'

'Gran's right, Bert,' said Ma. 'I've been thinkin' that myself.'

'Why? He hasn't done nothin' wrong. It wasn't him that stole that necklace.'

'Nah, but he's a Perkinski, isn't he? He's cousins to Sam. And you know the way them crushers think. They tar us all with the same brush even though we're innocent as newborn babes.'

'All right, all right,' Pa reluctantly agreed. 'I'll go and get him.'

'Nah, you're too poorly, Bert. I'll go,' said Ma.

'Go now, Liza,' said Gran urgently. 'Go now, before it's too late.'

33

Billy woke early, yawned, stretched, turned over and thrust his fist under his goose-feather pillow to snuggle it against his cheek before drifting back to sleep. But there was something under his pillow, something small and hard. Intrigued, he closed his fingers around it and pulled it out. To his amazement it was Lady Eden's thimble. How on earth had it got there, he wondered? And then he realized – the Eden girls must have been playing hunt the thimble and one of them had hidden it under his pillow.

He was sitting up in bed, turning the tiny gold cup round and round in his hand, thinking how pleased Pa would be because it was obviously worth a shilling or two, when Pearl came in carrying a jug of water for his morning wash.

'Look!' He held it up for her to see. 'Look what I found.'

Pearl put the jug on the table and turned to him

with a smile, but when she saw the thimble she cried out, 'Oh, Master Billy! Oh, how could you! Naughty boy! Give it to me.'

'Nah.' Billy put his hand behind his back, holding on to the thimble tightly. 'I found it.'

'Give it to me. Quick!' said Pearl, lowering her voice and looking anxiously at the door. 'Quick – before someone comes.'

'Nah!' Billy pushed her away. 'It's mine – I won it.'

'What is all the commotion?' complained Miss Jermyn, sweeping into the room. 'You will wake up the whole house with your caterwauling.'

Pearl rushed to the bed so that the governess couldn't see Billy, but he stood up and waving the thimble above his head whooped, 'Look! Look! I found it!'

'Why . . . why that belongs to Her Ladyship,' gasped Miss Jermyn. 'You stole it. You limb of Satan, you stole it.'

'No, I don't think he did, miss,' protested Pearl.

'Of course he did. How else would he have come by it? Go and tell Mr Pole to summon the police.'

'But, miss . . .' Pearl pleaded on the verge of tears.

'At once!' thundered the governess. 'And don't you dare!' she cried, grabbing Billy who, at the mention of the dreaded word 'police', had decided to make a run for it.

'I want to go home,' bawled the little boy, trying to squirm out of her grasp. 'I want to go home.'

'I'm sure you do,' snarled Miss Jermyn. 'But the only place you are going to is the police station.'

34

Ma had never been to Mayfair. The only parts of London she knew were Devil's Acre, where she lived, and Trafalgar Square, where she worked, so she had no idea where Stratton Street was. And neither, it seemed, did anybody else she met that morning.

'Stratton Street, my darlin'?' said a woman selling watercress. 'You sure you don't mean Sloane Street?'

'Nah, I don't.'

'Well, why don't you buy some of my nice cresses, my pet?' the woman held out her basket. 'Three bunches a ha'penny. All fresh from the market this mornin'.

'I haven't got no money for vittals,' retorted Ma, brushing past her.

'Stafford Street?' said a chimney sweep, leaning over his cart. 'That's the other side of Oxford Street, my ducky.'

'I said "Stratton".'

'Stratton?' The man stroked his blackened skin with a sooty hand. 'You sure it's in London?'

Finally Ma had the good fortune to meet a postman.

'Go straight down Piccadilly,' he said, pointing with the stick he used to knock on doors. 'You'll pass the Gloucester Coffee House, then the Duke of Devonshire's place – you can't miss it, it's an ugly building with a big brick wall in front of it. Then Stratton Street's next on your right.'

Ma didn't admit she couldn't read, nor could she tell her left from her right, but after a few more wrong turnings she finally reached the street where the Edens lived and, pausing to straighten her battered straw hat and adjust a ragged shawl around her shoulders, she knocked on the front door.

It was opened by Norris Pole, who informed her in icy tones that beggars were to use the area entrance or better still, he added, looking scornfully at her shabby skirt and down-at-heel boots, not at all.

'I am not a beggar, you stuck-up beanpole,' she snapped, hands on hips. 'I'm Billy's ma and I've come to get him.'

'You are too late.'

'Too late? What d'you mean? It's early. It's no more'n six o'clock.'

'I mean, Billy no longer resides here.'

'He no longer what?'

'He does not live here any more.'

'Where's he gone?'

'He has been apprehended.'

'Been what?'

'Arrested.'

'Copped? My Billy? What for?'

'A serious misdemeanour.'

'Can't you talk normal like the rest of us?'

'He has committed a crime.'

'Nah, not Billy.' Ma shook her head. 'He couldn't. He wouldn't. He's too sappy, bless him.'

'Nevertheless he stole a thimble from Her Ladyship, an item of considerable value, for which he will be soundly punished.'

And before Ma could stick her boot in the door the butler slammed it shut.

Ma ran all the way back to Devil's Acre, bumping into people and sometimes falling over herself in her haste.

'Bert! Bert!' she cried, stumbling up the steps of the caravan, panting heavily. 'They've copped Billy.

They say he stole some pesky thimble from that woman.'

'Where is he?' said Pa, trying to get up.

'In the lock-up. The crushers've got him.'

'Right, I'm goin' to . . . Aargh!' Pa groaned, bent double with pain.

'You can't go, Bert, you're too poorly. Oh, what're we goin' to do? Billy, my poor little Billy,' wailed Ma, her eyes welling with tears. 'I knew we shouldn't have let them toffs take him. I knew it.'

Jem was now faced with a dilemma. He had promised his mother that he would never see or speak to his Uncle Rudd again after the failed attempt to steal the Star of India from the Edens, but he was quite sure that if anyone could help them save Billy and Sam it was Rudd Jupp. His uncle knew everyone in the criminal world – he would know who had stolen the sapphire necklace and if he didn't he would soon find out. But . . . Jem chewed his lip in an agony of indecision – he had promised his mother, promised with his fingers uncrossed that he would never see or speak to his uncle again. And he could not, dared not break a promise like that, for who knew what terrible thing would happen to him? Unless . . .

'Ned,' he said as they set off from Devil's Acre the day after Billy's arrest, 'who do we know who could help us save Billy and Sam?'

'Don't know.' Ned shrugged.

'But there must be someone, maybe even someone in our family who's a leary bloke.'

But Ned wasn't listening. He had seen a particularly big rat scampering along the gutter and pulling his catapult out of his pocket he took aim at it.

Jem gave him a push so hard it nearly knocked him over.

'Pack off!' Ned rounded on him angrily. 'I could've got it if you hadn't—'

'Just listen, will you!' snapped Jem. 'I said, who do we know . . . ?'

'I already told you, I don't know nobody.'

'Course you do. A sharp bloke, one of the best cracksman in London. He came to Gran's birthday party.'

'Oh . . .' At last the penny thudded home. 'Oh, Uncle Rudd, you mean.'

'*Uncle Rudd?*' Jem stopped and looked at his brother in amazement. 'Lor', Ned, you're right. I hadn't thought of him. What d'you think we should do?'

'Go and see him, of course.'

'Nah.' Jem shook his head doubtfully. 'Nah, I don't think so.'

'Why not?'

'I don't think Uncle Rudd likes me.'

'You cracky or somethin'?' Ned stared at him, puzzled.

'Tell you what, you go on your own.'

'*What?*'

'I said . . .'

'Nah, I'm not goin' into St Giles on my own – not for Sam, not for Billy, not for no one,' retorted Ned, for Pa had warned them not to go into that rookery – 'On account of you'll never come out alive.'

'So you're makin' me go with you to see Uncle Rudd?' said Jem.

'Yeh, you got to.'

'Oh, well, I don't have no choice then, do I?' And grinning from ear to ear Jem led the way to St Giles.

'Where's Uncle Rudd live?' whispered Ned as the two boys stole through the dark and filthy alleyways of the infamous rookery, hunching their shoulders and huddling together in a vain attempt to make themselves inconspicuous.

'Just off Church Street.'

 205

'And where's that?' said Ned, hardly daring to lift his eyes from the rugged cobblestones lest he meet the baleful gaze of a potential murderer or kidnapper.

'Don't know.'

'You *don't know*? You mean we've come all this way and—'

'You'll have to ask someone.'

'Not me.' Ned shook his head vigorously.

'You're lily-livered, you are,' growled Jem. And going up to an old woman slouching in a doorway dressed in an assortment of rags he said, 'Where's Church Street, missus?'

The woman looked him up and down and pointed to a dark passageway. 'Go down there,' she said. 'You can't miss it.'

'I don't like this,' Ned whispered as the two of them groped their way along the rat-infested passageway and emerged into a courtyard piled high with rotting refuse and dung. 'And I don't like the look of them blokes over there neither.' He nodded at three men in billycock hats, who were lounging against the wall eyeing the boys in much the same way that a pride of lions eyes two tasty little antelopes. 'I think we should go back.'

The boys turned to run, but the men were faster.

In an instant one of them towered over them, barring their way, a cruel expression on his face, an even crueller knife in his hand, which he fingered lovingly as if he was itching to use it.

'Not seen you two in the Holy Land before,' he said. 'What brings you to these parts, eh?'

'They're up to no good, you ask me, Grind,' said another, his face and arms bearing the deep scars of recent stab wounds.

'Pigs' narks by the look of them,' said the third, glaring at the boys with hard, unforgiving eyes. 'Come to spy on us, I reckon.'

'Got any of the ready, have you?' said Grind, running his hand over the boys' jackets. 'A shillin', a tanner? You wouldn't want to leave without givin' us a little somethin' to remember you by, now would you?' He leered at them while the other men sniggered.

'We haven't got no money, guv. We haven't got nothin',' said Jem as the three men circled him and Ned, licking their lips in anticipation.

'Nothin'? Oh, that's a pity. We don't like brats that come visitin' us with nothin',' said Grind, pressing the tip of his knife against Jem's throat.

'W-we're not v-visitin' you, guv,' stammered Ned, watching in horror as a tiny drop of blood

trickled down Jem's neck. 'W-w-we've come to see our uncle.'

'Oh yeh? Bob's your uncle, is he?'

'Nah, he's called Rudd, R-Rudd Jupp.'

The name had the most amazing effect on the men, for in a flash they changed from menacing predators, ready to slit the boys' throats and toss their bodies into the sewers, to forelock-tugging, hat-raising toadies.

'Rudd Jupp?' said Grind in awe.

'Yeh,' Jem nodded. 'D' you know him?'

'Know him? Course I know him.' Grind swelled with pride. 'And he knows me.'

'Would you take us to him?'

'It'd be my pleasure,' grinned the man, pushing the knife back up his sleeve and motioning Jem and Ned to follow him.

It was clear the artful old woman had deliberately given the boys the wrong directions, for as Grind led them back down the passageway and across the street she called out, 'I want half what you took off them.'

'I didn't take nothin',' Grind shouted over his shoulder, 'on account of they're Rudd Jupp's nephews.'

'Rudd Jupp? Oh, sorry, sorry, my duckies. I didn't realize, I didn't know . . .'

Jem nudged Ned as the old woman burbled apologies. 'Seems our uncle's uncommon popular in these parts. I don't reckon nobody'll dare lay their paws on us now.'

Grind walked quickly down the street, through another passageway and across a courtyard until he came to a rundown public house, its paintwork peeling, its door hanging by one hinge.

'Stay close to me, don't look at no one and keep your traps shut,' he said, pushing the door open.

Although it was still early morning the bar was already crowded with men and women in various stages of inebriation, from tipsy to comatose. Some were chattering, arguing, laughing, singing, drinking and falling about like rag dolls. Others lay dead to the world on tables, under tables, clutching empty bottles, their coarse faces deformed and bloated, their brains numbed by gin and porter.

'Mornin', Grind,' snuffled the landlord, a thuggish man whose nose had been broken so many times he looked like a Pekinese.

'Mornin', Fowler,' said Grind, making a furtive sign with his thumb and third finger.

The landlord nodded. 'The party you're lookin' for is there,' he said. 'You can go in.'

Grind elbowed his way through the crowd and looking over his shoulder to make sure he wasn't observed he leaned against a wooden wall panel, which slid open just wide enough for a man to squeeze through.

'Quick!' he urged the boys, pushing them into a small courtyard where a dozen or more fighting dogs, many of them half starved, all of them trained to be vicious, were chained to their kennels. As soon as they saw the intruders the dogs set up an ear-splitting clamour and strained to get at their ankles.

Beyond the first courtyard was a second, where a dozen or more loutish men were leaning on a wooden enclosure watching two magnificent cocks fighting to the death, their red-gold feathers puffed up as they raked and tore at each other.

'Go it! Go it, Joey!' cried a man as one of the cocks began to weaken.

'That's the ticket, Scarlet!' yelled the man next to him as the other cock forced the loser to the ground, pecking and clawing it mercilessly until it lay fluttering helplessly in a pool of blood.

There were shouts of approval, money changed

hands and then two more unfortunate birds were thrown into the ring.

'In here,' Grind said to Jem and Ned, opening the door to an outhouse. Most of the occupants were gathered around tables, gambling with cards or dice, but they all looked up sharply when Grind and the two boys came in, their eyes suspicious, for there wasn't a man among them who wasn't a murderer, kidnapper, burglar, area sneak, shoplifter, fence, confidence trickster or forger, and all were on the run from the police.

The women were no better, for many of them made their living by luring some unsuspecting man back to their room, where he was set upon by their fellow conspirators, beaten, robbed, stripped and hurled down the stairs.

'Who're them brats, Grind?' growled a giant of a man with the bruised and battered face of a prize fighter.

'They say they're Rudd's nephews.'

'What?' came a cry of surprise from a darkened corner.

All eyes turned to look as a youngish man with a small, wiry body and the face of a fidgety ferret stepped forward to greet the boys, his head continually jerked to one side in a nervous tic, his eyes darting everywhere as if he expected someone or something to leap on him at any moment.

'Ullo, Uncle Rudd,' beamed Jem.

'I found them, Rudd,' said Grind. 'They were wanderin' around lost and I saw some ugly customers threatenin' them so I thought I'd best get them to you before they got hurt. I hope as how I did the right thing.'

'I'm much obliged to you, Grind,' said Rudd, managing a quick smile between his tics.

'That's all right, Rudd. You know I only did it cos you and me are mates and I'd never ask no favours in return, although if you happened to have a job comin' up . . .'

'Matter of fact I have, Grind. A plummy one.'

'Well, you know I make a good crow, Rudd.'

'I know that, Grind. And I'll bear you in mind.'

'Thanks, Rudd, that's very civil of you,' said Grind. And he walked away, well pleased with the turn events had taken, for Rudd and his partners in crime lived like lords on the proceeds of the gold, silver and jewels they had stolen – until they gambled and drank themselves back into poverty.

As the worst of London's low life settled back down to cards and dice, Rudd threaded his way through the tables and dismissing his cronies with a

flick of the hand he motioned to Jem and Ned to take their places.

'They've copped Billy – and Sam and his girl for that necklace, Uncle Rudd,' said Jem.

'So I do hear.' The man nodded gravely. 'It's a bad business.'

'Did you nick it, Uncle Rudd?' asked Ned.

Rudd's nervous tic went into overdrive and he gave Ned a baleful look. 'Nah, I did not. I wouldn't hardly let them cop my own flesh'n blood for it if I'd done it, would I? Although,' he added, his face relaxing into a sly grin, 'I'd have liked to get my paws on them sparks and that's the truth. Lor' knows I've tried often enough, haven't I?' he said, winking at Jem.

Jem flushed and gave a sideways glance at Ned. His mother had told him not to tell his brothers that he had helped – or tried to help – his uncle steal the Star of India. But Ned seemed not to have noticed.

'Course, that varminty Craddock thinks I nicked it, tried to arrest me he did, but I told him I was nowhere near the Edens' house that night. Matter of fact,' Rudd's grin turned positively wolfish, 'I was in clink at the time for bein' lushed and disorderly.'

'What'll happen to Billy and Sam?' asked Jem.

'They'll be tried and found guilty – course they will,' he said, waving aside Jem's protests. 'Then they'll be put in clink for a bit before they go to Australie. They'll be shipped out at different times to different places so they won't never see each other again.'

'You mean Billy'll be all on his own in Australie?' said Ned in a small voice.

'That's about it.'

'But he didn't do it, Uncle Rudd,' Jem blurted out angrily. 'Billy's so sappy he couldn't pinch a walking stick off a blind man.'

'I know that, son.' Rudd glanced nervously around the room, his tic working ten to the dozen. 'It was an inside job, always is,' he whispered. 'Ten to one a footman cracked that crib. Footmen!' His eye-balls swivelled angrily in their sockets. 'Thievin' varmints the lot of them,' he spat. 'Whoever did it'll lay low for a bit till he thinks the coast's clear, then he'll move on. He'll leave the Edens, you mark my words, get a job in another place and nick somethin' else.'

'But the crushers—'

'Can't prove nothin', Jem. Whoever nicked that necklace hasn't got it no more, that's for sure. It's already cut up into smaller sparks. I reckon right

this minute it's probably four rings, three bracelets and a stickpin. As for that thing you put on your finger they say Billy pinched . . .'

'Man says it's called a thimble,' said Ned helpfully. 'Women use them to—'

'Yeh, well, somebody put it under Billy's pillow so he'd get copped.'

'Why'd they do that?'

'Cos Billy must've seen or heard somethin' and they were frightened he'd start blabbin' about it.'

'You mean the cove that pinched the necklace pinched the thimble as well and put it under Billy's pillow?'

'That's right.'

'How long d'you think Billy'll have to stay in Australie, Uncle Rudd?'

'Well, it's like this,' the man sighed, 'the toffs don't like havin' their stuff nicked, so they got to make an example of anyone who tries. I reckon Sam and Billy and the girl'll get –' he leaned back, staring at the grimy ceiling pensively – the best part of fourteen years.'

'Fourteen years?' Jem yelped. 'Crimes, we'll all be dead by the time they come back.'

'*If* they come back. It's a horrible cruel place, I do hear.'

'How long'll it be before they go?'

'Could be just a couple of months, so we'd best get movin'. Here's what you've got to do . . .' Jem and Ned leaned forward eagerly, straining to hear, for their uncle was so used to being spied on by plain-clothes detectives and their paid informers he rarely raised his voice above a hoarse whisper, even if he was discussing the weather. 'You've got to watch the Edens' house like hawks. Find out as much as you can about the coves that work there, where they come from, where they go on their days off, that kind of thing. Best way to do it is get matey with one of the servants.'

'We already have. She's called Mrs Maltby,' said Jem eagerly.

'She's the cook, Uncle Rudd,' explained Ned. 'We go down the area every day when no one's about and she gives us jammy grub like mutton pies and dove tarts and . . .'

'Yeh, yeh, right,' said Rudd impatiently, his head jerking twice as hard as usual. 'Now listen, you've got to tell me what all them flunkeys look like. I don't mean they got two eyes, a conk and a kisser; I mean a proper description. I know most of the cracksmen in London, so . . .'

'So when you tumble to the one that nicked the

necklace you'll nab him, Uncle Rudd?' Ned was so excited at the prospect of saving Billy from transportation his voice rose until he was shouting.

'One step at a time, Ned. One step at a time,' hissed Rudd, putting a rough hand over the boy's mouth to silence him. 'We're dealin' with a fly customer here. If he gets wind we're on to him he'll –' Rudd waved an imaginary magic wand like a conjurer – 'disappear into thin air.'

35

Sam, Dolly and Billy were sent to trial the following week – Sam and Dolly to the Old Bailey, Billy to a special court for children.

'But I didn't pinch the varminty fimble,' whined Billy. 'I found it. I keep tellin' you, I found it.'

'You found it under your pillow?' said the magistrate.

'Yeh.'

'But you did not put it there yourself?'

'Nah.'

'Who do you think put it there?'

'One of them Eden girls. They were playin' a game.'

'We have questioned Sir Edmund's daughters and all of them have sworn on the Holy Bible that they have never put a thimble, or indeed anything else, under your pillow.'

'Then someone else did it.'

'Are you suggesting that some other person or

persons stole the thimble – a very fine gold thimble, I might add, studded with turquoises – and put it under your pillow?'

'Yeh.'

'And who, in your opinion, might that have been?'

Billy thought about the people in the Edens' house who might have done such a spiteful thing. 'I reckon it was old Jermyn.'

'And who is "Old Jermyn"?'

There was a hurried discussion among the clerks sitting around a table in the well of the court and much riffling through reams of paper before one of them said, 'Your Honour, Miss Jermyn is the governess in Sir Edmund's establishment. She is a woman of excellent character and her employers speak very highly of her.'

'I see.' The magistrate turned back to Billy, who was standing in the dock gazing vacantly at the ceiling and dreaming about pork pies. 'Why do you think Miss Jermyn put the thimble under your pillow, boy?'

'Cos she's a right old trout.'

'That is hardly a reason.'

'She had it in for me, guv.'

'And why did the governess "have it in" for you?'

'Cos she said I ate worms and she made me wear nesties and—'

'Yes, yes, that will do.' The magistrate silenced him with an impatient gesture. 'Billy Perkinski, I find you guilty of this wicked crime and I sentence you to transportation to New South Wales for the term of fourteen years.'

'Wales?' said Billy, his eyes lighting up. 'I got an uncle lives in Wales. Can I go and stay with him?'

'Not Wales, you foolish child. *New South Wales.* It is a province of Australia.'

'Australie?' Billy cried out as if he'd been hit. 'Nah, nah,' he sobbed as he was led away, 'I don't want to go, don't want to go to Australie.'

36

Mercifully Alice did not have cholera, nor any of the fearful diseases prevalent at that time, and after a short break in the country she was sufficiently recovered to return to London with her parents. But the news of her nursemaid's arrest upset her greatly.

'They can't send Dolly to prison, Mama. They can't,' she cried. 'And poor Billy too. You must do something. You must stop them.'

'Don't distress yourself, darling,' said Lady Eden, stroking her daughter's pale cheek to calm her.

'But Dolly didn't steal your necklace, Mama. She wouldn't steal anything from anyone.'

'Dolly was very foolish, Alice. She betrothed herself to a man who was a thief. Had we known, Papa and I would have prevented it and she might well still be with us. As for Billy,' Lady Eden sighed, 'there is no doubt that he stole my thimble. Poor child, he was proud of what he had done. He had no idea it was a crime.'

'I cannot begin to express my very deep regret at what has happened,' said Sir Edmund, who was sitting on the edge of an upturned orange box in the Perkinskis' caravan. 'The temptation was too much for the boy. I should have foreseen it. It was foolish, most foolish of me.' He gnawed his lower lip, one of his habitual gestures when he was anxious or unhappy. There was no doubt in his mind that Billy had stolen the thimble and time and time again he scolded himself for having taken a child from such a deprived background into the abundant wealth of his Mayfair home.

'It's not your fault, guv,' said Ma miserably.

'On the contrary, madam, I cannot but feel that it is.'

'Nah, you did it for the best, guv,' said Pa, sitting up. 'You wanted to give him a good life and – argh!'

'May I enquire as to the state of your health, sir?' said Sir Edmund, looking anxiously at Pa as he doubled up, clutching his stomach and groaning.

'It's as you see me, guv. My bread basket aches somethin' chronic. If this goes on much longer, I'll drop off the hooks.'

'I wonder — would you permit me to send my doctor to examine you? He is an excellent man. We were fearful that our youngest daughter Alice had contracted some malignant disease, but a physic prescribed by Dr Lacey effected a speedy cure.'

'Nah!' Pa exclaimed in alarm. 'I don't need no fizzy. I don't—'

'Yeh, he does, Guv. He needs some medicine — proper medicine,' said Ma, cutting him short. 'Only we can't afford no quack ourselves.'

'My dear lady, I should be delighted to bear any expenses incurred. It is the least I can do.' Sir Edmund got to his feet. 'I shall arrange for Dr Lacey to visit your husband without delay.'

37

Getting Mrs Maltby to talk about her fellow servants presented no problem. In fact, after a while Jem and Ned began to fear she would never stop.

'Now Milly – she's our kitchen maid – and Minny, the scullery maid, are twins. Their father took off before they were born – I suppose the thought of two in one go frightened him away – and their mother died three years ago, God rest her soul, so Lady Eden took them in, poor little mites. Pearl, the housemaid, comes from Whitechapel way. She can be a bit lippy at times but she's a hard worker. Then there's Signor Agnelli and Mam'selle Victorine. They're foreigners . . .' Mrs Maltby gave the boys a knowing look. 'Very fidgety they are, like a couple of cats on hot bricks, not –' she leaned forward and lowered her voice, 'not sensible like us English. She came down to the kitchen the other day, that Mam'selle Victorine, and . . . Here!' the

cook suddenly stopped, a suspicious look appearing in her eye. 'Why d'you want to know all this?'

'Cos . . . er . . . cos Billy used to talk to us about Dolly and them other people,' said Jem.

'Ah, poor Billy.' Mrs Maltby's face fell. 'I hear he got fourteen years. Of course he should never have done such a thing. Wicked it was. And as for Sam and Dolly . . .'

'But they didn't do it. They didn't. It was one of the ser—' began Ned. But Jem shut him up with a warning look and an elbow in the ribs.

'What about the two mouldy pates?' he said.

'You mean our footmen, I suppose?' Mrs Maltby folded her arms over her substantial bosom and settled down for some more gossip. 'Well, Ralph's a decent enough fellow, but that new one, Maurice –' she pursed her lips – 'he worked for Lord and Lady FitzHubert but he got chucked out – some nonsense about a dog, she's soft about that animal, so they say. Sir Edmund and Lady Eden took Maurice on, they're kind-hearted like that, but if you want my opinion they shouldn't have. He's up to a move or two, that man. I can see it in his eyes. I know Mr Pole doesn't trust him.

'Now Mr Pole's only been here a short time. He took over when our other butler was sacked – the

silly man used to smoke cigars in the pantry at night because Lady Eden didn't allow smoking, and he'd leave the window open to get rid of the smell and one night a thief got in, a boy . . .'

Jem turned white and stared at the ground.

'You all right, son?' said Mrs Maltby.

Jem nodded, not trusting himself to speak.

'Anyway,' continued Mrs Maltby, 'as I was saying . . . What was I saying?'

Ned, who had been half asleep, shook himself awake and said, 'Mr Pole . . .'

'Oh yes. Mr Pole worked for a duke before he came here. Very snooty about it he is. Makes it quite clear the rest of us are beneath him. And as for Miss Jermyn —' the cook's chins wobbled with indignation — 'we're not good enough to clean her boots just because she was governess to the children of a French count — or he might have been Italian or Spanish, they're all the same. The way Miss Jermyn talks you'd think she'd worked for the Queen of England instead of — Oh dear, I can hear Mr Pole scolding Minny. Here, take this,' she said, hastily wrapping a loaf of bread and a piece of cheese in a cloth and putting it into Jem's outstretched hands. 'Go on! Go on!' she hissed, shooing him and Ned away. 'And don't tell anybody I've been tittle-tattling about the servants. If Her Ladyship was to hear, I'd lose my job.'

'You were right, Uncle Rudd,' Jem said that evening as the three of them sat, heads close together, around Rudd's usual table in the Crown and Anchor. 'It *is* one of the footmen. The cook good as said so, didn't she, Ned? It's a bloke called Maurice.'

'Maurice?' Rudd shook his head. 'Nah, never heard of no cracksman called Maurice. Course, he's probably given himself another moniker. What's he look like?'

'His hair's white and—'

'I know that, you nincompoop. Every footman's hair's covered with lard and white powder. I want to know what his clock's like.'

'It's . . . er, well, it's . . .' Jem struggled to find the words to describe Maurice's handsome face. 'It's – you know. It's just a face.'

Rudd's nervous tic went wild. 'That the best you can do?' he snapped.

'He's got a big forehead,' said Ned hastily, for his uncle was well known for his quick and frequently violent temper, 'and a small conk.'

'And he's got somethin' in his chin like this.' Jem

pressed a cleft into his chin with his middle finger. 'It's a . . . What's it called, Ned?'

'A dumplin'.'

'Yeh, that's it. He's got a dumplin' in his chin.'

'You pullin' my leg?' barked Rudd, his face darkening.

'He means a dimple,' volunteered a young woman sitting at the next table.

'Eavesdroppin' again, Lily?' Rudd rounded on her angrily.

'Nah, I'm not,' she bridled. 'But I can't help hearin' them two brats screechin' their heads off, can I? I'm not deaf, you know.'

It was quite obvious from the way Rudd reached out and pinched Lily's cheek that she was his girl. 'All right, all right, my pet, don't get crotchety,' he said. 'Now, about this footman . . .' he turned his attention back to his nephews. 'He doesn't sound like nobody I know.'

Jem's shoulders slumped. 'So you don't reckon he lifted the necklace, Uncle Rudd?'

'Nah, I'm not sayin' that. He could be new to the business. Or he could've come from somewhere else, somewhere out of London.'

'So now what do we do?'

'Follow him. Follow him everywhere on his time

off – not too close, mind – and let me know where he goes, what he does, who he meets. Same goes for all the other flunkeys.'

'Crimes, we can't be everywhere at once!' Ned protested.

'D'you want them to send Billy to Australie or not?' said his uncle hotly.

'Couldn't you help us?' asked Jem.

'Me? Lor', son, if I was to even walk past the Edens' house, old Craddock'd cop me on suspicion. I can't step out my own front door – if I had one – but that varmint drags me up before the beak and I'm back in chokey again. I can't make a decent livin' with him breathin' down my neck all the time. Nah, I'm tellin' you straight, if you want to help Billy you've got to do it on your own. But be careful. You're not dealin' with toolers and buzzers here. You're dealin' with pros. And they can get nasty, very nasty. So watch yourselves or you'll come a mucker.'

38

The fields of Tothill in Westminster had rarely been a happy place for beings on two legs or four. Men had fought bloody battles to the death there, witches had been burned there, bears and bulls tormented and killed in the name of sport there, and hundreds of victims of the Great Plague were buried there. Given such a morbid history, it was the perfect site for a prison.

Built in the shape of a shamrock – the wing on the left for boys under seventeen, the other two for women – the Tothill Fields prison operated on the 'silent system'. No talking, laughing, singing or whistling was permitted by day or night. In addition prisoners were to look straight ahead at all times. A whispered word, a favourite song hummed absentmindedly, a glance to the left or right resulted in punishment, which could be a night or two in solitary confinement, a flogging or going without food.

Despite cramming three prisoners into cells

designed for two, with no water, no lighting, no lavatory – except for one zinc pan – no heating in winter and only a small hole in the wall for ventilation in the heat of the summer, Tothill Fields was considered a better prison than all the others and it was through its immense and forbidding iron gates that a very frightened Billy was conveyed after his brief appearance in court.

He was immediately given a bath, a uniform – a three-piece suit in iron grey, check shirt, sturdy boots and a woolly cap with ear flaps – and a midday meal. But even an ample serving of cold tinned mutton, potatoes and bread couldn't stop him whimpering, 'I didn't do it. I didn't do it.'

'Silence!' said the warder, standing over him.

'I want to go home.' Billy pushed the food away. 'I want to go home. I want my ma. I want—'

'Silence!' thundered the warder. 'Another word and you'll be punished, my lad.'

39

Dr Lacey was one of the most eminent physicians in London and, therefore, one of the most expensive. He charged twenty guineas for a visit to a patient's house and five guineas for pills and potions.

'Devil's Acre?' he exclaimed in answer to Sir Edward's request. 'Good heavens, sir, that is an infamous slum.'

'I am aware of that. I have been there myself. I should not presume to ask you to visit such a disreputable neighbourhood, Doctor, had I not done a great wrong to a man living there and for which I am most anxious to make amends.'

Dr Lacey sighed, a very audible sigh to convey his displeasure. But many years before, when he was a young man, he had made a mistake, a grave error of judgement that might have jeopardized his career had Sir Edmund not stood by him. 'Oh, very well,' he said. 'I shall go and see this . . . this . . . What did you say his name was?'

'Perkinski. Bert Perkinski.'

'Devil's Acre,' Dr Lacey muttered to himself as the butler showed him out. 'Devil's Acre . . . Upon my word, I shall be lucky to escape with my life, let alone my wallet.'

40

Maurice, the Edens' new footman, had one weekday afternoon and every other Sunday afternoon off. Freed of his uniform for a few hours, his larded, powdered hair concealed under a hat, he ran lightly up the area stairs and headed down the street.

'There he goes,' whispered Jem, peeking round the corner. 'I'll follow him while you—'

'Nah!' Ned shook his head vigorously. 'You always get to do the interestin' bits. You stay here and I'll follow him.'

'Oh, all right, all right. We'll toss for it. Got a coin?'

'Course I haven't.'

'Well, I have.' And Jem pulled a farthing out of the purse he hid under his waistband.

'Here, where d'you get that from?'

'Nicked it from Gran when she was sleepin'. I'll toss and you call. Heads, I follow Maurice; tails, you stay here, right?'

'Right,' said Ned.

The coin flew up into the air, turning over and over.

'Well, come on, plaguy quick. Is it heads or tails?' Jem cried. 'Oh, too late.' He pounced on the farthing as it fell to the ground. 'It's heads. That means I go.'

'But you didn't give me enough time. I was goin' to say tails.'

'Wouldn't have made no difference, you ninny. Tails means you stay.'

Ned leaned against the railings, his hands stuffed deeply in his pockets, scowling. Why was it, he wondered gloomily, that he always seemed to lose in any contest with his brother, even when they tossed a coin? A thought suddenly penetrated the inner recesses of his brain and he shot forward.

'Oy!' he yelled. 'Oy, that wasn't fair. You cheated. You . . . !'

But Jem had gone.

41

Jem dogged Maurice's footsteps from a safe distance, darting into doorways when the footman turned, as he did frequently, to cast nervous glances up and down the street as if he sensed he was being followed. With Jem in pursuit, Maurice came at length within sight of a public house called the Running Footman, a watering hole popular with many servants in the vicinity.

Maurice quickened his pace as he drew near and Jem could almost sense his relief that he had reached his destination safely, but just as he was about to push open the door a man emerged from an alleyway, laid a hand on his shoulder and swung him round to face him as easily as if the footman were no more than a toy.

Jem, watching from behind a pillar, saw the terror in the footman's face as he tried in vain to free himself from his assailant's vice-like grip. The two began arguing violently and Jem edged forward to hear what they were saying. Suddenly the other man drew a murderous knife from his sleeve and looked about to plunge it into Maurice's chest when three crushers appeared, swinging their truncheons and looking about them with a keen eye for trouble.

As soon as he saw them the man quickly put the knife back up his sleeve, snarled something at the petrified footman, pushed him roughly aside and melted into the crowd.

'What did the bloke say to Maurice, d'you know?' asked Rudd when Jem repeated the incident to him.

'He said, "You struck lucky this time, you rat. But next time . . ."'

'And what did Maurice do then?'

'Went into the pub, sat in a corner starin' at the door like a mouse starin' at a cat and . . .'

'Yeh?'

'And then I didn't see him no more.'

'What d'you mean?'

'I went down an alley to bog and when I came back he'd scarpered,' Jem admitted, shamefaced.

'He must've got out the back way or through the cellars,' Rudd murmured, more to himself than to Jem. 'And what about the other man, the one what attacked him?'

'Never saw him again.'

'What was he like? Tall, short, hairy, bald?' Rudd prompted his nephew, knowing that Jem was not the most observant of boys.

'Big. Not as big as Pa, of course —' in Jem's estimation nobody had the impressive physique of his father — 'but shoulders like that —' he stretched his arms wide — 'and I couldn't hardly see his face for whiskers.'

'D'you reckon Maurice knew him?'

'Oh yeh, he knew him all right.'

'Good, good.' Rudd nodded, his chin pulling his head down, his tic pulling it to one side so that he looked as if he was agreeing and disagreeing with his nephew at the same time. 'Keep watchin' him, Jem. Maurice is up to somethin', and from the look of it it's goin' bad for him.'

Ned was peeved.

'It's all right for you,' he complained. 'You're havin' all the fun. All I'm doin' is traipsin' all over London after varminty maids meetin' their blokes or visitin' their grans. I've spent hours'n hours watchin' them canoodlin' in the park or takin' some old crone for a walk. I don't see the point, straight I don't. Why've I got to follow them when we know Maurice is the bloke that 'arf-inched the necklace?'

'Cos you never know.'

'Never know what?'

'That's the point,' insisted Jem. 'You never know what.'

42

All the boys in Tothill Fields wore numbers, badges and marks on their left sleeve to show what their crime had been and the length of their imprisonment. As well as a yellow waistcoat and a yellow collar attached to his jacket identifying him as a thief, Billy sported a yellow ring around his arm, which meant he was condemned to transportation, and a large number one, for first-class prisoner, together with a badge informing his fellow inmates that he was sentenced to more than two years.

Such an impressive array of bits and bobs marked Billy as a master criminal in the estimation of the other prisoners, the majority of whom were nine or ten years older than him, and his arrival caused quite a sensation.

'He's only five,' the boys whispered to each other in awe, 'and he's already a top cracksman.'

'What did he nick?'

Nobody was quite sure. To justify such a severe

sentence it had to have been something that belonged to an aristocrat, and one of high rank at that. What the boys didn't know they made up and the story grew more and more ridiculous with every telling: Billy had stolen a mother-of-pearl snuff box belonging to an earl, a countess's silver bracelet, a duchess's emerald ring, the Lord Mayor of London's gold chain of office . . . By the time the story had been around the prison twice, Billy was credited with having stolen the jewels from the Queen's crown. In fact, he had stolen the crown itself . . . 'And the old girl was wearin' it at the time,' whispered one credulous boy into the ear of another.

'Lor', he must be brilliant.'

The only person who resented Billy's imagined achievement was a short, squat, thuggish boy called Zed Stoke. Stoke's huge head with its tiny, vacant eyes and slack, blubbery mouth looked as if it had been rammed into his shoulders by a sledgehammer and his bulging biceps were covered in hideous tattoos. In his fifteen years on earth Stoke had been imprisoned twenty times, mostly for stealing from or assaulting old men and women too weak to defend themselves, but as none of them came from the middle or upper classes he was always given a light sentence.

Because of his unruly behaviour in prison, however, he had been flogged, deprived and shut up in a cell by himself more often than he could remember. But every punishment was another badge of honour as far as Stoke was concerned and that, plus the ability to use his fists to advantage, ensured he was treated with respect and fear by the other boys. He was number one in Tothill Fields, the self-styled 'king' – until Billy arrived.

Stoke was almost choked by his bitterness and resentment of the newcomer, doubly so when he finally saw the little boy. 'He's just a baby,' he scoffed.

'But he stole the crown jewels, Stoke,' said the other boys. 'And they're boatin' him to Australie for it.'

Stoke had never been transported, never even been sentenced to transportation. Nor had he wanted to – until that moment. But the thought that this pretty little blue-eyed, golden-haired 'baby' had achieved what he hadn't, and was being hailed as a hero for it, made his blood boil.

On his first night behind bars Billy was put into the prison dormitory, a huge room which stretched the entire length and width of one block. Unfort-

unately there were twice as many boys as iron beds in this grim barracks, so the less fortunate had to sleep on skimpy mattresses on the floor.

As a mark of their admiration, all the boys vied with each other to persuade Billy to take their bed.

'Take mine. It's close to the door.'

'Nah, take mine. It's close to the window.'

'Nah, take mine.'

'He's sleepin' here,' said Stoke, silencing them. 'Hughie –' he nodded at the boy in the bed next to him – 'get out and let Perkinski sleep in your bed.'

Obediently Hughie slid on to a mattress on the floor and motioned to Billy that he should take his bed.

Stoke leaned on his elbow for a while, staring at Billy. Finally he bent over and whispered in his ear, 'I've been copped twenty times. What about you?'

'Never,' sniffled Billy on the verge of tears.

Stoke made a derisive sound. 'So what did you nick? Was it old Vicky's crown?' He waited with bated breath, for he knew if the answer was yes he could never compete with a thief of that calibre.

'I didn't nick nothin',' Billy wailed, raising his voice.

'Shh!' Stoke warned, pointing to the warders at

each end of the room. 'If they hear you blabbin',
you'll be in for it.'

'I didn't nick nothin',' whispered Billy. 'I found
it.'

'Found it? Found what?'

'A fimble.'

'A thimble?' Stoke tapped his ear wondering if
he'd heard right. 'Did you say "a thimble"?'

'Yeh.'

'Where d'you find it?'

'Under a pillow.'

'Whose pillow?'

'Mine.'

'Where was the pillow?'

'On a bed.'

'Whose bed?'

'Mine.'

'*You slept in a bed with a pillow?* Crikey, you a toff or
somethin'?'

'Nah. But I lived with toffs.'

'Where?'

'Opposite Green Park.'

'Mayfair? You lived with real toffs and all you
nicked from them was a pesky thimble?'

'I didn't nick it. I keep tellin' you, I found it,' Billy
cried in exasperation.

'Get out of Hughie's bed, you little varmint,' growled Stoke, grabbing Billy by the leg and dragging him down to the floor.

'What's wrong, Stoke? What's happenin'?' hissed the other boys. 'Where's Billy?'

'On the floor with the rats and roaches where he belongs,' said Stoke. 'A thimble!' he jeered. 'He says all he's in for is findin' a thimble. I ask you!'

'A thimble.' As the word was passed around the dormitory the boys began to snigger. 'A thimble! And he didn't even nick it, he found it.'

'Who's talking?' cried out one of the warders, getting to his feet.

'It's the new boy, sir,' Stoke called back. 'He won't stop jabberin'. He's keepin' us all awake, sir.'

The warder strode down the room, banging a stick against his legs.

'Another word out of you, four-eight-three,' he said, for all prisoners were called by their numbers, 'and you will be—'

'But it wasn't my fault,' protested Billy. 'It was—'

'Silence! I shall report you to the governor for talking and answering me back.'

'Serves you right, you pesky brat,' snarled Stoke as the warder walked back to his place. 'Fimble!' He

 245

sniggered. 'Fimble – that's a good name for a little toerag like you.'

In the dim recesses of his loutish brain Stoke's hatred for the little boy grew like a poisonous fungus, until it filled his every thought. Billy had to be punished. Billy had to be taught a lesson.

And Stoke set about it with a vengeance.

43

Despite the cruel fate that had befallen Billy in his adopted home, the women of Devil's Acre were still eager to sell their children for a sovereign or two, for children were easy to come by but money was not, and they swarmed around Dr Lacey's carriage as it drove into the courtyard where the Perkinskis lived, shouting, 'Take my boy this time, guv. Take him! He's honest. He won't nick nothin' from you.'

The two liveried footmen got down and stood looking around them uneasily, unsure whether to help the doctor make his way through the unruly crowd or stay with the carriage, for he had warned them that if they turned their back on it even for a moment the horses would disappear together with the wheels, lamps and upholstery.

'Out of my way!' grunted the doctor, pushing the women aside. 'I have twelve children of my own. I assure you I have no need of more.'

Pa Perkinski was stretched out on the floor on a

pile of straw covered by a dirty piece of linen when Dr Lacey went in, stoically resisting the temptation to put a hand over his nose, for the smell in the caravan was rather worse than the worst pigsty.

'So, sir,' he said to Pa, 'what ails you?'

'Eh?'

'What is *wrong* with you?'

'Me? Nothin'. Nothin' at all,' said Pa breezily.

'He's got the collywobbles, guv,' said Ma, pointing to her stomach, 'and he can't keep his grub down.'

'And his lower regions?'

'Oh, there's nothin' wrong with them, guv, cos after's he's brought all his grub up there's nothin' left to go down.'

'Mm,' said the doctor, looking at Pa thoughtfully. 'Be so good as to lift your shirt, sir, that I may examine you.'

'What, in front of them?' said Pa coyly, nodding at Ma and Gran.

'Lawks a mercy, I've seen your belly often enough, Bert,' cackled Gran. 'And a nasty sight it is too.'

'Come, come, sir,' said the doctor testily. 'I have no time to waste. Lift your shirt.'

Pa had secretly sworn that he would not let the

doctor find anything wrong with him for doctors, as everyone knew, gave their patients foul-tasting medicine, which invariably killed them, or, if that failed, put them into a hospital from which they only emerged in a coffin. He did his best, therefore, to stay silent even when Doctor Lacey pummelled and probed his stomach and belly. But when the man's bony fingers dug a little too deeply into a particularly sensitive spot, Pa let out a great roar of agony.

'It is just as I thought,' said the doctor, straightening up.

'Is he . . . Is he goin' to croak, guv?' asked Ma fearfully.

'Croak? If you mean by that, is your husband about to die, madam, the answer is no. He is suffering from a painful disorder of the stomach, but one that the correct medication will cure. I shall send my page with it. Good day to you.'

And he hurried away.

44

Tothill Fields prison was not far from Devil's Acre and on her way to work the streets Ma stopped there every morning, her head bowed, her bony hands pressed against the walls of the fortress, as if by touching them she was also comforting Billy.

As darkness fell she plodded home, bone weary from her efforts to sell the few buttons, ribbons and combs on her tray, and lingered there once more, stroking the bricks and murmuring, 'Night night, Billy. Sleep tight, my tulip.'

On the other side of the wall stood another woman, equally grieved.

In many ways Dolly was a model prisoner. She never broke the rules, never uttered a word, barely lifted her eyes from the ground, knitted endless socks without complaint, twiddled straw in and out of her fingers for hours to make bonnets or baskets and always bobbed a curtsy to the matrons and warders.

'It's because she was brought up in the work-house. She's used to obeying orders,' they said to each other, nodding their approval. 'She's a good girl. If only . . .'

If only she would stop crying. For no matter whether she was working, eating, exercising or sitting in chapel, Dolly wept.

'Stop snivellin', you stupe,' hissed the more strident of her two cell mates when the warders were out of earshot. 'It won't get you out of here. We've all tried it, haven't we, Queenie?' She grinned at her companion. 'Oh, I'm sorry, so sorry, Your 'Onour, I didn't mean to do it,' she squealed in an affected voice, locking her hands over her heart and rocking back and forth in an agony of remorse. 'Just let me go free and I promise on my baby's life I'll never do it again. Sob, sob . . .' She threw back her head, cackling. 'Never works though, do it, Queenie?'

'Nah, they got hearts of stone, them lot. Don't matter if you grizzle your head off, here you are and here you'll stay, miss, till they boat you to Australie.'

'And then you'll really have something to snivel about,' said Queenie, clearly enjoying her role as messenger of doom.

But Dolly did not weep because she had been wrongfully imprisoned. She was used to being deprived of her freedom through no fault of her own. She had been born in a workhouse, had spent the first fifteen years of her life there, bullied and abused, and might well have died there of starvation or some foul disease if Lady Eden had not accompanied her husband on one of his visits and, seeing the girl comforting a sick friend, said, 'I think she would make an excellent nursemaid, Edmund.'

From that moment Dolly's life had changed. From a sad-eyed waif with sallow skin and hollow cheeks, she blossomed into a beauty. Her hair grew thick and lustrous, her skin glowed, and nothing – not Miss Jermyn's waspish rebukes nor Mr Pole's constant criticism – could suppress her joy. Sometimes she felt she'd burst with happiness. And now Lady Eden, the very person who had saved her life, the woman she worshipped, believed she was a thief, that Dolly had repaid her kindness and generosity by stealing her beautiful sapphire necklace.

The girl bent her head and wept tears of shame.

45

In her free moments, when she wasn't eating, sleeping or taking lessons, Alice could be found in the house or garden sketching – chairs, lamps, vases, trees, flowers, squirrels. And people. Most of all, people – her mother, father, sisters, visitors, servants.

'She has inherited the gift from my brother,' Sir Edmund told his dinner guests proudly. 'Several of his paintings are in the Summer Exhibition at the Royal Academy and I'm quite confident Alice's will hang there some day too.'

Alice had the keen eye of the true artist. She never missed a detail – Milly's squint, Minny's buck teeth, Signor Agnelli's bald spot, the dimple in Maurice's chin, the heart-shaped mole on Miss Jermyn's neck, the tiny nicks in Mr Pole's left earlobe as if it had been nibbled by a mouse.

'It's time you had lessons, my darling,' said her

father, looking through her work one evening. 'I shall engage a tutor for you. No doubt my brother will advise me of a suitable one.'

'Oh when, Papa, when?' cried Alice delightedly.

'In October when I return from the country.'

'But October is so far away. It's two whole months.'

'Then you must be patient, miss,' her father smiled. 'Patience is a virtue.'

Unfortunately it was one Alice did not possess. Two whole months – and she had already drawn and painted everything and everyone in the house and garden.

'Mama, may I go and draw people in the street?' she asked.

'Certainly not. But if you promise to be neat and tidy you may sit on the drawing-room window seat.'

Although the drawing room was at street level it was not as good as actually being in the street, thought Alice ruefully, but after a while she began to realize its advantages – her paper didn't blow away or get soaked in a summer shower, people didn't stop and look over her shoulder making irritating comments and, most importantly, she could draw without her subjects being aware of it.

At first she sketched the other people who lived

in the street: ladies and gentlemen dressed in their finery, getting in and out of carriages or walking sedately, their footmen in tow. But after a while she grew bored – they all looked the same, the men in their tall top hats, the women in elegant gowns, and she turned her attention to others – the girl selling milk, a yoke across her shoulders with two heavy pails suspended from either end, the muffin man, his basket full of those teatime treats wrapped in a piece of flannel to keep them warm, the crossing sweeper with his white hair and nut-brown, leathery skin, the hurdy-gurdy man cranking out popular tunes, the nursemaids leading or carrying small children, the footmen walking dogs, the letter carrier in his scarlet frock coat delivering mail six, sometimes twelve times a day, knocking on doors with a rat-tat! for a letter or an urgent rat-tat! rat-tat! for a telegram.

'I do not know why you waste so much time sketching these common people,' said Georgiana, coming in unexpectedly one day and riffling through the rapidly growing pile of street scenes.

'And I do not know why you waste so much time looking at yourself in the mirror,' retorted Alice.

'I shall report you to Mama for insolence,' exclaimed Georgiana, flouncing out of the room.

'Do so,' muttered Alice, turning back to the window.

She leaned forward eagerly. There were two boys standing on the corner, one short and stocky, the other an inch or so taller. With swift, deft strokes Alice began to sketch them. The shorter one amused her. Despite his ragged clothes and grimy face he had a bold stance, his chin tilted up, his shoulders back as if he owned the world, or at least London. The other looked ill at ease, as if he had grown too quickly and didn't know what to do with his long arms and legs.

Sketching them was not easy for they kept darting back and forth, peering round the corner and disappearing again. Was it a game they were playing? Alice wondered. Or were they hiding from someone?

They were there again the next day. And the next. But never for long. Alice began to notice that whenever a servant left her own house one of the boys went after them. They were very discreet, looking up at the sky or bending down to tie a non-existent bootlace if the man or woman glanced back, but there was no doubt about it, thought Alice, those two boys were following the Edens' servants.

46

In her day the *Warrior* had been a proud man-of-war, a sturdy seventy-four-gun ship that had helped defend her country in numerous sea battles, including Trafalgar and Cadiz. But with increasing age, she had become a leaky hulk lying off Woolwich Dockyard, rotting from stem to stern, one of many floating prisons in London and Portsmouth. A good storm would have sunk her, which would have been a kind fate. As it was she sank lower and lower into the filthy, sewage-laden water of the River Thames, creaking and groaning under the weight of hundreds of prisoners, most of them the most dangerous, crime-hardened men garnered from all the jails in the kingdom.

Had Sam Perkinski been found guilty of murdering a man or assaulting a woman or injuring a child, especially if they were of his own class, he would have been sent to Pentonville or Brixton for a year or

two, depending on the leniency of the court, to work the crank or do shot drill or tread the mill. But as he had had the audacity to steal a sapphire necklace from one of the aristocracy – a relative of the Queen, no less – Sam was sentenced to fourteen years in Australia and sent to the *Warrior* to await deportation.

For his 'heinous' crime the young man was confined in the lowest of her three decks, the hottest, darkest and dirtiest, filled with hundreds of hammocks slung so closely together there was not an inch of space between one lice-ridden man and his flea-bitten neighbour.

All night long they tossed and turned, crying out in rage or despair, but Sam lay on his back, staring at the ceiling only a foot or two above him, seething. For the first time in his life he had given up crime, gone straight, found a respectable job. And how had society rewarded him?

He clenched his fists, cursing.

'Let them rot in hell,' he shouted into the foul, fetid air.'

'Yeh, best place for them,' growled the man next to him. 'What you in for, mate?'

'Nickin' some sparks – which I didn't,' muttered Sam, 'but I wish I had now. Wish I'd nicked everythin' in that blasted house – their gold and silver, their furniture, their carpets, the paper off their walls . . .'

'You're right,' said a man on the other side. 'Why should them toffs have everythin' and we got nothin'? Why can't they share some of it with us, seein' as how they got so much?'

'Share . . . Huh!' the first man scoffed. 'The likes of them wouldn't share a crust of bread with you if you was layin' in the gutter starvin'.'

'When I get out of here,' said Sam, 'I'm goin' to rob them blind, the whole lot of them. I'm goin' to work with my Uncle Rudd and . . .'

'Rudd? Not Rudd Jupp?'

'Yeh. You know him?'

'One of the best cracksmen in the business,' said the man admiringly. 'I wouldn't mind comin' in with you if Rudd'd have me.'

'And me,' said the other man. 'We could crack some jammy cribs with Rudd Jupp.'

'Right.' Sam nodded. 'Soon as I get back from Australie we'll—'

'Australie? You bein' boated to Australie? Blimey, mate, we'll all dead before you get back – *if* you do.'

47

Forbidden by Miss Jermyn to stare out of the nursery window – apparently it was something young ladies did not do, according to the governess – Alice could barely wait to go down to the drawing room every afternoon to see if the two boys were still there.

Sneaking a peek one morning before breakfast when Miss Jermyn was temporarily indisposed, the little girl was shocked to see the boys run across the road when they thought nobody was looking and down the area steps. Were they burglars? she wondered, her heart beginning to pound. Were they going to break into the house in broad daylight?

She turned to run – she would tell Mama, and Mama would send for the police – but in her haste she nearly bowled over Pearl, the housemaid, who had come in to sweep and dust the room as she did every morning.

'Ooh, Miss Alice!' she cried, grabbing the door

jamb to steady herself. 'Whatever are you doin' in here at this time of day?'

'Sorry, sorry,' babbled Alice. 'Pearl, there are two boys – they ran down the area steps – I saw them – they've been watching our house – they mean to do us harm, I know it – I must tell Mama.'

'No.' Pearl caught the girl's arm as she made to run past. 'No. Beggin' your pardon, miss, but you can't.'

'Can't?' cried Alice, pulling herself free. 'How dare you!'

'They're not burglars, miss,' Pearl whispered. 'They're . . .' she dropped her voice even lower, 'they're poor Master Billy's brothers.'

Alice stared at her open-mouthed.

'It's true, miss. They come here every day and Mrs Maltby gives them grub – food, cos they're very poor and she feels sorry for them, what with poor Master Billy being in that awful place and their father poorly and can't work. But if Mr Pole was to find out, Mrs Maltby'd get the sack.'

Pearl searched Alice's face anxiously but when Alice said nothing she went on, 'If you think it best, miss, I'll tell Mrs Maltby that she mustn't . . .' she hesitated. A housemaid, even a chief housemaid, was inferior to a cook and would never dare to tell her what she must or must not do – 'I mean I'll *suggest* that she stop givin' them boys grub.'

'No,' Alice said firmly, her mind made up. 'No, Pearl, I think she should. It's the least we can do for Billy's family. And I won't tell Mama and Papa. I won't tell anyone, I promise.'

48

Billy had never been in a garden, had no idea how to mend a torn trouser leg or repair a boot and as for carpentry, he was more likely to break a stool than make one. And so, along with all the other boys who had no skills other than picking pockets, he was put to work in the oakum room, a large barn-like structure filled with rows and rows of benches.

Picking oakum was a gruelling, tedious task. The prisoners were kept at it for five hours a day, untwisting lengths of old rope, hardened and black with ships' tar, watched by warders standing on a raised platform or sitting on high stools.

Every boy was given a pound of smelly rope to unravel and as they worked the air became thick with brown dust which settled on their clothes and hair and in their lungs.

On the walls of the room hung placards on which were printed encouraging texts from the Bible, such as, 'Be sober, be vigilant, because your adversary the devil as a roaring lion walketh about, seeking whom he may devour.' Since few of the boys could read, these heart-warming words were lost on them. Equally useless was the text 'Swear not at all'. As one boy protested, 'Blimey, we're not even allowed to talk so when could we bloody well swear?' – for which misdemeanour he was put on half rations for a week.

But despite the threat of punishment the boys did talk, making signs to each other or whispering so quietly it sounded more like a sigh. Since their lives were a monotonous round of work, exercise, school, chapel, eat, sleep, with no variations on that theme, the main topic of their snatched conversations was invariably their imprisonment.

'How long you in for?' one asked of another.

The boy next to him stopped 'twiddling' rope for a second and laid three fingers on his knee.

'Three weeks?'

'Months.'

'What for?'

'Pinchin' a coat and an umbrella from my master,' came the reply. 'What about you?'

'One week for knockin' on someone's door and runnin' away. And him –' he nodded at a boy in front – 'he got a month for nickin' six plums from a

garden and him –' he jabbed an elbow in the ribs of the boy on his other side – 'he got three weeks for spinnin' a top in the street, cos a toff said it was annoyin' him.'

And so they whispered among themselves to while away the leaden hours. But nobody spoke to Billy as he sat at the end of a row, head down, shoulders hunched, his small fingers fumbling with the steel-like rope. Nobody paid him any attention as he muttered to himself, 'Can't do it. Can't do it. It hurts,' as the harsh fibres dug into his flesh, drawing blood. But little by little his pile began to grow and by the time the warders shouted, 'Stop!' he had unravelled his pound of rope.

The boys stood up and row by row they shuffled forward to have their fibre weighed.

'Oy, Fimble,' whispered Stoke, who was sitting behind Billy. 'Want a biscuit?'

Billy turned eagerly and as he did so Stoke nodded and winked at the boy in front.

'Chew on that!' jeered Stoke, pushing an old button in Billy's mouth.

Billy's face fell – it was so long since he had eaten one of Mrs Maltby's soft, buttery shortbreads or spicy ginger nuts – and it fell even further when he

turned back to discover his pile of fibre had disappeared.

'Number four-eight-three, move sharp!' shouted a warder impatiently. 'Bring your work here to have it weighed.'

'I've lost it. He nicked it,' cried Billy, pointing at the boy sitting in front of him.

'Blaming others again, four-eight-three? The governor shall hear of this.'

As Billy was led away to be punished yet again he heard Stoke laughing. 'Poor Fimble,' he jeered. 'Poor little Fimble.'

49

Jem had devised a secret signal to let Mrs Maltby know that he and Ned were waiting in the area – he scratched at the kitchen door. Anybody on the inside hearing the noise would assume it was a stray dog and ignore it, for there were many sick and starving animals wandering the streets of London. If Mrs Maltby did not appear within a few minutes, it was a warning that Mr Pole or one of the other unsympathetic servants was in the vicinity and the two boys crept back up the steps, crouching low lest they be seen from the kitchen window.

More often than not, however, the door was opened a crack and a parcel thrust at them with a 'There you go, my pets,' and a smile. They were amazed, therefore, when the door opened one day in response to Jem's furtive scratch and a girl stood there, staring at them with unabashed curiosity.

'Scarper!' Jem hissed at Ned and they turned to run.

'No.' Alice reached out and caught Ned's sleeve. 'Stay! I want to talk to you. I'm not going to hurt you.'

The suggestion that a girl, any girl, especially a small one, could hurt them stopped Jem in full flight and he glared at her.

'What d'you want?' he demanded gruffly.

'I know who you are,' said Alice, not at all fazed by Jem's belligerent attitude. 'You're Billy's brothers. And our cook gives you food.'

'Nah, she doesn't.' Jem denied it hotly, for he and Ned could be flogged for begging.

'Don't be silly,' said Alice. 'I know she does.'

Jem took a deep breath – first the girl had suggested she could hurt him and now she was calling him silly – but before he could explode she went on, 'I don't mind. And I'm sure Mama wouldn't if she knew. But I should like to know why you keep following our servants – and don't say you don't,' she held up her hand to silence Jem's vehement protests. 'You hide round the corner,' she nodded in the direction of Piccadilly, 'and every time someone leaves our house you go after them. And if you don't tell me why,' she folded her arms and tilted her chin even higher than Jem's, 'I shall order our cook not to give you any more food – ever.'

Jem was about to say he didn't want any more of her varminty food – ever! – when he caught Ned's eye. Of course they needed the food Mrs Maltby gave them; they needed it badly. Swallowing his pride with an effort, Jem muttered, 'All right. It's like this . . .'

Alice listened to his story wide-eyed. 'So you really think that our footman took Mama's necklace?' she said when Jem had finished.

'No doubt about it.'

'And that he will leave soon and go to some other house and steal from them?'

'Yeh, that's what Uncle Ru . . .' began Ned. But Jem cut him short with a warning look.

'That's what our Uncle Roger thinks,' he said, for the less Alice knew of their relationship to a thief the better.

'I know about your Uncle Rudd,' said Alice, grinning. 'Billy has told us all about him. He is a . . . what did Billy call him . . . ? A *master cracksman*.'

'Yeh, he is,' Jem couldn't resist praising his uncle. 'He's a real fly bloke.'

'So what can I do?' said Alice.

'Do?'

'To help.'

'Oh. Oh well.' Jem had been about to say,

'Nothin'. What can a *girl* do?' but he had a feeling the one standing facing him would not take kindly to such an answer, so he said, 'Keep your eyes and ears open.'

Alice frowned. 'But I always keep my eyes open, except when I am sleeping. And as for my ears . . .'

Jem sighed. The toffs seemed to have such trouble understanding plain English.

'I mean watch Maurice and let us know if he does anythin' funny,' he explained with ill-concealed impatience.

'What do you mean by "funny"?'

'Well, like . . . er . . . like . . . er . . . Look we've got to go. We've got work to do.'

'Wait.' Alice pushed the door to for a moment and returned holding a parcel. 'Mrs Maltby asked me to give you this.'

'Where is she?' asked Ned, for he had developed a soft spot for the motherly cook.

'Engaging Mr Pole in idle chatter while I talk to you,' said Alice. And she closed the door with a sly grin.

50

Dr Lacey's page was a boy of twelve. Normally he walked to patients' houses with a basket of medicines on his arm, but since Devil's Acre was too dangerous for a stranger to walk in alone, and too far from the Harley Street surgery anyway, he went in the doctor's carriage with a burly coachman and two footmen for protection.

His arrival was greeted with jeers and catcalls.

'Crimes, what d'you call that?' cried an urchin, pointing at the page's patent-leather pot-shaped hat.

'A football,' cried another, and before the page could stop them they had knocked the elegant hat off his head and begun kicking it around in the mud and dung.

'Lor', look at them,' said a girl, fingering the rows of silvered buttons on the page's tight-fitting jacket. 'Bet they're worth a bit.'

'Oy, stop that! Stop that, you hear!' shouted the

coachman, getting down from his seat and cracking his whip menacingly.

The girl giggled and ran away, but not before she'd ripped off two or three buttons and stuffed them down her bodice.

'Come on, Cyril,' grunted the coachman, laying about him with his whip to keep the other children at bay. And leaving the two footmen to guard the carriage, he followed the page up the steps of the caravan and waited while the boy went inside.

'Physic from Doctor Lacey for a Mister Albert Perkinski,' proclaimed the page, reaching into his basket and producing a large bottle filled with a blue liquid.

'Oh crikey,' exclaimed Pa, who was lying on the floor as usual, clutching his stomach. 'Just what I thought – it's rat poison.'

'You are to take the dosage as written on the label,' said the page, handing it to him.

'Right,' said Pa. 'I'll do that. Thanks. Goodbye.'

'What's dosage?' asked Ma.

'The amount of medicine Mr Perkinski has to take,' explained the page.

'So how much is that?'

'Two spoonfuls. One in the morning and one . . .'

The page hesitated and looked about him. 'You do have a spoon, don't you?'

'We did. But it got nicked.'

'But we've got a knife,' said Gran.

'No. No, that won't do at all. I think Mr Perkinski should take . . . er . . . one gulp – one good gulp, morning and night,' said the page, well pleased that he had solved the problem.

'Go on, Bert,' said Ma when the boy had gone. 'Take your medicine.'

'Not me.' Pa pushed the bottle away. 'I'm not takin' that. And I'd like to see the person who can make me.'

'Right, Gran,' said Ma, nodding at her.

'Gran?' Pa laughed. 'Gran? You think that little old lady can make me – Argh!' he cried as Gran clambered on to his chest and held his nose tight. 'Argh!'

'There you are, Bert,' chuckled Ma, pouring one 'good gulp' into his open mouth. 'Feelin' better?'

51

Maurice had disappeared.

'Upped and offed in the night, just like that, not a word to no one,' huffed Mrs Maltby. 'Course, I'm not surprised. I never liked him, wouldn't trust him as far as I can throw him.'

'Where's he gone?' said Ned.

'I don't know and I don't care. We're better off without him, that's for sure. And here's another bit of good news – two bits, in fact: Mr Pole's leaving, going to work for a duke in Ireland. Real pleased with himself he is – "I have been offered a position more in keeping with my experience and ability,"' she mimicked the butler's soft, breathy voice. 'And Miss Jermyn's given in her notice too. Says she's got to look after her old mother in Dorset – though I'm surprised an old boot like that ever had a mother,' she laughed, giving the boys a wicked wink. 'Course, it's hard on Her Ladyship, what with Sir Edmund being away. But it's my opinion,' she lowered her

voice, 'she's a better judge of character than him. He's got a kind heart, a bit too kind for his own good sometimes. Her Ladyship'll take on a much better butler and governess than he would – Oh Lord, here comes Pole. I must go.' And she shut the door, quite forgetting to give Jem and Ned their bag of scraps.

'So Maurice has made his move already,' said Rudd when he heard. 'A mite too quick, I'd say. A mite stupid too, leavin' in the night like that. Shows he's up to somethin', just like I said. But where's he gone? That's what we got to find out.'

Rudd slunk through the streets of Mayfair to the Running Footman, his collar well up, his cap well down, his eyes on the pavement. He knew the area well, for it was these handsome three- and four-storey houses he plundered for gold, silver and jewellery – but always under the cover of darkness. By day he stayed hidden in the rookery, safe from the sharp-eyed Craddock and his plain-clothes detectives.

The popular pub was a hotbed of gossip. No one discussed the foibles and indiscretions of their own employers, of course, for every footman and valet was anxious to convey the impression that the

household he worked for was the crustiest of upper crust, but engaging in tittle-tattle about other servants, especially if that involved maligning them, was a favoured pastime.

Rudd was not known in the Running Footman, nor did he want to be, but he needed the help of its regular clients if he was to track down the runaway Maurice.

It is amazing how a jovial manner and, more especially, a generous wallet will open men's hearts and mouths and though it pained Rudd to pay for yet another round of gin and porter, after an hour or so of idle chatter with his new drinking companions the information he was seeking finally emerged.

'Maurice?' said one, in answer to Rudd's seemingly casual enquiry. 'No, there was no footman at the Edens called Maurice.'

'Course there was,' said another. 'Tall, good-looking, really fancied himself. Used to come in here of a Thursday.'

'Oh. Oh, him. But I thought he worked for Lord and Lady FitzHubert.'

'He did till he got the push – somethin' to do with a dog.'

'You talkin' about Maurice Vartle?' said a man at the next table who had been eavesdropping.

'Yeh. Know him, do you?'

'Course I do. He was with that gang that did the big robbery in Kensington a while back — stole a mint of money from a bank. But when the crushers began to close in he turned Queen's evidence and told them everything, so he got off while the rest of the gang went on a nice, long boat trip to the other side of the world. Meanwhile Maurice took up as a footman and was doing quite nicely thank you, till one of the gang escaped and came back — Swanny Turps. Big, hairy bruiser. Swore he'd get revenge on Maurice for squealing.'

'That Turps sounds like the bloke I saw with Maurice,' said Jem some hours later when his uncle told him and Ned about his visit to the Running Footman.

'So now Maurice is runnin' for his life,' said Rudd. 'And we've got to find out where he's runnin' to.'

'How're you goin' to do that?' asked Ned.

Rudd bent towards the boys, lowering his voice so they could barely hear him. 'I got eyes and ears

everywhere, I have,' he said. 'If Maurice is in London, I'll find him.'

'Well, you'd better do it plaguy quick, Uncle Rudd,' Jem said. 'Cos if Swanny Turps finds Maurice again he'll –' he made a slashing motion across his throat – 'top him.'

52

Great-aunt Hildegarde was unwell – an unheard-of event, for she so resented paying doctors' bills that she did her utmost to keep healthy, taking a short walk twice a day, washing infrequently, eating sparingly and drinking the polluted water not at all.

'I understand she is suffering from an attack of gout,' said Lady Eden.

'What is gout, Mama?' asked Edwardina.

'A severe pain in the big toe – It is not amusing,' Lady Eden scolded her daughters as they burst into giggles. 'We must pay her a visit.'

Immediately the laughter died away to be replaced by cries of horror.

'But we have never been to Great-aunt's home.'

'She has never invited us.'

'You know how she dislikes visitors.'

'We should be most unwelcome.'

'Nevertheless we must go,' said Lady Eden firmly. 'I have received a letter from your papa in which he expresses concern that Lady FitzHubert is unwell and requests that we call upon her to express our sympathy.'

'Papa is too soft-hearted,' muttered Henrietta.

'Indeed!' huffed Georgiana. 'Great-aunt would not visit one of us even if we were dying.'

'Girls, I find your remarks distasteful,' scolded their mother.

'But must we all go, Mama?' wailed Thomasina. 'Do you not think Great-aunt would be most displeased if we all went?'

'I am sure it would tire her, Mama.'

'And make her feel even worse.'

'Yes, you are probably right,' Lady Eden nodded. 'Perhaps just one of you should accompany me.'

'I think it should be Alice,' said Georgiana.

'Why?' said Alice.

'Because you are the youngest.'

'Oh, Mama, no!' protested Alice. 'That isn't fair.'

'Do not be so selfish,' snapped Georgiana. 'It is your Christian duty to visit the sick.'

'Oh, and I suppose it is *your* Christian duty to stay here?'

'Children, children, please. This is most unseemly behaviour,' said Lady Eden, frowning. 'Alice, you will accompany me to Great-aunt

Hildegarde's this afternoon and there is nothing more —' she raised a hand to silence her — 'nothing more to be said.'

Although Great-aunt Hildegarde lived just around the corner in Arlington Street, Alice had never been to her house. Nor had she any desire to. In fact, she was very angry that she had been coerced into accompanying her mother while her sisters lolled under the shade of the cherry trees in their garden, sipping lemonade.

'Do not look so sulky, Alice,' her mother reprimanded her. 'It is most unpleasant in a young lady. One cannot always do what one wants. One has to learn to be unselfish.'

'Yes, Mama. Sorry, Mama,' said Alice. And she took her mother's outstretched hand as they mounted the steps to Great-aunt Hildegarde's house, followed at a discreet distance by Stephen, their new footman.

It was customary for footmen to go ahead to inform the house of the intended visit of a friend or member of the family, but in this instance Lady Eden had decided to flout the rules of etiquette for she knew that if Great-aunt Hildegarde was made aware of their visit she would send word that she was not at home.

A butler opened the impressive front door with its huge gold knocker in the shape of a lion's head, a knocker that was hardly ever used. 'Yes?' he growled, without the slightest hint of decorum.

For one moment Lady Eden lost her self-possession and took a step back, for she had never been spoken to with such disrespect; nor had she ever seen such an appalling creature masquerading as a butler.

Alice too was shocked and she stared at the man, repelled by his pockmarked skin, his bushy eyebrows, his nose criss-crossed with a mass of bright red veins and, most repulsive of all, the huge warts on his chin.

'I have come to see Lady FitzHubert,' said Lady Eden, regaining her composure.

'I regret that Lady FitzHubert is unable to . . .' began the butler in a surly voice.

'Indeed?' said Lady Eden, sweeping past him with Alice in tow.

'But Lady FitzHubert—'

'Will be delighted to see her niece and great-niece, I am quite sure,' said Lady Eden. And she handed him her parasol with an imperious gesture.

'But Her Ladyship is unwell.'

'Which is precisely why we have come to visit her. Now, shall you show us up or must we find our own way?' said Lady Eden with a confidence she didn't feel, for she had only been to the house once before, shortly before her marriage to Sir Edmund, and she had no idea where Great-aunt Hildegarde would be found.

For a fleeting moment the butler's mouth tightened and his eyes flashed fire. Alice gripped her mother's hand more tightly, but the man gave them a bow that was more insolent than obsequious and said, 'And who shall I say wants to see her?'

'Lady Eden and Miss Alice.'

'Very well,' he said, walking up the grand staircase. 'Wait there.'

'Such impudence,' muttered Lady Eden under her breath. 'Come, Alice,' and taking her daughter's hand she followed the butler up the stairs.

Great-aunt Hildegarde occupied a room on the second floor at the back of the house. She had had her bed moved close to the window so that she could bang on it with her walking stick if a cat or squirrel had the temerity to intrude on her property. Sir Lancelot lay on a cushion by her side, his paws twitching, his eyelids fluttering as he dreamed of his one glorious glimpse of freedom, when he had chased dogs, cats, rats and mice all over Devil's Acre.

'There's a Lady Eden and Miss Alice to see you,' said the butler, opening the door. 'I tried to tell them you were indisposed but . . .'

'We were saddened to hear of your indisposition, Aunt,' said Lady Eden, going into the room before the old woman could gather her wits and order them out. 'I do hope you are feeling better today. Thank you, my man. That will be all,' she said icily, dismissing the louring butler with a wave of her hand. 'Alice —' she turned to her daughter, who was carrying a bouquet of pinks. 'Alice!' she repeated in a louder voice, for the little girl was staring at the butler's receding back with a puzzled frown on her face.

'Oh — oh, sorry, Mama.' She hurried forward with the bouquet.

'Flowers,' sniffed Great-aunt Hildegarde, waving them away. 'I have a garden full of them. I hardly need more.'

'But you do not have pinks, and pinks are much prettier than any of the flowers in your garden,' said Alice, looking out of the window. 'Oh . . . Oh, Great-aunt, there is a young man out there. He has his

hands folded behind his back and he is looking up at the sky.'

'I am perfectly aware of that, child. I do have eyes in my head,' snapped Lady FitzHubert. 'The young man is Cecil, my husband's ward. He wastes a great deal of his time gazing at the sky instead of getting on with his work.'

'But what is he looking at?'

'I have absolutely no idea.'

'Is it the clouds?'

'I have just told you . . .'

'Or is it birds, do you think?'

'For goodness sake!' Lady FitzHubert huffed. 'Have your parents never told you that children should be seen but not heard?'

'No, never, Great-aunt. Papa and Mama encourage us to ask questions, provided they are sensible. And my questions are always sensible . . . Well, nearly always.'

'Indeed!' huffed the old woman. 'And how, may I ask, is your "adopted" son, Parthenope?' she said smugly, for she knew, as everyone did, that Billy was in prison.

'Unfortunately he has been apprehended for a crime,' said Lady Eden, flushing.

'Just as I warned you and Edward, Parthenope,

but you chose to ignore me. I told you no good would come of taking that wicked little gutter urchin into your home, but—'

'Billy is not wicked,' protested Alice. 'I do not believe that he stole Mama's . . .'

'And how is Sir Hubert?' asked Lady Eden, placing her hand firmly on her daughter's shoulder to stop her chattering.

'My husband is on an extended tour of our estates in Scotland. He is not expected to return until . . . Aah!' Lady FitzHubert winced as a sharp pain pierced her big toe.

'Would you like me to place a cushion under your foot, Aunt?' said Lady Eden.

'Certainly not, Parthenope. You will oblige me by staying well away from my foot.'

'Is it horribly painful, Great-aunt?' asked Alice, peering at the old woman's big toe, which was swathed in bandages.

'It is.'

'As bad as toothache? I have had toothache.'

'It is considerably worse than toothache.'

'Is it as bad as earache? I have had earache.'

'Be quiet, Alice. You are tiring your great-aunt,' said Lady Eden as the old woman glowered at her.

'I was only doing my Christian duty, Mama,' protested Alice.

'Oh?' snapped Great-aunt Hildegarde. 'And what exactly is that?'

'Visiting the sick and expressing my sympathy.'

'And you think asking endless questions is a suitable expression of your sympathy, do you?'

Alice shrugged. 'I could do something else, if you like. I could read to you. I could come here every afternoon and read to you.'

Lady Eden stared at her daughter in disbelief. If Alice had announced an intention of sailing around the world in a leaky bathtub, her mother could not have been more amazed.

Great-aunt Hildegarde was also taken aback. 'Do you think I cannot read, child?' she demanded.

'No, but sometimes it is tiring to read,' said Alice, looking pointedly at the lorgnette suspended from the old woman's neck, 'and my eyes are much younger than yours.'

'Do not imagine that by feigning affection for me you will thereby inherit any of my fortune, child,' said the old woman severely.

'Oh, I don't,' said Alice airily. 'I shall be a famous artist when I grow up and people will give me a great

deal of money for my paintings – much more than you have, Great-aunt Hildegarde.'

Lady Eden opened her mouth to utter a string of abject apologies for her daughter's bluntness, but the old lady motioned her to be silent. For a long moment she looked intently into Alice's face as if she was searching for something – a memory, perhaps, a reminder of the girl she herself had once been, eager, irrepressible. Then she nodded and said, 'Be here tomorrow at three sharp. But do not stay longer than one half-hour and do not expect anything to eat or drink. Is that understood?'

'Perfectly.' Alice grinned – and was rewarded with the ghost of a smile from her great-aunt.

'Really, Alice, I cannot understand you,' said Lady Eden as she and her daughter walked back to Stratton Street. 'One minute you are distressed at having to visit your great-aunt and the next you are offering to visit her every afternoon to read to her. What is the explanation for this extraordinary behaviour?'

'It is because I felt sorry for her, Mama.'

'And there is no other reason?'

'No, Mama. What other reason could there be?'

Lady Eden looked at her thoughtfully. Clearly

her clever little daughter had something on her mind. But what was it?

'Oh look, Mama,' cried Alice, distracting her mother from further questioning, 'there's the man with the dancing dogs. May we go and watch, just for a moment?'

53

Life in prison was tough for all the boys but doubly so for Billy, who in the short time he had been with the Edens had grown accustomed to the pleasures of good food, and plenty of it, and a soft, warm bed he didn't have to share with an army of fleas, lice and bugs. But he could have endured the hardship of Tothill Fields had it not been for Zed Stoke.

From sunup to sundown Stoke made Billy's life a misery. By day he punched, pinched and kicked the little boy until he was covered in bruises and by night he tormented him with horror stories about transportation.

'Reckon you'll be goin' to Australie pretty soon, Fimble,' he'd whisper, leaning over the side of his bed and shaking Billy awake. 'You'll be goin' on a nice boat trip, you will.'

The other boys would be awake now, listening, for they enjoyed the nightly entertainment.

'Know about them boats, do you, Fimble?' Stoke

said. 'They put all the prisoners in the hold, that's in the bottom, where it's all dark and freezin'. It's so freezin' your fingers and toes turn blue and drop off, then your nose, then your ears, then . . .'

The other boys giggled, but Billy trembled so violently they could practically hear his teeth chattering.

'Then,' continued Stoke, warming to his story, 'when you're 'arf dead and can't hardly move they throw in snakes, hundreds of them, huge snakes, long as this room and thick as . . . thick as . . .' he had to stop and think about it '. . . thick as that column old Nelson's standin' on in Trafalgar Square. And they eat people. They eat them very, very slow, startin' at the feet and then the legs and then the . . .'

'I'll tell J-Jem about you,' stammered Billy. 'I'll tell J-Jem and he'll come and give you a right walloper if you don't leave me alone.'

'Oh?' sneered Stoke. 'And who's J-Jem when he's at home?'

'He's my brother. And he's bigger than you and strong, strong as a . . . as a . . .'

'Snake?' suggested Stoke. And the other boys roared with laughter.

'What's goin' on?' shouted the warder, striding towards them.

'It's four-eight-three, sir. He's keepin' us all awake again, sir,' snivelled Stoke. 'He won't shut up, sir.'

'Right, you're up before the governor in the morning, four-eight-three.'

And poor Billy was punished yet again – deprived of food and shut in a dark cell for hours on end, where he cried and cried and cried.

54

Slowly but surely Pa was getting better, although he never stopped complaining that Dr Lacey's medicine had a most disgusting taste and given the choice he'd rather drink the contents of a cesspit. Not that the food Pa ate was much better – soup which was nothing more than hot water with a potato and some tired cabbage leaves or withered carrots in it, a piece of bread from a soggy, grey 'quartern' loaf, a stale pastry sold half price by the bakery at the end of the day and a maggoty apple, all washed down with the dirty water from a rain barrel. Nevertheless, the time finally came when he was able to keep most of this unappetizing fare down.

'You can thank the quack for makin' you better, Bert,' said Ma with feeling.

'And Sir Edmund for payin' him,' added Jem.

'Yeh, yeh, I do,' Pa nodded. 'But I'm not thankin' her for nothin',' he said, giving Gran a sour look.

'Specially not that confounded bread poultice. Bread poultice!' He spat out the words angrily. 'Look what it's done to me.' He lifted his shirt to show his chest and belly, which were now completely hairless. 'I look like a plucked chicken.'

'Don't worry, Bert,' said Gran. 'I got a real stunnin' gypsy remedy for makin' hair grow. All you got to do is rub in some pigeon droppin's and . . . Nah! Nah! Don't get snaggy, Bert,' cried the old lady. 'It was just a suggestion.

Although Pa was on the mend, he still wasn't well enough to go back to his work as part-time porter at Covent Garden market and occasional prizefighter, and the Perkinskis relied heavily on Mrs Maltby's handouts. Which was why Jem and Ned still scratched at the kitchen door of the Edens' house every day, eagerly awaiting their food parcel. One morning Alice opened the door to their signal.

'I did what you told me,' she said. 'I kept my eyes and ears open.'

'Oh yeh?' Jem peered over her shoulder to see if there was any food on the kitchen table for them.

'Mama and I visited my great-aunt Hildegarde yesterday.'

Jem sighed. Why did girls always chatter on

about nothing, he wondered, especially when there were important things to do, like taking food home to Ma and Pa and rescuing Billy and Sam and Dolly?

'She is an elderly lady and rather unwell,' continued Alice.

Jem shuffled impatiently from one foot to the other. If it weren't for the food he hoped to get, he would have told the girl to shut up and stop wasting his time in no uncertain terms.

'She lives on Arlington Street,' said Alice.

'Who cares?' thought Jem. And he opened his mouth wide in a jaw-breaking yawn.

'Her proper name is Lady FitzHubert.'

Jem froze in mid-yawn and Ned audibly choked.

'Fitz'Ubert?' he exclaimed. 'Crimes, she didn't tell you about us, did she?'

'Tell me what?' said Alice.

'About the dog . . .'

'About nothin'.' Jem gave Ned a look that should have turned him to stone. 'Look, get on with it, will you?' he snapped at Alice.

'Well, Great-aunt Hildegarde has a new butler, a frightful man. He was odious to Mama and me . . .' Seeing the puzzled expression on the boys' faces, she explained, 'He was very rude. And he did his best to prevent us from seeing her.'

'So what's the point of . . . ?' began Jem impatiently.

'I am getting to the point,' said Alice, glaring at him. 'Stop interrupting me.'

If anyone else had spoken to Jem in such a curt way he would have given them a biff on the nose. But he had a queasy feeling that Alice would have given as good as she got, so he kept his fists clenched behind his back.

'The butler was a very ugly man. His skin looked like a burnt crumpet, his eyebrows were so big one could barely see his eyes, his nose was the colour of a plum and the warts on his chin were . . .'

Jem thought he would explode if he she didn't get to the point soon.

'I could hardly bear to look at him. But just as he was leaving the room I noticed something very odd about his left ear . . .' Alice paused for dramatic effect. 'He had tiny bits missing from the lobe as if a mouse had been nibbling it.'

Jem and Ned exchanged looks.

'Bits?' said Ned.

'Yes.'

'Missin' from his ear?'

Alice nodded.

'Oh,' said Ned.

But Jem could contain himself no longer. 'You've made us stand here for 'arf an hour listenin' to you jabberin' about your pesky aunt and all you got to tell us is her butler's got bits nibbled out of his ear by some varminty mouse, you stupe!'

'But Mr Pole, the man who used to be our butler, had identical bits missing from the lobe of *his* left ear. So Norris Pole and Great-aunt Hildegarde's new butler are one and the same man,' retorted Alice. 'Now do you understand, you . . . you stupe?'

55

'She's a sharp one and no flies,' said Rudd admiringly when Jem told him Alice's story. 'So it wasn't Maurice that nicked the Star of India after all,' he smiled, although the constant jerking of his face made it look more like a snarl. 'I might've known Silas Fox'd be behind it. Best cracksman in London, he is . . . after me, of course.'

'Silas Fox?' Ned looked confused. 'Who's he?'

'Norris Pole. Leastwise that's what he called himself when he worked for the Edens. He was Cuthbert Goodbody when he did the job on the Earl of Clarendon, Ivan Ironside when he gulled the Marquess of Bath, Boris Stakowski . . . Blow me tight, I can't keep up with that bloke; he's changed his name and the way he looks so many times. Master of disguise he is, a real stunner. It's not so much what he puts on his mug, though he was on the stage for a bit so he knows all about make-up, it's the way he acts. He kind of gets into another person's skin, he walks and talks like them. I once spent a whole evenin' in the Crown and Anchor, chattin' up what I thought was a scrumptious poppet, and all the time it was Silas – or Sly, as he's known. Laughed so much he nearly wet himself. Mind you, I didn't find it so funny,' added Rudd, a touch sourly.

'So this bloke Sly nicked the Star of India?' said Jem.

'That's right. And I reckon Billy must've seen or heard somethin', so Sly put that thimble under Billy's pillow to get him copped before he could blab,' said Rudd. 'He always works it so that some poor devil gets collared for the job while he goes free. Nobody never suspects Sly, not even the crushers. So now he's gone to work for Lady Fitz'Ubert so he can get his hands on her diamond tirara . . . and he will, I wager you. Him and his missus.'

'His missus?'

'Woman by the name of Freda. Up to the nines is Freda, just as leary at disguisin' herself as Sly. They always work as a team.'

'Wonder who that could be?' said Ned.

'Must be one of the maids – the Edens've got dozens of them,' said Jem.

'Nah, she won't be at the Edens no more,' said Rudd. 'She'll be workin' alongside Sly at Lady

Fitz'Ubert's, just waitin' for the moment to 'arf-inch that tirara.'

'So it's someone who worked at the Edens and now . . . Oh! Oh lor'!' cried Jem. 'I know who it is.'

'Who? Who?' Ned clutched his arm.

'S'obvious. It's Dolly.'

'Dolly? Nah, it can't be.'

'I think Jem's right,' said Rudd. 'Dolly – or Freda as her real name is – and Sly were plannin' to make it look like Sam had pinched the necklace . . .'

'That's why Dolly – er, Freda – was encouragin' Sam,' said Jem excitedly, 'pretendin' she was spoony on him and wanted to marry him.'

'Only it all went wrong and Freda got nailed as well as Sam. Well, I'll be blowed.' Rudd gave a wry chuckle. 'So there is justice in this world after all. But who's Sly workin' with now that Freda's gone? That's what I want to know. Well,' he leaned towards the boys and whispered, 'there's only one way to find out. Someone's got to get into the Fitz'Uberts' house.'

'Break in, you mean?' said Ned nervously.

'Don't be soft,' snapped his uncle. 'I mean someone's got to live in the house, be there all day, every day so's they can watch Sly, find out who

he's workin' with and then wait till they make their move.'

'Alice,' said Jem and Ned together.

'Yeh, she's up to snuff,' agreed Rudd. 'And Sly wouldn't be suspicious, seein' as how she's one of the family.'

But when Jem and Ned put the proposal to Alice the next morning she shook her head.

'I have persuaded Great-aunt to let me visit her every afternoon to read to her. She would never, never permit me to stay there. Nobody ever stays in Great-aunt's house except a few servants.'

'That's it!' said Rudd. 'One of you two's got to go and work there as a servant.'

'Doin' what?' said Ned doubtfully. 'We don't know how to cook or clean or . . .'

'You'd have to be a bootboy.'

'What does he do?'

'Cleans boots, of course, and other dirty jobs that no one else wants to do. And he works for next to nothin' and sleeps in the coal cellar and eats scraps.'

'Ned'll do it,' said Jem.

'Me?' Ned rounded on him angrily. 'Why me? Why don't you . . . ?'

'Cos Lady Fitz'Ubert knows me. She doesn't know you.'

'She does. She saw me.'

'Nah, not up close like me. I was talkin' to her in her carriage but you were standin' right at the end of the street, miles away, pretendin' to be Bobby Grimes.'

'Looks like you got to do it, Ned,' said his uncle.

'But what if she doesn't want a bootboy?'

'Tell her you'll do it for a bit of grub and somewhere to sleep. She's the meanest moll in London. She'll take you on if she doesn't have to part with any of her money.'

'But . . .'

'Look,' said Jem, putting a hand a Ned's shoulder, 'd'you want to help or not?'

Ma flew into a panic when Ned told her.

'Nah,' she cried, hugging him hard. 'I'll lose you as well as Billy. That man's a devil – Sly Fox. I've heard tell of him. He'll 'arf-inch that woman's diamond tirara and make it look like you did it. Then you'll be boated to Australie too and I'll never see neither of you no more.'

'I'll do it,' said Pa, struggling to his feet. 'I'm well enough now.'

'What, you a bootboy?' scoffed Gran. 'Bit big for it, aren't you?

''Sides, everyone knows your mug,' said Ma.

'Ma's right,' agreed Jem. 'Everyone knows you're Bert the Beast, the best prizefighter in London — leastwise you used to be before you got the collywobbles. Sly Fox'd tumble to it the moment he clapped eyes on you.'

'I got to do it,' said Ned, though his heart failed him at the thought. 'I got to help Billy and Sam.'

'You're a brave boy, my tulip,' said Ma. 'I'm real proud of you.'

56

'And if them snakes on the boat don't get you, the crocodiles will. Heard about the crocodiles in Australie, have you?' Stoke bent down and prodded Billy hard to make sure he hadn't fallen asleep. But the little boy lay scrunched into a tight ball on his hard mattress, his heart pounding like a drum.

'I said, have you heard about the crocodiles?' whispered Stoke, prodding Billy again.

'N-n-nah.'

'Crimes, I thought everybody knew about them. You're a real dummy, you are,' scoffed Stoke, turning to the other boys, who all laughed appreciatively. 'They're the biggest, fiercest, viciousest in the whole world. They got teeth like this.' Stoke stretched his arms as wide as they would go.

'Nah.' Billy plucked up the courage to contradict the bully. 'I've seen crocodiles in Punch'n Judy shows and they're small, real small, like this.' He held his hands a few inches apart.

'That's cos they were English crocodiles, fat'ead!' jeered Stoke. 'The ones in Australie are a hundred, a thousand times bigger. Soon as they hear there's a boat comin' in with a load of prisoners they all rush down and wait with their mouths wide open. Then when you get off the boat they —' he made a loud snapping sound with his teeth — 'bite you to bits.'

'Let me out!' screamed Billy, hurling himself at the door. 'Let me out! I won't go! I won't . . . !'

'You again, four-eight-three?' barked the warder. 'I've had just about enough of this caterwauling every night. I'm takin' you to the guv'nor right now.'

'Poor little Fimble,' chuckled Stoke as Billy was dragged away. 'I don't reckon he'll live long enough to get to Australie at this rate.'

Lady Eden was patron of many charitable institutions, including the Society for the Welfare and Rehabilitation of Female Prisoners. It was while attending a meeting of this society that she came to hear that Dolly was gravely ill. Grieved to the point where her heart was breaking, Dolly had been put to bed in the prison infirmary, where she lay scarcely breathing.

 *305*

'I understand that she refuses to eat or drink,' said Lady Ridgeway, who was President of the Society. 'The doctors despair of her.'

Lady Eden uttered a cry of horror. 'How terrible! Oh dear, that is too distressing. I must see her.'

'Visitors are not permitted, Lady Eden.'

'But surely they would make an exception in this instance? Would you use your influence, dear Lady Ridgeway?'

'I will see what I can do, Lady Eden. I will do my best.'

57

Ned was so nervous as he walked up the steps to Lady FitzHubert's house his knees were knocking like castanets.

'I'll be close by if you need me,' Jem had said, taking up a position on the corner of Arlington Street and Piccadilly with Ma's tray of knick-knacks hanging round his neck as if he was a street seller.

Ned had never done anything without his brother beside him. They had slept, eaten, worked, played and squabbled together all their lives and Ned would rather have been scrapping with him, even if it meant another black eye or bloody nose, than be on his own. He felt frightened and forsaken as he lifted the heavy knocker and let it fall with a resounding thud.

After what seemed a dog's age Ned was on the point of running back to Jem and saying, 'There's no one there, let's go home,' when the door was

opened by Silas Fox in a butler's uniform that had clearly seen better days.

'No beggars,' he growled.

'I'm not a beggar, guv. I'm . . . er . . . I'm . . . er . . .'

'Spit it out, I haven't got all day.'

'I'm lookin' for work.'

'Glad to hear it,' said Silas. 'Go and look somewhere else.' And he made to shut the door.

'I'm willin' to work for nothin', guv. All I want's somewhere to kip at night and a crust or two,' said Ned, as Rudd had instructed him.

Silas looked at him thoughtfully, stroking the thick, black hairs on a particularly large purple wart on his chin.

'You've got no home?' he asked.

'Nah, I haven't, guv.'

'No mother or father?'

Ned shook his head.

'No brothers, no sisters?'

'Nah, no one.'

'Where've you been living?'

'In the gutter most times or shop doorways or under bridges.'

'Hmm . . . Go down there.' Silas indicated the basement area. 'I'll see if Her Ladyship wishes to take you on.'

Ned hurried down the steps and waited anxiously by the kitchen door. What if Lady FitzHubert didn't want him? he fretted. What if Sly Fox suspected it was a trap? What if . . . ? In a nervous frenzy he pounded on the door with his fists.

'All right! All right!' came a shrill voice. 'No need to break it down . . .' and the next moment it was opened by the fattest woman Ned had ever seen. Every part of her wobbled, from her three chins to her breasts as big as footballs and her huge belly. Her bright red hair was loosely stuffed under a lace cap and her face so heavily lined she looked like a prune's grandmother.

'So you're the party Mr King was telling me about,' she said, running a bloodshot eye over Ned. 'Huh! You don't look as if you could do a decent day's work.'

'Yeh, I could,' he protested. 'I could do anythin' and I don't want nothin' for it.'

'That's lucky, because you won't get anything. All I get is a few coins from the skinflints up there . . .' She jabbed a finger at the upper storeys, where Sir Hubert and Lady FitzHubert lived. 'Well, don't hang around on the doorstep. Come in, come in,' she said, pulling Ned into a dark and gloomy kitchen. 'You can start with that.' She pointed to the kitchen range, a monstrous piece of furniture that seemed to fill half a wall. 'I want it scrubbed and polished – and done properly, mind.'

'Oh, I'll do it proper, Your Ladyship.'

The woman threw back her head and roared with laughter, revealing so many black teeth it looked as if she had a mouthful of coal.

'That's the first time anyone's called me "Your Ladyship",' she guffawed. 'My name's Mrs Wellborne and I'm the housekeeper here. That means I'm in charge of all the other servants – only we've only got one, she's Becky. She's upstairs sweeping the carpets, at least she should be. I'd better go and see.' And she lumbered away, her huge hips swaying from side to side.

Ned was wondering how to clean and polish the kitchen range, never having seen one before, when a girl not much older than him rushed in, her hair dishevelled, her face red and sweaty.

'My broom,' she muttered, looking wildly round the room. 'My broom. Where is it? Where . . . ? Oh!' She jumped when she saw Ned. 'Who're you?'

'N— I mean, Nick. My name's Nick. I'm the new bootboy.'

'You goin' to work here?'

'Yeh.'

'What they payin' you?'

'Nothin'.'

'Same as me then. But at least I've got a roof over my head and a bit of bread in my mouth . . .'

'Becky!'

'Lor', I can't stand here jabberin' or that old crab'll be after me. Gets at me day'n night. She's always yellin' . . .'

'Becky, where are you, you lazy little baggage? Get yourself up here this minute,' came a strident voice from above.

'Comin', Mrs Wellborne. I'm comin',' Becky shouted back. 'Now where is that confounded broom?' she muttered, running round in circles.

'That it?' asked Ned, pointing to a pole with a few bristles on it propped against the wall.

'Oh yeh. Thank you, Nick,' said the girl, grabbing it. But before she could run away Ned said, 'You got to help me now.'

'What?'

'That.' He nodded at the range. 'Mrs Wellborne says I've got to clean it. But I don't know how.'

'You never done it before?' said Becky, amazed.

Ned shook his head. 'What's it for anyway?'

'Cookin', of course. That bit in the middle's the boiler, that's for boilin' water, and them doors on either side are ovens and the underneath's where they put the coal and coke for the fire so that . . .'

'Yeh, yeh, all right, how'm I supposed to clean it?' said Ned, who had never cleaned anything in his life.

'You got to scrub it inside and out – you'll find the scrubbin' brush in the scullery.' She indicated a small room off the kitchen with a large sink. 'Then you got to polish the outside – you'll find the white-wash and polish in the scullery too.'

'And what about them?' Ned nodded at a huge pile of dirty saucepans and pots on top of the range.

'They've got to be washed and dried and polished and hung up on their pegs. The soap and cloth's in . . .'

'Yeh, I know,' Ned said, with a deep sigh. 'In the scullery.'

58

Accompanied by a footman, Alice visited Lady FitzHubert every afternoon, arriving promptly at three and leaving at half past on the dot. Once she met Sir Hubert's ward on the stairs and smiling sweetly she held out her hand and said, 'Good afternoon, I am Alice Eden, Lady FitzHubert's great-niece.'

'And g-g-good day to you,' stammered Cecil, taking Alice's firm little hand in his own white, limp one. 'I am—'

'I know who you are. Tell me,' she leaned towards him, 'what do you do in the garden? I have seen you looking at the sky so intently.'

Immediately Cecil's eyes lit up.

'I'm an astronomer . . . Well, not a proper one yet but I am learning,' he said, his stammer quite disappearing in his enthusiasm. 'I have a telescope, just a small one, which belonged to my dear papa and I read a great deal about the heavens and . . . oh, d-d-dear.' He stopped dead at the shrill sound of a bell. 'That will be Lady F-F-FitzHubert.'

'It is because I am late,' said Alice, lowering her voice and stifling a giggle. 'It does not do to displease Great-aunt. She can be very grumpy.'

'Miss Alice, I b-b-beg of you not to inform her of our conversation,' said Cecil anxiously. 'Any m-m-mention of my love of astronomy causes her g-g-great aggravation.'

'Do not worry,' said Alice. 'I shall not say a word.'

And she hurried up to the old lady's room.

At her mother's suggestion Alice had taken several books with her – *Pride and Prejudice* by Jane Austen, *Cranford* by Mrs Gaskell and *The Pickwick Papers* by Charles Dickens. But Lady FitzHubert would have none of them.

'*The Pickwick Papers?*' she exclaimed in disgust. 'Sheer nonsense! Why would I wish to hear of the ridiculous escapades of a group of very silly men? Read to me from *The Times*, if you please, the financial pages. I am particularly interested in stocks and shares.'

The financial pages, Alice quickly discovered, were unutterably boring and several times her great-aunt snapped, 'Speak up, child, you're mumbling. Are you asleep?'

'Sorry, Great-aunt. My throat is getting dry. May I please have a glass of water?'

'If you must,' she said grudgingly. 'Call for Mr King.' She indicated a long sash hanging by the side of the fireplace.

Alice tugged on the bell pull and taking her place by Lady FitzHubert's chaise longue she began to read again. But the butler did not come in answer to her call and after a few minutes Alice said, 'Great-aunt, my throat is very dry. I really must have some water.'

'That wretched man! He is quite the worst butler I have ever had. Call for him again, child.'

'Great-aunt, if I may I will go down to the kitchen and get a glass of water myself,' said Alice.

'You most certainly may not. Go to the kitchen, indeed! That is no place for a lady.'

'But I am not a lady yet,' said Alice, 'and I do know how to pour a glass of water.' And before Lady FitzHubert could stop her she had gone. But if she had turned at the door she would have seen something quite amazing, something no one had seen for many a year . . . Lady FitzHubert was laughing.

59

Jem had found a good position outside the Bath Hotel on the corner of Piccadilly and Arlington Street from where he could keep an eye on the FitzHuberts' house as well as attract people to buy the knick-knacks on his tray — boot laces, matches, combs, brushes, razors, shirt-studs, kettle-holders, all of which were second, if not third or fourth hand.

'Take a look at this, ladies'n gents,' he shouted, holding up a clothes brush. 'You'd pay five shillin's for an article jammy as this if you were sappy enough to buy it from one of them flash shops in Regent Street. But I'm not askin' for five shillin's. I'm not even askin' for four shillin's or three. And why not, I hear you say.'

'Why not?' came a voice from behind him.

'Cos I'm a . . .'

'. . . bloke with a heart of gold? Lor', I wish I'd had a hot dinner for the number of times I've heard that one.'

'Cos I believe in treatin' people fair'n square.'

'Oh yeh? Pull the other one.'

Jem didn't bother to turn round. There was always someone in the crowd who, with nothing better to do with his time, liked to provoke street traders.

'I'm not askin' for two shillin's for this plummy article,' cried Jem, waving the brush in the air.

'And you wouldn't get it neither.'

'I'm not even askin' for one shillin' . . .'

'Cos it ain't worth it.' A hand reached out and grabbing the brush held it up for everyone to see. 'On account of it ain't got no bristles. Not a one!'

Jem snatched the brush back and spun round. A boy about his age stood there, similarly dressed in a battered wideawake, a frayed jacket, trousers with one leg missing and boots held together with string. From his shoulders was strung a tray on which was a tempting assortment of sweets – almond toffee, black balls, bullseyes, squibs, treacle rock, peppermint rock, Gibraltar rock, rose acid and Wellington Pillars.

'You're on my pitch, toerag,' snarled the boy, glaring at him.

'It isn't your pitch, knocker-face,' retorted Jem.

''Sides, I was here first. I've been here since seven o'clock.'

'Seven o'clock? Pah! I've been on this pitch for nigh on three years, so you,' he jerked his thumb, 'hook it or else.'

'Or else what?'

'Or else I'll knock your block clean off your shoulders.'

Now Jem was faced with a dilemma. Although he was aching to flatten the impudent sweet seller, he knew it would not be a quick, easy victory, for the two boys were equally matched and any prolonged fight would be bound to attract the attention of the policemen who patrolled the streets, truncheons at the ready. Right or wrong, he would be arrested, taken before a magistrate and given a severe whipping or prison sentence, a punishment to be avoided at all costs, especially as he had to stay at his post to help Ned.

'Well?' demanded the sweet seller, squaring up to him. 'You goin' or am I goin' to give you a right leatherin'?'

'All right, all right. But first I want some of them,' Jem pointed to the almond toffees. 'How much're they?'

'Three for a farthin'. But since it's you, fat'ead, I'll

make it two for a farthin',' sniggered the boy, grabbing the only coin Jem had earned that day and putting two of the toffees in his outstretched hand.

Jem walked away, his head down, pretending to ignore the boy's taunts. Popping one of the toffees in his mouth he started chewing it, but on the instant he uttered a terrible cry and fell to the ground, his tray of trinkets spilling all over the pavement.

In a trice a crowd gathered round, staring at him as he writhed in agony.

'Whatever is the matter, my dear?' said a woman, bending over him.

'P-p-poison,' gasped Jem, clawing at his throat in a frenzy as if trying to tear something out.

'*Poison?*' The word spread through the crowd like wildfire.

'Who? Who has poisoned you?' said the woman.

'Him.' Jem pointed to the sweet seller with a trembling hand and opened the other one to show her the almond toffee. Then with a last long, gurgling sigh his eyes rolled back in his head and he lay still.

'Oh my goodness, he's dead,' cried the woman, wringing her hands. 'You!' She turned on the sweet seller. 'You have killed this poor innocent child with your vile confections.'

'They ain't vile,' protested the boy, backing away. 'I ain't done nothin' wrong. It's not my fault the toerag's croaked.'

But the crowd would have none of it.

'Murderer!' they shouted. 'Villain! Monster!' And, 'After him!' as the boy, seeing he was about to be lynched, took to his heels, speeding down the street with a dozen or more angry men and women in hot pursuit.

The moment they were out of sight Jem sprang up and began gathering all his bits and pieces from the pavement and putting them back on his tray.

'Well I never,' exclaimed the woman, staring at him in amazement. 'I thought you were dead.'

'Yeh, I was. But I'm all right now. I reckon I just got a bit of toffee stuck in my throat,' Jem grinned. And resuming his place on the sweet seller's pitch he held up the brush with no bristles and shouted, 'Take a look at this, ladies'n gents. I'm not askin' a shillin' for it. I'm not even askin' sixpence . . .'

'Where you been?' Jem demanded angrily as his brother dragged himself up the street late that night. 'I been waitin' and waitin'.'

'And I been workin' and workin',' said Ned. 'I had to wash a pile of pots and pans, scrub and polish the

range, wash the floors, clean the windows, whiten the front steps, carry coal, clean boots, scour the . . .'

'Crimes, haven't they got no other servants?'

'Just Sly, only he calls himself Mr King now. Then there's a girl, Becky, and a fat old customer called Mrs Wellborne.'

'That all?'

'There was a footman called Luke, but he was given the boot for bein' lazy.'

'Right, I'll see you here same time tomorrow. Now keep your eyes open, Ned, and . . . Ned! Ned!' Jem shook his brother, but Ned was so tired he slumped to the ground, dead to the world.

60

The women's hospital in Tothill Fields was little better than the prison itself – overcrowded, damp, dirty, its grimy windows closed and barred to keep the prisoners in and fresh air out.

Dolly was asleep when Lady Eden was escorted to her bedside by a nurse who kept bobbing her head and curtsying as if she was royalty.

'May I have a few moments alone with Miss Medway?' said Lady Eden.

The nurse looked doubtful. 'It's not allowed, Your Ladyship. I got to stay here.'

'I give you my word that I shall not do or say anything that contravenes the rules of this prison,' said Lady Eden, giving the nervous woman her most radiant and disarming smile.

'Very well, Your Ladyship, I'll leave you,' she said, curtsying again. 'But only for a few moments.'

When the nurse had gone Lady Eden gazed for some time on Dolly's gaunt face and murmuring,

'My poor child,' she took the girl's hand and stroked it.

Dolly woke and seeing her former mistress she tried to struggle upright, crying, 'Oh, M'Lady . . . Oh, M'Lady, I didn't do it. I didn't!'

'Do not distress yourself, my dear,' said Lady Eden, gently pushing her down. But Dolly would not be comforted.

'I didn't steal your necklace. You got me out of the workhouse, you gave me a home and I was so happy, so happy . . .' The girl choked and began to cough, a hard, rasping cough that came from deep in her lungs.

'Dolly, please, calm yourself,' Lady Eden urged her.

'I'd kill myself before I'd do anything to hurt you, M'Lady. I swear on my life, I swear I didn't steal your necklace. Neither did Sam. Sam loves me – he'd given up the bad life for me, he was doing an honest job. We're innocent, M'Lady, we're innocent. You must believe me. Please!'

'Time's up, Your Ladyship,' said the nurse, coming back.

'Thank you,' said Lady Eden. But as she turned to go she bent down and whispered in Dolly's ear, 'I do believe you, my dear. And I shall do everything in my power to make others believe you too.'

'Well,' said the nurse when Lady Eden had gone, 'that was a real lady and no mistake. They say her husband's cousin to the Queen herself. Fancy her visitin' the likes of you.'

But Dolly was so happy that Lady Eden believed she and Sam were innocent she ignored the woman's rudeness.

'Nurse,' she said, 'could I have something to eat, please? I'm very hungry.'

'No, you can't. It ain't supper time yet. You'll wait like everyone else. Just because you got friends in high places don't signify you can lord it over us, miss. You're still a prisoner and don't you forget it,' huffed the nurse. And turning on her heel she stomped away.

'Oh, Edmund, it was so frightful,' said Lady Eden. 'All those poor women lying on miserable straw mattresses like animals. And the sheets and blankets . . . I could scarcely believe my eyes. They were so thin, so grey with age there was no warmth or comfort left in them. Poor Dolly. We must get her out of that dreadful place.'

'But, Parthenope,' said Sir Edmund, 'just because

Dolly says she and Sam Perkinski are innocent, it does not mean they are.'

'Edmund,' said Lady Eden firmly, 'I looked into that girl's eyes. She is not a criminal and I am absolutely convinced that neither she nor Sam stole my necklace.'

'Then who did, my dear?'

'That is something for Detective Inspector Craddock to find out.'

'But be reasonable, Parthenope. The case is closed. You cannot expect the police to . . .'

'On the contrary, Edmund, I expect you to use your position and influence to persuade them to reopen the case. I am quite sure there has been a grave miscarriage of justice and it must be reversed before it is too late and poor Dolly and Sam and little Billy are transported to Australia.'

61

Alice was so eager to see Jem the following morning, she had opened the door and was halfway up the area steps before he had even started down.

'Great-aunt Hildegarde has a housekeeper, a frightful woman . . .' she began.

'I know. Ned told me. She's called Mrs Wellborne.'

'She is *not*,' Alice said emphatically.

'What d'you mean?'

'I met her on the stairs yesterday when I went down to fetch a glass of water from the kitchen. She tried to avoid me, she looked the other way, but I saw her neck, Jem. I saw her neck!'

'What about it?' Jem frowned.

'She has a mole on it.'

Jem rolled his eyes in despair. He had hoped for something useful, something that would help him and Rudd, and all this stupid girl could talk about was moles.

'So has my gran,' he said. 'She's got dozens of 'em, big black hairy ones all over her . . .'

'No, no, this woman has one mole, a heart-shaped mole, on her neck . . . And so did Miss Jermyn.'

'Miss Jermyn?'

'She used to be our governess, but she left shortly after Silas Fox. Don't you see what that means?'

'Course I do,' protested Jem, suddenly realizing. 'I twigged that long before you. Your old governess is Sly's wife, Freda.'

'So Sly and his missus are both in Lady FitzHubert's house now,' said Rudd.

'And Alice told me Sir 'Ubert's away too,' said Jem. 'He's in Scotland – wherever that is – so Sly and Freda've got the place pretty much to themselves.'

'Well, you tell Ned to be careful. Tell him to watch out for thimbles under his pillow,' said Rudd, with a grim attempt at humour.

 327

62

Scotland Yard was one of a row of dingy little houses in Whitehall Place that had been acquired as the headquarters for the Metropolitan Police. The front of the house was divided into two offices adequate for the Commissioners but the servants quarters at the back had been converted into a police station for 'A' Division and the recently formed Detectives Department. So cramped was this side of the house that piles of books, clothes, blankets, saddles and other horse paraphernalia were heaped in the garrets and every available corner.

Swearing under his breath, for he was an orderly man, Craddock made his way through this mess. But he had another reason to be irritated that morning, for he had just been informed by one of the Commissioners that he was to re-investigate the theft of the Star of India.

'Sir Edmund and Lady Eden are not satisfied,' said

the man. 'They now believe that Dolly Medway and Sam Perkinski may be innocent of the crime.'

'Based on what evidence, sir?' asked Craddock, trying to keep the anger out of his voice, for he had several urgent cases to solve, including two savage murders.

'That you must find out for yourself,' said the Commissioner, waving him out of his office with a peremptory gesture.

Now, Craddock was an honest man, honest with everybody he dealt with and, most importantly, honest with himself. He knew his irritation came not from resentment against Sir Edmund and Lady Eden for forcing him to reopen the Star of India case but from guilt that he had not handled it appropriately in the first place; he had been too quick to jump to conclusions instead of engaging in his usual patient, punctilious enquiries. He had been convinced that Rudd Jupp had stolen the jewels and when that rogue had produced a rock-solid alibi for the night of the crime he had been so vexed he had allowed himself to incriminate the next, most obvious culprits.

But who had led him to accuse Dolly and Sam, he wondered, as he was driven to Stratton Street in the back of a hansom cab? Who had first pointed the finger of suspicion at them?

'May I have permission to speak with your butler, Sir Edmund?' he asked when once again he found himself in the Edens' morning room.

'Mr Haydon?' said Sir Edmund, looking puzzled.

'I was referring to Norris Pole, sir.'

'Mr Pole is no longer in our employ, Inspector. He left some weeks ago. He is now working for the Duke of Connemara in Ireland.'

'Has anybody else left your service recently, sir?'

'Indeed they have. Miss Jermyn, the governess. And Maurice Vartle, the footman. The latter disappeared in the middle of the night, never to be seen again.'

'Ah,' said Craddock, tapping the side of his nose.

'Yes, indeed, Inspector,' said Sir Edmund gravely. 'While I would not wish to cast aspersions on anyone and I am most certainly not advising you on how to conduct your investigation of this case . . .'

'Nevertheless you think it would be wise of me to track down Maurice Vartle, sir. And I agree with you. His sudden disappearance is decidedly strange – servants do not give up a good position in a well-established house on a whim – which suggests he

may have been involved in the theft of Her Ladyship's necklace, if not the perpetrator of the crime. You also mentioned that someone else had left your service, the governess . . .'

'Miss Jermyn. I understand she has gone to care for her elderly mother in Hinton St Mary, in Dorset.'

'Do you have her address, sir?'

'I do not, but since Jermyn is an unusual name I imagine it would not be too difficult to find her in a small village.'

'You're going on a nice holiday, Jenkins,' Craddock said to his detective sergeant when he got back to Scotland Yard.

'Oh right, sir. Thank you, sir. I could do with a bit of rest.'

'Good man.' Craddock grinned. 'You're off to Ireland and then to Dorset. As fast as you can. I want you back here by Monday at the latest, is that clear?'

'Yes, sir. Quite clear, sir,' said the sergeant. And muttering 'Holiday . . . bah!' under his breath he stalked away.

63

Like any conscientious miser, every night Sir Hubert opened the big, iron safe in his study and took out all the gems, rubies, emeralds and sapphires, stroking them lovingly as if they were his precious pets. But the one he cherished the most was the diamond tiara, a magnificent diadem. He held it up, marvelling yet again at its myriad stones as they glittered in the candlelight. After an hour or so of this gloating he put everything back in the safe, locked it, locked the door of his study and, having checked and double-checked that the butler had put out all the fires and lamps in the house and shut and bolted every door and window, he went to bed.

In his absence, Lady FitzHubert took over these duties. But whereas her husband always downed a tot of whisky before retiring for the night, she preferred a glass of hot milk.

'Mrs Wellborne takes it up to Her Ladyship's bedchamber,' Becky told Ned as they worked side by

side, scrubbing the cold, stone floor of the kitchen with soap and water and vinegar to clean off the candle grease. 'They say all the thieves in London've tried to get them sparks, specially the tirara, but they haven't got no hope. Her Ladyship keeps the keys of the safe and the study down her bosom and she sleeps very light, sometimes she hardly sleeps at all, so if anyone was to try to get them off her, she'd know. 'Sides, that varminty dog of hers sleeps by her bed'n he'd kick up a shindy if anyone was to go near her. Nah, I don't reckon nobody's never goin' to get that tirara, no matter how hard they try . . . Oh dear,' she muttered, trembling at the sound of heavy footsteps on the stairs, 'that'll be Mrs Wellborne. I'll be well for it if she hears me chatterin'.'

64

Ned was creeping out of the house to see Jem one night when he barged into Cecil on the stairs.

'Oh!' exclaimed the young man, nearly dropping his candle in his fright. 'Who the d-d-devil are you?'

'Ned . . . I mean, Nick. I'm the new bootboy.'

'And what are you d-d-doin' up and about so late?'

'I'm . . . er . . . I'm just walkin' around cos I can't sleep.'

'Well, Nick, you can carry this for me,' said Cecil, putting a small telescope in the boy's arms. 'It is an instrument for l-l-looking at the stars.'

'What d'you want to look at them for?'

'Because they are wonderful, marvellous, fascinating,' enthused Cecil, opening the double doors that led into the garden.

'They don't look wonderful to me.'

'That's because you've never l-l-looked at them properly,' said Cecil, adjusting the lens and handing

the telescope to Ned. 'Put it to your eye, close the other one and tell me what you see.'

'Cor!' exclaimed Ned. 'I can see a thumpin' great diamond. It's all glittery.'

'Beautiful, isn't it?' Cecil's eyes shone as brightly as the star Ned was staring at, entranced. 'It's called Sirius, the Dog Star.'

'What, that star? You mean it's got a name?'

'That one does.'

'And then he told me the names of some of the others, Jem,' Ned said to his brother when he finally met up with him later that night. 'He told me there were thousands of them and he goes into the garden every night and looks at them.'

'You mean he stands outside gawpin' at stars when he could be kippin'?' said Jem in disbelief.

'That's what he said.'

'Blimey!' Jem shook his head, clearly unimpressed with Cecil's hobby. 'He must be off his nut.'

65

Alice was upset. She had told Jem that Silas and Freda Fox were in Great-aunt Hildegarde's house and he had told Rudd Jupp. She knew Rudd was a clever thief – Jem now boasted openly about his uncle's prowess – but she feared that neither Rudd nor the boys were doing anything to prevent Silas and Freda from stealing her great-aunt's jewels.

'Nah, we got to wait,' said Jem, when Alice pressed him.

'Wait for what?'

'For them two to make a move.'

'Oh really!' Alice stamped her foot in frustration. 'Then it will be too late.'

Unable to contain herself any longer, Alice decided to take matters into her own hands. She would warn Great-aunt Hildegarde and her great-aunt would inform the police and they would arrest Silas and Freda. But things did not go according to plan. Her great-aunt listened to her with increasing impatience, finally interrupting her with a snort of rage.

'Goodness me, child, I have never heard so much foolishness. My butler and my housekeeper are dangerous criminals in disguise, you say? I beg to inform you that they both came to me with the very best character references.'

'But . . .'

'I blame these . . . these fairy tales on the ridiculous books you read,' spluttered the old woman indignantly. 'They fill your head with stuff and nonsense. I wonder your mama permits you to read them. As soon as I am well enough I shall take it upon myself to visit her and express my disapproval in the strongest terms.'

66

'I spoke to the Duke of Connemara's chief steward, sir,' said Sergeant Jenkins, standing stiffly to attention in Craddock's office the following Monday, his black top hat under his arm. 'He informed me that they hadn't taken on a new man or woman for the past year. And as for Miss Jermyn, the only lady I found of that name in Poole was a spinster who got very shirty when I asked her where her daughter was.' The sergeant winced at the memory. 'She gave me a nasty blow with a rolled umbrella,' he added, pointing to a bruise on his cheek. 'You'll forgive me saying so, sir, but you sent me on something of a wild goose chase.'

'But where have the geese flown to and what are they doing now? I wonder,' mused Craddock, tapping his chin thoughtfully.

'What about Maurice Vartle, sir? Have you found him?'

'I have indeed, Jenkins. I found him in a dark alley with his throat cut.'

'So we can eliminate him from our enquiries, sir.'

'Why?'

'I beg your pardon, sir, I don't quite understand you. You just said Maurice Vartle was dead . . .'

'Just because he's dead, Jenkins, doesn't mean he didn't steal the Star of India. In fact, it's more likely that someone wanted that necklace so badly they murdered him for it.'

'And who do you think that someone is, sir?'

'If I knew that, Jenkins,' said Craddock testily, 'I'd have them behind bars, wouldn't I?'

67

Alice waited until she and her mother were alone before confiding in her, because she was afraid that if she blurted out her suspicions in front of her sisters they would laugh at her, especially Georgiana. As luck would have it, Lady Eden asked Alice to accompany her to the dressmaker one afternoon.

As they drove along Piccadilly in their carriage Alice decided the moment had come to speak. Unfortunately their route took them down Park Lane and as the entrance to that fashionable street was very narrow a vast number of omnibuses, carriages, donkey carts, cattle, sheep, poultry and of course people were all jostling to get through, which resulted in a horrendous traffic jam.

Lady Eden was so vexed by the delay that it was not until their horses were finally trotting along that she gave her full attention to what Alice was saying . . . and then she was doubly vexed.

'Oh, Alice,' she exclaimed, 'why didn't you tell me all this before?'

'So you do believe me, Mama?' cried Alice eagerly.

'Do you realize, child, the terrible danger you put yourself in?' said her mother in a stern voice. 'You will not go to your great-aunt's to read to her again . . . No, Alice, you will not,' she said, raising her hand to silence the little girl. 'I shall send her a note saying it is no longer convenient.'

'But, Mama,' said Alice, 'we cannot leave Great-aunt alone with those dreadful people.'

'I shall pass on the information you have given me to Detective Inspector Craddock. He will know what to do.'

'Oh, thank you, thank you,' said the little girl, throwing her arms around her mother's neck.

'Alice,' said Lady Eden pushing her gently back on to her seat, for it was considered very ill-mannered to display any emotion in public or, for that matter, in private, 'I am deeply disappointed that you chose to associate with criminals and street urchins rather than confiding in your papa and me.'

'Sorry, Mama,' said Alice, looking contrite.

'But I am proud that you are such a clever,

observant child,' said her mother, her face softening, 'and that you may yet have saved Dolly and Sam and even little Billy from an undeserved and cruel fate.'

68

'Heard the good news, Fimble?' whispered Stoke. 'There's a boat goin' to Australie tomorrow and you're goin' to be on it. All them snakes'n crocodiles'll get you and . . .'

'Two-seven-five, you talkin'?'

Stoke sprang up in alarm. He had been so engrossed in pouring his nightly phial of poison into Billy's ear he hadn't noticed the warder walking towards him.

'Me, sir? Nah. Nah, course I wasn't, sir.'

'Don't try to gammon me, two-seven-five. I heard you.'

'Well, yeh, sir . . . Yeh, you're right, sir, I was, sir, cos Fimble . . . I mean, four-eight-three, sir, he's goin' to be boated to Australie in the mornin' and the poor little nipper's feelin' crawly mawly, so I was just tryin' to cheer him up, sir.'

'That's uncommon civil of you, two-seven-five,

but in future keep your trap shut or I'll have you up before the guv'nor.'

'Yeh, sir. Sorry, sir. I won't do it again, sir,' grovelled Stoke. But as soon as the warder had gone back to his place, the bully leaned over the side of his bed again and hissed, 'Just a few more hours, Fimble. Just a few more hours.'

69

Jem was standing in his usual place on Piccadilly with his tray of knick-knacks, trying to persuade an elderly woman to buy a blunt razor, when Ned came running up, panting.

'Got some news,' he said, tugging at his brother's arm.

'Pack off!' hissed Jem, pushing him away.

'But it's important,' insisted Ned.

'Can't you see I'm busy? Oh, drat!' Jem exclaimed as the woman put down the razor and walked away. 'Now see what you done. I'd nearly got her to buy it. I kept tellin' her she had hairs on her chin thick as pigs' bristles and—'

'I heard Mrs Wellborne talkin' to Becky and she said the old man's comin' back tomorrow.'

'What old man?'

'"Sir" Ubert, of course.'

'"Sir" Ubert's comin' back? Why didn't you say so before, you block'ead! That means Sly'n Freda've got

to pinch that tirara tonight. It's their last chance with just the old girl in the house by herself.'

'What'll I do, Jem?'

'You got to stay awake and soon as you see anythin' dodgy, open the front door and wave. Me'n Uncle Rudd'll be waitin' outside and we'll run in and . . .'

'Catch the pair of them red-pawed.'

'That's about it.' Jem grinned. And tucking his tray under his arm, he set off at a run for Seven Dials.

'Uncle Rudd,' Jem cried, bursting into the back room of the public house where Rudd and several other villainous-looking men were invariably engaged in an illegal game of hazard, 'I got somethin' to . . . Aargh!' he choked as someone grabbed him by the back of his jacket and lifted him off the ground, swinging him back and forth like the pendulum of a clock.

'And who might you be?' grunted a gin-sodden voice in his ear.

'Let him go, Biffa. He's Rudd's sister's brat,' said one of the men, pausing for a moment before throwing the dice.

'Where's my uncle?' said Jem, picking himself up from the floor.

The man with the dice gave him a cunning look. 'Let's just say he's busy tonight.'

'Oh crimes!' muttered Jem.

'Well, some people might call it that,' the man chuckled.

'When'll he be back?'

'When the job's done, of course. Now hook it. We don't want pesky brats gettin' under our feet, do we, Biffa?'

'Nah,' growled Biffa, 'we don't.' And opening the door, he helped Jem on his way with the toe of his boot.

70

Ned had been very tempted to tell Becky about Silas and Freda Fox, but Jem had warned him not to. 'She might be workin' with them,' said his brother. Ned doubted that. There was something transparently honest about Becky, and when he had let slip that he was not averse to removing the odd purse or silk handkerchief from someone's pocket she had been visibly shocked.

Their chores for the day finally done, they had settled down for the night on the kitchen floor, Becky in one corner, Ned in another, when the housekeeper came in.

'Becky, have you warmed the milk for Her Ladyship?' she demanded.

'Yes, it's in the pot on the stove, Mrs Wellborne.'

'Right. Now you two get to sleep,' she said, pouring the milk in a glass. 'And I don't want to hear another sound out of either of you, or you'll feel my slipper on your behinds.' And so saying, she picked up the candle from the kitchen table and ambled away, leaving them in darkness.

Jem flew through the streets, more excited than afraid. Of course it would be dangerous to tackle Sly Fox and Freda without Rudd's help – the two were vicious criminals who would stop at nothing to get what they wanted – but the thought of taking them on single-handedly elated Jem. If he succeeded – *when* he succeeded – not only would Sam, Dolly and Billy walk free but also he would be a hero, he would be the boy who had saved the FitzHuberts' tiara from falling into the hands of thieves. The police would give him a huge reward, the prime minister would give him a medal and the Queen would knight him . . . Sir Jem Perkinski. Nobody would give Rudd Jupp a second thought after that. The whole Perkinski tribe would look up to Sir Jem Perkinski . . . but first he had to stop Sly and Freda.

When he got back to Arlington Street he was so out of breath he had to bend double to get rid of the stitch in his side. After a moment or two he had recovered enough to squeeze between the railings of the FitzHuberts' residence and he crouched low, waiting for the moment when Ned would throw open the door and give him the signal. And then . . .

And then what? Jem had no idea. If his Uncle Rudd had been there . . . No, he didn't need Rudd, he told himself sternly. He could do this on his own.

Ned waited until Becky had fallen asleep and all sounds in the house had ceased before stealing up the stairs to the entrance hall. There were various large, lumbering pieces of furniture in heavy oak and mahogany, but the best one to hide behind, Ned decided, was a grandfather clock, since it was in a dark corner from where he could see anybody coming down the stairs and going into Sir Hubert's study. Fortunately there was a full moon that night and its bright light shone through the stained-glass windows on either side of the front door, casting a ghostly glow over the interior.

Ned was trembling so violently from fear and excitement that his legs gave way and he sank down on his haunches, hugging his knees to his chest. The clock chimed the quarters. Although the noise was deafening and Ned began to dread the whirring sounds that warned the mechanism was working itself up for yet another blast, it also helped to keep him awake.

As the hours ticked noisily by, Ned's initial agitation subsided and he grew bored. Jem had been

wrong, nothing was going to happen that night, he thought as he fidgeted and scratched and shifted from one position to another in a vain attempt to get comfortable. He was on the point of giving up and going back to join Becky on the kitchen floor when he heard a noise. Someone was coming down the stairs.

Ned's heart began to pound so loudly he was quite sure whoever it was would hear him, but the grandfather clock stirred itself into life at that moment, announcing to the world that it was three o'clock.

As the last thunderous chimes died away, Ned peered round the clock and saw the butler standing at the foot of the stairs, looking up, an anxious expression on his face. A minute later the house-keeper came down, grinning from ear to ear, holding up a bunch of keys.

'Well done,' whispered Sly. And crossing to the study, he unlocked the door and went in while Freda stood outside, looking around suspiciously as if she could sense someone watching her. Ned stopped breathing and his heart obligingly stopped beating. But just as he thought he would explode, Sly came out of the study with a leather bag.

'Get everything?' whispered Freda eagerly.

Sly nodded. 'Everything, including . . .' He showed her the tiara, a piece of such dazzling beauty that even in the moonlight the diamonds flashed like a thousand stars.

Drooling, Freda reached for it greedily.

'Keep it safe, my dear,' whispered Sly, 'while I deal with Cecil.'

'Be quick,' said his wife as she went back up the stairs, hugging the tiara to her like a baby.

'It will be the work of a moment,' said Sly.

'Make sure Cecil doesn't see you.'

'He won't.'

Ned knew he should have run to the front door and opened it for Jem, who would be waiting for his signal, but he allowed curiosity to overcome common sense, and waiting till Freda had gone back up the stairs, he eased himself out from behind the grandfather clock and followed Sly.

As he peered round the door, he could see Cecil standing in the middle of the garden, gazing up at the sky through his telescope, completely unaware of the butler gliding across the lawn towards him. Ned watched, spellbound, as Sly crept up on Cecil like a cat stalking a bird, but before he could shout a warning to the unsuspecting young man Sly had

drawn out a cosh and brought it down hard on Cecil's head.

As Cecil slumped to the ground with a groan, Sly hurried to the end of the garden and threw the bag over the side wall. Then he turned and with scarcely a glance at the inert body of Cecil made his way back to the house.

Ned had seen many crimes committed on the streets and alleyways of Devil's Acre, but the sight of a harmless young man being brutally attacked in the garden of one of the noblest houses in London shocked him and he let out a cry of horror.

Sly's head snapped up, and when he saw Ned standing in the doorway, his face ashen in the moonlight, he gave a snarl and leaped towards him.

Jem shrank into the shadows as the constable on the beat plodded by. Every fifteen minutes Jem heard the man's heavy boots as he trudged up the street, stopping now and then to look up at windows or peer into dark areas. Once or twice he yawned, for it was tedious work protecting the houses of the very rich.

Jem, by contrast, was becoming more and more tense. What was happening in the house? Had Sly and Freda committed the robbery yet? And where was Ned? Was he keeping watch or lying on the kitchen floor fast asleep? Just as Jem thought he'd go off bang if something didn't happen, he heard a cry of alarm.

'Ned?' He sprang up. 'Ned – that you?'

The front door stayed determinedly shut, the windows closed and in darkness. The only hope of getting in was through the back . . . But how? All the houses in Arlington Street were impressive double-fronted properties with three storeys and a basement. Nevertheless, they were terraced, which gave Jem a problem, for the only way he could get into the FitzHuberts' garden was through the gardens of the adjoining houses.

He ran to the corner of the street and looked left and right. There was no constable in sight, but it wouldn't be long before he plodded round again. All Jem had to do was climb over the garden wall of the last house in the block. But it was very high, much too high for him to get over unaided.

'Oh crikey!' he groaned.

'What's up?'

Jem spun round. A man towered over him, a thuggish man with deep cuts and scars on his face and a cruel expression in his eyes.

'Oh, it's you,' said the man.

'Grind?' said Jem.

'That's me. Jem, innit? What're you doin' in these parts?'

'Tryin' to get over that wall.' Jem pointed.

'Oh? Somethin' of interest on the other side, is there?'

'Yeh, my brother Ned.'

'Well, I won't ask what he's doin' there, same as you won't ask me what I'm doin' here,' said Grind with a cunning grin, patting his bulging pockets. 'Come on, I'll give you a leg up. Plaguy quick, nipper, before a crusher comes. And remember, next time you see your Uncle Rudd tell him what I done for you and he owes me a favour.'

At the sight of Sly's cold-blooded attack on Cecil, Ned turned on his heel and sped through the drawing room and across the hall. But there was no time to open the front door to warn Rudd and Jem – Sly would have been on him before he had slid back the first of the many bolts. Hesitating for only a moment, Ned flew up the stairs, his heart hammering, his mind in turmoil. Things weren't going according to plan. Rudd and Jem should have been there to help him, 'Oh Lor'!' he gasped, taking the stairs two at a time. 'What'll I do now?'

'Freda!' yelled Sly, bounding up the stairs after him. 'Freda . . . the brat . . . stop him!'

Freda, who had been sitting on the edge of her bed waiting anxiously for her husband, stumbled to her feet and lumbered on to the landing where she collided with Ned.

'What the devil . . . !' she exclaimed, falling on her back, her feet in the air.

'Stop him!' bellowed Sly. 'Stop the brat!'

'Is it Cecil?'

'No, it's the bootboy. He saw me. He saw me cosh Cecil. Stop him!'

Ned hurtled up to the top landing. He had never been anywhere in the house except the servants' quarters and he was confused. Where could he go? Where could he hide?

'Lor', I wish Jem was here,' he muttered, looking at all the closed doors.

Getting over the walls that divided the first house on Arlington Street from the second and third was easy. Jem was a strong, agile boy and all he had to do was climb one of the many trees and clamber over each wall until he reached the FitzHuberts' garden.

He stood for a moment looking up at the house. He could hear muffled sounds from the inside, a man's voice raised in anger, then a woman's . . . His heart missed a beat. The garden door was open!

Jem ran. But in his haste he didn't notice the inert body of Cecil stretched out in the grass and he tripped over it, falling hard.

'Blimey!' he cried, picking himself up. 'Looks like someone's been wiped out already!'

There was a kerfuffle on the landing below Ned. Sly, who had fallen over the prostrate body of his wife, was swearing heartily and his oaths redoubled as Freda, in attempting to struggle to her feet, tripped him up yet again.

'God damn you, woman!' he cursed. 'That boot-boy'll squeal on us to the crushers if he gets away.'

'Gets away?' Freda sounded calmer than her irate husband. 'There's no way he can get away, my dear. Not from up there.'

'You stay here while I go up and flush him out.'

'I'll be ready for him this time, my dear,' said Freda, taking the cosh her husband handed her.

Near to fainting with fear, Ned ran the length of the landing and opened the very last door. By the light of the moon he could make out a small bed and a chest of drawers with a jug and basin on it.

He could hear Sly opening doors as he searched

for him. The man was getting nearer and nearer. It would only be a matter of minutes, seconds, before he found him. Ned ran to the window and looked down. Too far to jump; he'd break his neck. There was no escape that way. And then he saw a movement. He peered into the darkness. Was someone there? Yes, yes, he could see them now . . .

'Help!' he shouted. 'Help me!'

'Ned?'

'Jem?'

'What you doin' up there?'

'Sly'n Freda're after me. They're . . . Oh Lor'!'

At that moment the door flew open and with a cry of triumph Sly pounced on Ned and dragged him away from the open window.

'Got you, you pesky varmint,' he gloated, shaking the boy like a dog with a rat until he slumped unconscious to the floor. 'And now . . .' Sly reached into his sleeve and pulled out a murderous dagger, 'I'm going to finish you off.'

Jem had never been in a such a grand house before. He stood in the entrance hall of the FitzHuberts' residence, wondering which way to go, when he heard a sound close by and peering into the shadows he made out a small girl hunched in a dark corner between a cabinet and an umbrella stand.

'You Becky?' he whispered.

She shrank from him in alarm.

'I said, "Are you Becky?"'

She nodded, wide-eyed with fear.

'Go'n get the crushers, Becky. Tell them there's been a murder . . . oh, and tell them someone's tryin' to steal the FitzHuberts' sparks. Well, go on,' Jem snapped, pulling the terrified girl to her feet. 'Plaguy quick or it'll be too late.'

'I've got him,' crowed Sly.

'Well done,' said Freda, waddling into the room.

'I'll slit his throat and we'll wrap his body in a sheet and hide it.'

'No, no, my dear,' said his wife, putting a restraining hand on his arm. 'Why not throw him out the window?'

'Eh?' Sly frowned.

'We can tell the police that he and Cecil were in on this together.'

'Ah, I begin to see what you mean. We'll say we caught them both red-handed in the study stealing the FitzHuberts' jewels . . .'

'They ran off in different directions,' said Freda,

picking up the story. 'While you went after Cecil I followed the bootboy up here, and in trying to escape through the window he fell to his death.'

'But the third accomplice, someone waiting in the garden next door, escaped with the jewels.'

'Which you will go and hide now before we call the police, my dear.'

'Mrs Fox, you are a genius,' beamed Sly.

'Oh, I try my best,' said Freda modestly.

'Right, you take his legs and I'll take his arms,' said Sly, picking up Ned's lifeless body. 'At the count of three we shall hurl this little varmint to his death. Are you ready?'

'Ready, my dear.'

'One . . .'

They swung the body back.

'Two . . .'

Ned's eyes flickered.

'Be quick, my dear, he's coming to,' barked Freda.

'One more swing,' said Sly. 'One, two, thr—'

But before Sly could say, 'Three!' Jem shot into the room, shouting, 'Get your dirty paws off my brother!' grabbed Ned and held on tightly.

'Oh, it's you again, you toerag,' snarled Sly. 'Well, I've just about had enough of your interfering.' And,

putting his hands round Jem's throat, he squeezed so hard the boy's face turned purple. But just when Jem was sure he'd die there came the sound of a rattle being sprung followed by another and another.

'Police!' whispered Freda.

Suddenly the street was alive with policemen, dozens of them, all springing their rattles and shouting as they converged on the FitzHuberts residence.

'Don't worry, my dear,' Sly whispered to his wife. 'We'll come out of this squeaky clean. It's those two,' he nodded at Jem and Ned, 'who'll swing for this crime, not us.'

71

'Here they are, sir. Here are your villains,' said Sly, hauling Jem and Ned down the stairs by their ears. 'Mrs Wellborne and I have caught them for you.'

'Well done, Mr . . . er . . .'

'King, sir. Mr King, butler to Sir Hubert and Lady FitzHubert. And may I introduce this very brave lady, sir. She is the housekeeper.'

'Pleased to meet you, sir, I'm sure,' said Freda, attempting to drop a curtsy, although it was quite impossible with her huge belly.

'Well done, both of you,' said Detective Inspector Craddock. 'We have been anticipating a major crime in this area and I am not at all surprised that the Perkinski brothers are involved. Where there's trouble you can be sure of finding a Perkinski,' he added, glaring at them.

'But it wasn't us, guv,' cried Jem.

'It was them two,' said Ned. 'They 'arf-inched the tirara and . . .'

'They were goin' to chuck him out the window and . . .'

'They near throttled him. Only when they heard . . .'

'QUIET!' thundered Craddock.

'It's a pack of lies, sir, as I'm sure you realize. They couldn't tell the truth if you paid them,' said Sly, with a curl of the lip.

'Perhaps you would be good enough to tell us the truth, Mr King,' said Craddock.

'Certainly, sir. I was woken from sleep shortly before three o'clock and upon hearing a noise I came downstairs in time to see these two boys emerging from Sir Hubert's study with a large bag. Since it was obvious they were engaged in foul play, and it is the duty of a butler to protect his master's property, I followed them and witnessed a violent scene in the garden. Master Cecil, a charming young man who is the ward of Sir Hubert, was standing on the lawn looking up at the sky, as is his custom . . .'

'Looking up at the sky?' Craddock interrupted him. 'Is the young man not quite right?'

'He is an astronomer, sir.'

'Ah,' Craddock nodded. 'That would explain it. Pray continue, Mr King.'

'Master Cecil was standing on the lawn, minding

his own business, when this thug –' he pointed at Jem – 'no doubt believing that Cecil would try to stop him, crept up on the poor fellow in a most cowardly way and dealt him a cruel blow to the head.'

'It wasn't Jem,' shouted Ned. 'He's tellin' whoppers. It was him. He—'

'SILENCE!' roared Craddock. 'Jenkins, keep that boy under control.'

'Yes, sir,' said the sergeant, tightening his grip on Ned.

'Pray continue, Mr King,' said Craddock.

'The boy then ran to the end of the garden and threw the bag over the wall where, I have no doubt, an accomplice was waiting. The FitzHuberts' heirloom will be miles away by now,' said Sly, shaking his head in consternation. 'The boy himself tried to climb the wall, but seeing me in hot pursuit he ran back into the house.'

'And I chased that little varmint up the stairs,' said Freda, pointing at Ned. 'He thought he'd escape by getting out the window, but I caught him just in time.'

This was too much for Ned. Giving Jenkins an elbow in the ribs and a sharp kick on the shins, he wrenched himself free from the sergeant's grasp and

hurled himself at Sly, screaming, 'It was you. You did it! You did it!'

Sly fell back under the impact, and before he could grab it his wig fell off, revealing a head completely devoid of hair. Ned in a rage lunged at the man's face. As everyone watched in amazement, Sly's huge, bushy eyebrows and whiskery warts came away in Ned's hands, revealing a very ordinary face beneath.

'Uncle Rudd said he always wears a disguise,' Ned said, looking as pleased as punch with himself.

'Well, well, well,' said Craddock, stroking his chin. 'What have we here?'

'Silas Fox, guv,' piped up Jem. 'And that's his wife, Freda.'

'Stop her!' Craddock barked at his policemen as Freda turned to run. But her false breasts and huge belly slipped down to her knees and she stumbled and fell.

'And I'll wager she looks different without this,' laughed Jem, ripping off the woman's bright red wig.

'Mr and Mrs Fox.' Craddock gave them a wry smile. 'I've heard a great deal about you but never had the pleasure of meeting you in the flesh. I would never have connected you, Mr Fox, with the glacial

butler who served Sir Edmund and Lady Eden. And you, Mrs Fox –' he turned to her – 'were, no doubt, the fearsome governess, Miss Jermyn. Truly,' he chuckled, 'you should both be back on the stage, although I imagine your current "profession" is far more lucrative. Well, come along, Mrs Fox, hand it over . . . The tiara, woman, the tiara,' he said testily as Freda opened her eyes wide in feigned innocence. 'We know you've got it. Or would you rather we searched you?'

Scowling and swearing, Freda turned her back, reached under her voluminous skirt and many petticoats, and produced the diamond tiara.

'They stole Lady Eden's sparks as well, guv,' said Jem.

'Thank you, Mr Perkinski, I had already worked that out for myself,' said Craddock tartly. 'And where is the Star of India now?' he asked the Foxes. 'No, don't bother to lie to me,' he snapped as they both began to protest vigorously. 'You stole it from Lady Eden – and a very convincing job it was too. You certainly had me fooled.'

Freda glanced furtively at her husband as if asking his permission to speak.

'Tell me where the necklace is and I'll do my best to see the pair of you are boated to Australia, instead of . . .' Craddock tied an imaginary noose around his neck.

Pole flinched and Freda muttered, 'Jonah's got it,' through clenched teeth.

'Jonah? Well, I never.' Craddock chuckled again. 'I didn't know that old rogue was still in the business. Still operating from that filthy garret off Crown Street, is he? Right, while my constables conduct you two to Scotland Yard I shall pay Mr Jonah a visit. And as for these boys . . .' He frowned at Jem and Ned.

'We weren't doin' nothin' wrong, guv,' said Ned.

'We were only tryin' to help, Your Honour,' said Jem.

'Be off, you little varmints,' growled Craddock, 'before I find a good reason to arrest you too.'

72

'There's just one thing that puzzles me in all this, sir,' said Jenkins when Sly and Freda had been bundled into the back of a police cart and the Perkinskis had gone, running down the street as fast as their legs would carry them.

'And what is that?' said Craddock.

'Something a bit rum, sir.'

'Which is . . . ?'

'Haven't you noticed it yourself, sir?'

'Get to the point, man,' snapped Craddock.

'Her Ladyship. Not to mention the dog. With all this shindy, you'd think they'd have woken up.'

'Ah, I fancy there is a good reason for that, Jenkins. Now . . .' He looked up at the two landings above him and frowned. 'I wonder which of those rooms is Lady FitzHubert's bedroom?'

'May I make a suggestion, sir?'

'Very well, what is it?'

'We ask the maid, sir, the little girl who told us about the burglary.'

'And where is she?'

'I believe she's in the kitchen, sir. She was rather frightened by all the hubbub and I told her to stay there where she'd be safe.'

'Go and get her, please.'

A moment later Jenkins returned with a still trembling Becky in tow.

'There's nothing to be frightened of now, child,' said Craddock gently. 'We simply want you to tell us which of all these rooms is Her Ladyship's.'

'I'll show you, sir,' said Becky. And she led them up to the first floor, where she stopped and pointed at a door. 'That's where she sleeps, guv, but you'd best not go in cos she don't like visitors, specially in the middle of the night.'

'I doubt she will object,' said Craddock and he opened the door to reveal Lady FitzHubert lying flat on her back, her mouth wide open, snoring fit to raise the dead.

'Cor, love a duck!' cried Becky in amazement. 'She always says she has trouble sleepin', and look at her now. And as for him . . .' she pointed at Sir Lancelot, who was snoring with equal enthusiasm, 'fine watchdog he is.'

'Drugged, both of them,' said Craddock. 'Was Her Ladyship in the habit of taking a drink before she retired for the night?'

'Oh yes, sir.' Becky nodded. 'Mrs Wellborne always took her a glass of hot milk . . .'

'. . . into which she poured some laudanum so that she could steal Lady FitzHubert's keys without fear of waking her. Clearly the plan was that Sly would attack Cecil – no doubt he was going to make up some cock and bull story about Cecil being the thief – and hide the bag of jewels in the next garden, from where he could retrieve them later. But the Perkinski boys forced them to change their plans at the last minute. Oh, they were clever rascals, Sly and Freda,' said Craddock, 'but not quite as clever as us.'

'You?' said Becky, summoning up the courage to contradict him. 'It wasn't you lot that copped them,' she said indignantly. 'It was Nick and the other boy.'

'Nick?'

'Our bootboy.'

'I think she means Ned Perkinski, sir,' said Jenkins. 'And if you don't mind my saying so, sir . . .'

'Yes, yes, I know what you're going to say, Jenkins – Jem and Ned deserve a reward,' said Craddock testily. 'Very well, I shall arrange it.'

73

'Mama, I do hope Cecil has recovered from the awful blow to his head that wretched man gave him,' Alice said as she and her sisters took tea in the drawing room.

'I understand he is fully recovered, my darling. In fact, I received a letter from Great-aunt this morning informing me that since Cecil is so interested in astronomy he has gone to Berlin to study under Professor Ecke.'

'What is astronomy, Mama?'

'The study of the sun, moon and stars.'

'How very boring,' said Georgiana.

'Georgiana finds studying all her dresses far more interesting,' muttered Alice in an aside. 'And what has happened to Dolly and Sam and Billy, Mama?' she asked aloud.

'They have all been released from prison.'

'Oh, how wonderful! Does that mean Billy will come back to us?' asked Alice.

'No, my dear. I know how fond of him you have grown — and, indeed, so have I,' said her mother gently as Alice's face fell, 'but your papa and I agree that Billy will be happier with his own family.'

'What about Dolly, Mama?' asked Thomasina.

'She and Sam are to be married. Sam has found a position with the Marquess of Salisbury's family and Dolly is to be nursemaid to their children.'

'And Great-aunt Hildegarde,' said Alice, 'is she well?'

'Unfortunately Great-aunt is still suffering somewhat from her ailment, but she says she would be pleased if you were to continue to read to her in the afternoons.'

Georgiana laughed out loud at that and was reproved by a stern look from her mother.

'Oh, Mama, must I?' sighed Alice. 'Great-aunt only wants me to read from the newspapers, the kind of newspapers that Papa reads, and they are so dreadfully dull.'

'You need not worry,' said Lady Eden, taking a letter from her reticule. 'Great-aunt says you may take any books you wish, including *The Pickwick Papers*,' she added with a twinkle in her eye, for Alice had told her of Lady FitzHubert's disapproval of that

particular book. 'And she would like you to take tea and dainties with her.'

'Tea and dainties?' echoed Georgiana, pouting.

'Great-aunt also has a gift for you, Alice. It is a token of appreciation for the role you played in apprehending Silas and Freda Fox – a gold locket set with rubies, which belonged to her mama.'

'A gold locket set with rubies?' snapped Georgiana, whose nose was now badly out of joint. 'That is not fair. I am the eldest. Great-aunt should give it to me.'

'I shall give it to Billy's mother,' said Alice, relishing the look of horror on Georgiana's face. 'Poor lady, she has no money to buy food for her family and . . .'

'Do not distress yourself, my dearest,' said Lady Eden. 'I have instructed Mrs Maltby to give the Perkinski boys a small parcel of nourishing sustenance whenever they require it. And tomorrow, Alice, you and I will pay the family a visit.'

74

For the third time in as many months the Edens' carriage drove into the Devil's Acre, to be greeted by the usual crowd of ragged residents, who gawped at Lady Eden and her daughter with ill-concealed envy.

'Bert! Liza!' shouted Old Mother Perry. 'It's them toffs again.'

Ma and Pa hurried out of the caravan, followed by the boys.

'Billy!' exclaimed Alice, leaping down from the carriage. 'Oh, I am so pleased to see you,' she said, throwing her arms around him and giving his dirty face a big kiss.

From the corner of his eye Billy could see Jem and Ned nudging each other and sniggering. To be kissed by a girl was bad enough, but to be kissed by a girl in front of his family and all the neighbours . . . Billy turned bright red and hid his face in his mother's skirts.

'You can come in, if you like,' Ma said to Lady Eden. 'Bert's tripes are better now and we've cleaned up the caravan. It's lookin' real jammy again.'

Even if she had known what the word meant, jammy would not have been Lady Eden's word for the indescribable mess that met her eyes as she stepped through the door followed by a footman carrying a large hamper. But she took her place politely on a rickety orange box, indicating to the footman that he should place the hamper on the floor and leave.

'Mrs Perkinski,' she said, 'I do hope you will not be offended, but I have brought you all the clothes I purchased for Billy. I have no further use for them, whereas he . . .'

'Lawks a mercy!' exclaimed Ma, riffling through the layers and layers of expensive materials. 'Fit for a prince, these are, ma'am. I can sell them at the market. They'll bring me in a good few guineas, I can tell you.'

Lady Eden nodded her approval. 'And Alice has something for Billy,' she said, looking at her daughter.

Alice opened her small reticule and took out a gold thimble set with turquoises.

'Blimey!' cried Ma, quite overcome.

Lady Eden laughed. 'As it is thanks to your boys that I have my necklace back,' she said. 'Sir Edmund and I thought the very least we could do by way of recompense would be to give this to you.'

'That's very kind of you, ma'am,' said Ma, who had already calculated how much she could get for it from the pawn shop. 'Billy,' she pushed him forward, 'say somethin'.'

But Billy looked woebegone and his lower lip began to tremble.

'What's the matter with you, you ungrateful little varmint?' said Ma angrily.

'I thought . . .' sobbed Billy. 'I thought it was going to be a pork pie.'

Billy woke that night, screaming in terror.

'What's up, my tulip?' said Ma in alarm.

'It's . . . it's two-seven-five,' he said in a trembling voice.

'Two-seven-five?'

'That'll be one of the prisoners at Tothill,' explained Pa, who had been in prison himself once, although, as he told anyone who bothered to listen, he had been totally innocent of the crime for which he had been convicted.

Billy dropped his voice to a whisper as if he feared

his tormentor might, by magic, overhear him. 'Zed Stoke.'

'And what did he do to you?'

Tearfully the little boy recounted the horrors Stoke had filled his head with night after night.

'Wait till I get my paws on him,' growled Pa. 'I'll—'

'I got an idea,' Jem interrupted him. 'I know how we can get even with Zed Stoke. Ma –' he turned to her eagerly – 'all them togs Lady Eden gave us . . .'

'Gave me, you mean,' retorted his mother. 'And what about them? You're not havin' any, if that's what you're thinkin'.'

'Just a few, Ma . . . It's all right,' he added hastily as Ma began to protest loudly, 'you'll get them all back. But I need them for my dodge.'

On a chill morning in late October the door of Tothill Fields prison opened and a boy came out, a short, squat, thuggish boy with tiny, vacant eyes and a slack, blubbery mouth. He looked round briefly as if he half hoped someone might be waiting for him, then he gave a shrug, thrust his hands in his pockets, lowered his head against the biting wind and trudged up the street towards the corner around which Jem, Ned and Billy were hiding.

'That him, Billy?' Jem hissed in his ear.

'Yeh.'

'Right. You know what you got to do.'

'Nah.' Billy hung back, trying to hide behind his brothers. He'd been more than willing when Jem had told him his plan, for there was nothing he wanted more, apart from a pork pie, than to see Zed Stoke get his comeuppance, but now that he was face to face with the bully again he was afraid. 'I can't,' he whined.

'Course you can. Now get goin' or I'll give you a jacketin' you'll never forget.'

Persuaded by Jem's encouraging words, the little boy stepped out of their hiding place, almost blundering into Stoke, who was walking along, his eyes glued to the pavement, a morose expression on his face.

He cussed Billy and was going to give him a slap for getting in his way, but just as his hand was about to connect with the little boy's head Stoke stopped dead, staring at him in amazement.

'Crimes!' he breathed, running his eyes over the little boy's splendid outfit – the cap with the feather, the brightly coloured kilt, the jacket with silver buttons, the frilly shirt, the tartan socks to the knees, the tartan scarf over the shoulder, held in place with a silver brooch. 'Crimes, who're you?'

'I'm lost,' said Billy, as Jem had primed him.

'Where d'you live?'

'I'm lost,' Billy repeated parrot-fashion.

'Can't you say nothin' else?'

Billy was about to say, 'Yes, I can,' when he remembered Jem's instructions.

'I'm lost,' he said for the third time.

Zed's beady little eyes lit up. 'A nincompoop as well as filthy rich,' he gloated. 'This'll be easy as fallin' off a log. Come with me, nipper,' he said, offering Billy his hand in an affectionate way. 'I'll take you home.'

'He's fallen for it,' Jem whispered to Ned as Stoke, with a furtive look to left and right to make sure no one was watching, led an unresisting Billy into a dark, narrow alleyway and without further ado began pulling off his clothes.

'Skinning', as it was called, was very popular with petty thieves. All they had to do was corner a defenceless well-dressed child, steal its fine clothes and hurry to the nearest dolly shop to sell them before the police appeared. Stoke was over the moon about his good luck. 'This lot'll make me rich,' he chuckled, peeling off Billy's jacket and kilt.

'And this is uncommon flash,' he laughed, taking off the little boy's cap and trying to stretch it over his own fat head. 'How do I look, nipper? Like a swell, I'll wager.'

Billy stared up at him wide-eyed. The sight and sound of Stoke filled him with horror. Every muscle in his body ached to run away, but Jem had made him promise he'd go along with the dodge on pain of death, describing that death in gruesome detail – including the removal of toenails – so Billy bravely stood his ground.

Now, if Stoke had not been as thick as two short planks he might have wondered why Billy didn't scream and struggle and try to get away as any normal child would have done. But somewhere deep in the recesses of his tiny brain he must have sensed that something was not quite right, for he bent down, peering intently into Billy's face.

'Here,' he frowned, 'haven't I seen you before?'

'I'm lost,' said Billy.

'I know you. I do. You're . . . Blimey, you're Fimble.'

'I'm lost.'

'Shut up sayin' that, will you?' shouted Stoke, who had finally begun to realize he was being

tricked. 'What're you doin' here? Why're you dressed like that?'

'Cos they're his togs, that's why,' came a voice from behind him. 'So give them back.'

Stoke spun round and let out a gasp. Like all bullies he only preyed on smaller, weaker children, and the sight of Jem, who was as big and strong as he was, made him uneasy.

'And who d'you think you are, tellin' me what to do?' he said.

'I'm Jem Perkinski. And that's my brother Billy. Now, give him back his togs or I'll . . .'

'Nah, I won't.'

'We'll see about that,' said Jem. And with a growl of rage he leaped at Stoke.

Billy was overjoyed to see his brother give Zed Stoke the good hiding he deserved. 'Bash him, Jem!' he shouted. 'Wallop him good'n proper!'

But then something peculiar happened. Although Jem was clearly the better fighter of the two and could have beaten Stoke with one hand tied behind his back, he suddenly fell down and hunched into a ball.

'Yah, lily-livered!' scoffed Stoke.

'Jem!' exclaimed Billy in horror. 'Jem, get up!'

'This your big, strong brother?' Stoke jeered at

Billy. 'Lor', he's as soft as you. He's no better'n a baby.' And picking up Billy's clothes he turned and sauntered away, whistling arrogantly. But at that moment Ned came hurtling round the corner, followed by two policemen.

'Jem, Jem, did he hurt you bad?' he cried, running up to Jem, who lay on the ground groaning.

'I . . . I tried to stop him. He's got . . . he's got Billy's togs,' gasped Jem, pointing with a trembling hand. 'He's nicked them.'

The policemen took one look at Billy, who was now turning blue in the cold air, and with shouts of 'Stop thief! Stop!' and swinging their rattles, they took off after Stoke.

Billy cheered and Jem sprang to his feet, grinning from ear to ear. 'Well done, Ned,' he said.

'They've nabbed him! They've nabbed him!' yelled Billy, as the two policemen marched past them with Stoke between them.

'Yeh, that's the last you'll ever see of him, nipper,' said Jem.

But Ned shook his head.

'Nah, he'll be out soon,' he said.

'Nah, he won't. He'll be on his way to Australie,' said Jem.

'Australie? Just for nickin' some togs?'

'And a thimble, Ned. Them toffs won't like him nickin' that thimble they gave Billy.'

'But he didn't nick it.'

'Oh yeh he did.' Jem gave his brother a wicked wink. 'They'll find it in his pocket.'

A Note from the Author

Crime and Punishments

If you were caught committing a crime at the time when the Jammy Dodgers were working the streets of London, you could be whipped, sent to prison, hanged or transported to Australia, Bermuda or Gibraltar.

Children as young as six were put in prison for very minor offences, such as sleeping rough in doorways, throwing stones at a street lamp, climbing over a wall, knocking on doors and running away, and even spinning a top in the street. Two sisters aged ten and twelve were actually hanged for stealing apples from an orchard.

Food to Go

The streets of London were noisy with the incessant shouts of 6,000 street sellers: 'Watercress. Nice and fresh!' . . . 'One a penny, two a penny, hot cross buns' . . . 'Hot spiced gingerbread nuts. If one'll warm you, what'll a pound do?'

Many Victorians lived on nothing but fast food.

It was easier and cheaper to buy pea soup, fried fish, eel pies, baked potatoes and muffins from a street seller's painted wooden tray than to prepare the food at home, especially if home was one small room shared with nine or ten other people, with no space or money for pans, plates or cutlery.

Ice cream, called 'penny ices', was sold on the streets of London, but it was slow to gain popularity, probably because there were many cheap imitations which, according to one disgusted customer, 'tasted like stewed tripe with a little glue'. And although in 1847 Fry's launched the first chocolate bar, chocolate was a luxury only the rich could afford.

Cures

While wealthy Victorians paid to consult doctors of varying degrees of competence and honesty, the poor relied on traditional remedies. These contained ingredients such as creosote, which is now used to preserve wood, and boa-constrictor droppings as cures for tuberculosis. If these remedies failed, it was recommended that gas should be pumped up the patient's bottom, 'from where it would be sure to reach and clean the lungs'.

Leeches, which suck blood and look like very fat

 *385*

black worms, were thought to cure all manner of complaints, from tumours to whooping cough. To get rid of a headache, sufferers would attach several leeches to each side of their forehead and let them drink the 'bad blood' out.

Bloodletting was also popular. A doctor would sever a vein and let the 'poison' drain away with the patient's blood. It was not unusual for the patient's life to drain away as well.

Despite all this, the nineteenth century saw some amazing advances in medicine: anaesthetics (which were viewed with suspicion until Queen Victoria used chloroform during the birth of her eighth child), vaccination, radium (later X-rays and radiotherapy) the discovery of germs, which led to the the development of antiseptics, and the invention of the stethoscope (which started out as a wooden tube that the doctor could carry in his top hat).

King Cholera

The four major outbreaks of cholera in Britain between 1831 and 1866 killed 140,000 people. The disease struck suddenly and many victims died within the day. It was thought to be caused by poisons in the air, but a doctor called John Snow discovered in 1854 that the culprit was the filthy and contaminated water.

Until the mid-nineteenth century the contents of sewers and cesspits were emptied into the River Thames, along with animal dung, dead dogs, cats and rats and the bloody remains from slaughterhouses. The water companies then pumped this foul mix back to London homes and standpipes for people to drink. Small wonder they fell ill. But in 1865 a new sewer system was built, providing London with clean water, and 'King Cholera' disappeared.

A Glossary of Victorian Slang and Phrases

Neither Jem, Ned, Billy nor the author made up any of the words or expressions in this book, even the golopshus ones. They were all part of common speech in Victorian times.

Arf-inch	Half-inch, steal (rhyming slang for 'pinch')
Area	Small space in front of the basement of a house
Billycock	Round low-crowned felt hat
Bread basket	Stomach
Bull's Eye Lantern	paraffin lamp that emits light from a single round lens — usually stuck in a policeman's belt, leaving his hands free
Burnisher	Tool for polishing
Buzzer	Pickpocket
Canoodle	Kiss and cuddle
Chokey	Jail
Chump	Head, as in 'off your chump' — mad
Clock	Face
Cracksman	Housebreaker
Cracky	Crazy
Crank	Heavy revolving disk that a prisoner must push round a set number of times each day as a punishment
Crib	House, as in 'crack a crib' — break into a house
Crow	Lookout

Drop off the hooks	Die
Fence	Someone who buys stolen goods and sells them on
Fly	Clever/artful
Gammon	Persuade
Golopshus	Delicious
Gull	Someone who is easily tricked. Also to trick someone
Half-tester bed	Bed without footposts
Huzard	Gambling game played with dice
Hurdy-gurdy	Barrel organ, an instrument on which music is played by winding a handle
Jacketing	Beating
Leary	Clever/artful
Looney tic	Lunatic/mad
Lorgnette	Glasses on a stick
Lushed	Drunk
Moniker	Name
Mullock	Rubbish
Obstropolous	Awkward/stroppy
Pantaloons	Knee-length underwear worn by wealthy boys and girls
Pates	Head. Insulting in, e.g. 'mouldy pate'
Peg-tops	Children's game for two, where each player spins small tops to try to hit the other player's tops
Phaeton	Four-wheeled open carriage pulled by two horses
Narks	Informer/spy, as in 'pigs' nark' — one who spies for the police

Quality	Wealthy people
Queer	Ill or strange
Rattle	Instrument that makes a loud noise when whirled. Policemen used to carry these, and to raise the alarm they would 'spring' their 'rattle'
Ready	Money
Reticule	Small dainty bag
Rookery	Slum
Rum	Odd
Sappy	Foolish
Shot drill	Having to carry a cannonball as a punishment
Smelling salts	Strong-smelling mixture, inhaled in cases of faintness or headache
Snaggy	Irritable
Snakesman	Child who can wriggle through small spaces in order to let other people in to steal things
Snuff	Powdered tobacco, taken by putting a pinch in the nostrils. Also in 'up to snuff' – good enough; 'snuff it' – die
Sparks	Jewels/jewellery
Spliced	Married
Toady	Person making an effort to please
Tooler	Pickpocket
Touch someone	Succeed in getting money from someone
Tread the mill	Go on a treadmill as a punishment
Trotter cases	Shoes
Trucks	Trousers

Tumble to	*Detect/find out*
Varminty	*Rotten/offensive*
Wheel	*Cartwheel*
Wideawake	*Hat with a wide brim and shallow crown*

A selected list of titles available from Macmillan Children's Books

The prices shown below are correct at the time of going to press. However, Macmillan Publishers reserves the right to show new retail prices on covers, which may differ from those previously advertised.

BOWERING SIVERS

Jammy Dodgers on the Run	978-0-330-43663-2	£4.99
Jammy Dodgers go Underground	978-0-330-43664-3	£4.99

All Pan Macmillan titles can be ordered from our website, www.panmacmillan.com, or from your local bookshop and are also available by post from:

Bookpost, PO Box 29, Douglas, Isle of Man IM99 1BQ
Credit cards accepted. For details:
Telephone: 01624 677237
Fax: 01624 670923
Email: bookshop@enterprise.net
www.bookpost.co.uk

Free postage and packing in the United Kingdom